## Praise for
## *Ladies with Options*

"A treat . . . An engaging story of female bonding and finance . . . You'll cheer them on as they risk their wad to save their town."

—Sandra Dallas,
author of *The Chili Queen*

"In this lighthearted novel, an early '80s Minnesota ladies' investment group calling itself the Mostly Methodist Club finds itself upended by a pink-haired new member. She puts them onto a company developing new technology—run by a young man named Bill Gates."

—*Chicago Sun-Times*

"The eight ladies of the Mostly Methodist Club in Larksdale, Minn., who meet every Sunday to swap recipes, escape football, and occasionally invest a few dollars, are prompted by teenager Skye to look into those new companies run by, what are those names again, Bill Gates, Michael Dell, or something like that. You might be able to guess what happens next in Cynthia Hartwick's entertaining novel."

—*The Dallas Morning News*

"*Ladies With Options* by Cynthia Hartwick lists librarians and hairdressers and housewives as its heroes. . . . They gain what is, in modern society, the greatest of powers. They get rich."

—*Toronto Sun*

"Delightful and entertaining . . . a story to invest in."

—Lynne Hinton,
author of *Friendship Cake*

"Readers will certainly enjoy seeing small-town gals make good, but the real pleasure here comes from the snappy narration of Sophia, daughter to one of the Ladies and gossipy chronicler of matters both financial and personal. . . . A witty, thoroughly likable tale."

—*Kirkus Reviews*

"A can't-put-it-down, stay-up-all-night, page-turner . . . I laughed, loved, and triumphed with the Larksdale Ladies."

—Barbara Bretton,
author of *Girls of Summer*

"Electric."

—*London Free Press*

"Lively, insightful, and entertaining . . . her blend of humor and perspective on Middle America pays big dividends, both fun and bittersweet. . . . Hartwick's novel chronicle of a Minnesota ladies' investment group is neither Standard nor Poor . . . loaded with great one liners . . . Fabulous!"

—Pamela Morsi,
author of *Here Comes the Bride*

"Touching and laugh-out-loud funny."

—Jennifer Chiaverini,
author of *The Quilter's Apprentice*
and *The Quilter's Legacy*

# Ladies with Prospects

CYNTHIA HARTWICK

BERKLEY BOOKS, NEW YORK

A Berkley Book
Published by The Berkley Publishing Group
A division of Penguin Group (USA) Inc.
375 Hudson Street
New York, New York 10014

This book is an original publication of The Berkley Publishing Group.

This is a work of fiction. Names, characters, places, and incidents either are the product of the author's imagination or are used fictitiously, and any resemblance to actual persons, living or dead, business establishments, events, or locales is entirely coincidental.


Cover design by Judith Murello.
Cover illustration by Tsukushi.



PRINTING HISTORY
Berkley trade paperback edition / April 2004

Library of Congress Cataloging-in-Publication Data

Hartwick, Cynthia.
Ladies with prospects / Cynthia Hartwick.
p. cm.
ISBN 0-425-19421-3
1. Women—Societies and clubs—Fiction. 2. Women—Finance, Personal—Fiction. 3. Women—Minnesota—Fiction. 4. Female friendship—Fiction. 5. Investment clubs—Fiction. 6. Investments—Fiction. 7. Minnesota—Fiction. I. Title.

PS3558.A71555L335 2004
813'.6—dc22

2003062829

PRINTED IN THE UNITED STATES OF AMERICA

10 9 8 7 6 5 4 3 2 1

*For JJB and AMcC,*
*who made it possible*

PROLOGUE

# Up to Speed

Okay—the main lesson I learned during my brief, wacky career as a project manager is that nothing goes right if the whole team isn't on the same page from the outset. So let me bring you up to speed about the Larksdale Ladies. Don't worry—I promise this won't take over sixty seconds. It's easy enough to cover the Ladies' main claim to fame in just three words:

They made money.

More precisely, they made a *lot* of money. They did it two ways. First, they started an investment club that bought into a bunch of then-dinky tech companies with names like "Microsoft" and "Dell" years before most people even knew those companies existed. Second, they sold those stocks around 1990 to buy Larksdale's only (fairly) big homegrown company, Prairie Machine Tools.

They bought PMT, which was then an old-line cash-register manufacturer, to keep it from sending all its jobs down to

Mexico. At the time, the buy looked to be a slightly dumb act of charity or hometown boosterism. Turned out, though, that PMT owned a very useful technology crucial to a little doohickey, which went on to be sort of popular.

You may have heard of the doohickey.

It was called the Internet.

And by 1997, PMT software was running on something like 47 percent of all the world's Web servers.

The Ladies set up the company (renamed PMT Software) so employees could easily buy its stock. As tech stocks zoomed, that proved a great recruiting tool. Of course, it also meant the Ladies wound up owning only about a third of the company—but then, one-third of PMT's $24 million a year in net profits pretty well guaranteed the eight Ladies didn't need to lose any sleep over Social Security in their golden years.

Nothing like that extra million bucks a year to take the edge off your worries.

For a handful of small-town women who started investing because they feared Social Security would never pay enough to retire on, that was a happy ending, and it looked likely to go on forever. Only it turned out that along about 1999, the road to paradise started getting a little bumpy.

And that's where this story begins.

And me?

I'm in the story partly because my aunt Dolly was an original Lady and helped me join the group. Mainly, though, I'm in it because I'm writing it—and like most writers, I can hardly ever keep my nose out of anything.

CHAPTER ONE

# The Beginning

As PMT Software's most junior manager, I was doing what every other junior manager at every other software company was doing that sweltering June of the blazing late-nineties high-tech boom. I was working my butt off.

More precisely, I was starting the second eight hours of my usual sixteen-hour workday. Now, don't let that sound like I'm complaining. I liked my work—and *everybody* in those days worked as hard as I did, or harder. Besides, there were perks. We had free neck massages beginning at 4 P.M., free food in the cafeteria, a well-stocked and free snack room, and frequent distributions of goofy toys and sporting gear to raise morale during all-nighters. Larksdale, Minnesota, wasn't quite Silicon Valley—I don't recall anyone being given a free Porsche for joining the company, for example—but we weren't doing badly, at all.

By dour old Midwestern standards, the place was positively debauched.

But we did work a Silicon Valley schedule. The parking lot never emptied, even at 4 A.M. Most of the office lights, on all four floors of the PMT building, were still on at 11 P.M., six days a week. By that summer of '99, casual dress had reached even the executive suite, and though most of the senior people still had that slow, modest, courteous Midwestern manner about them, they (and we) were just as driven to win as any of our competitors from Palo Alto to New Delhi.

That day my back (nestled in a $1,000 Aeron chair) was doing okay, and my fingers were flying over the keyboard—but my eyes were feeling like sandpaper. I always knew I was tired when the air-conditioning started sounding loud. And that fateful Friday afternoon, June 2, it sounded to me like an F-16 taking off. I kept typing, though, because we were racing to beat a deadline, and if I finished testing some last-minute code changes before Floyd Higginsbottom walked in, my group would pick up hundred-dollar bonus checks to blow over the weekend.

At five o'clock, right on time, Floyd stuck his head into my cubicle and asked, "How's it going, Callie?"

Floyd was one of those straight-down-the-line, old-PMT middle managers who appear to be right out of *Dilbert*—but who prove to be both a lot nicer, and a lot smarter, than anybody expects. My fingers were still flying over the keyboard as I said—

"Thirty seconds, Floyd."

He kept politely quiet, and shortly I lifted my hands and held them aloft, like a rather showy concert pianist—

"Ta-dum!"

"You happy with it all?"

"Sure am, Floyd."

"I'm going to lock it down, then."

This meant all the code we'd written to that point would be

sequestered so it couldn't be altered; nobody could get inspired, reopen the file, and accidentally screw up everything. Floyd leaned in past me, entered his ID and a password I wasn't supposed to know, then accepted the program's offer to lock down the work.

He stepped back, embarrassed I think, to have gotten so close. Then he reached inside his shirt pocket for the moderately thick envelope I knew held bonus checks for the six programmers in my group. "Okay, then," he said. "Good job, Callie. We're five days ahead of schedule." He handed me the checks.

I tried to sound surprised—

"Hey! Thanks, Floyd."

Money always made Floyd uneasy; with the transfer done, he said in a happier tone, "Well, I'm off for some fishing."

Fishing was a hot time for old Floyd, so I wished him a lot of fun.

"I'll have my cell phone, and my Blackberry, and of course I'll log in from the cabin computer—and call you tomorrow."

I'd already switched over to my e-mail program. Typing, I answered—

"Swell, Floyd. See you Monday."

Believing Floyd was gone, I continued working, and was surprised when he reappeared at my desk. I felt vaguely nervous until he cleared his throat and muttered, "There's some kind of rumor about us and a takeover."

I relaxed. High-tech companies always have rumors flying. I tended to ignore them all, so I said—

"You mean we're buying Microsoft?"

He considered it carefully, realized I was joking, and looked relieved. "Yeah. Huh. Guess you're right. Silly rumor." Not exactly a guy to hammer a point, he added cheerfully, "See you Monday."

When I looked up, he was gone. I must have been more tired than I realized. Floyd, bless his heart, was so far out of the loop that if PMT insiders were the sun, he would be circling out beyond Pluto. Nice guy, and a heck of a programmer, but not exactly wired-in.

If Floyd had heard about it, the rumor had to be *huge*.

Still, being pretty clueless myself, I missed the warning signs. I picked up the envelope and, feeling like a plus-size Tooth Fairy, started on a slow stroll around the adjacent cubicles to hand out the checks. I spent about six minutes in the first four cubicles. I got squirted twice with water pistols—about average for the place in summertime—and had a few minutes of pleasant chat. Then I borrowed a water pistol from our youngest programmer, Janet Carter. It was a tiny thing, but I figured it would do the job—and I started toward Vince's cubicle.

In my best fantasy fashion, suddenly I was Gary Cooper in *High Noon*. I might have been expecting to get it in the back, but nobody was going to stop me from walking down Main Street.

As I neared Vince's doorway, I pressed myself closer to his cubicle wall and started edging forward. Even Gary Cooper wasn't crazy. Then I whipped around into the cubicle entrance . . . and got hit with another squirt-gun blast.

Vince was serious about his toys: *This* gun was a Super Soaker, and it caught me right in the chest.

I yelped—but I wasn't helpless, because I'd leveled Janet's water pistol, and I got him right between the eyes.

Alas, mine was a Pyrrhic victory, since I looked as if I'd been showering in my T-shirt; but at least I was ready with a snappy reply. I said—or rather, sputtered—

"What *the* . . . *How'd* you . . . ?"

Vince pointed past me. Turning, I saw a miniature PC video camera mounted on one of the cubicles, and realized if only I'd taken a different route I could have ambushed *him*. Of course, that was probably Custer's last thought, too.

"Oh, cool, money!" Vince had spotted the envelopes. He grabbed one out of my hand. "I hope it's, like, a zillion dollars."

"You wish," I said.

I hadn't taken a seat—and not just because of the water-gun welcome. I really liked Vince. Yes, it was a business necessity for me to be nice to him, since he was PMT's only certifiable genius, but I liked him, too. Vince was like Jimmy Neutron grown up, and over the hair gel, but still popping out genius ideas about once a minute. Ours was PMT's only group dealing primarily with hardware—radio-linked credit card processing machines. The only reason we could stay in that market was that Vince kept finding ways for us to leapfrog the competition. At least once a week he'd stick his head into my cubicle and yell, "Hey! You know what would be *really* cool?" Then he'd spin out some idea that I'd present to our manufacturing partners and they would pronounce brilliant. I'd long wondered why Vince stuck around PMT, when any venture capital firm would have backed his ideas with real money and made him rich. When PMT adopted his ideas, they gave him five hundred stock options, worth, since PMT was privately held, more or less nothing.

My friend Traci said Vince was staying because he was in love with me—but then Traci is the sort of stunningly beautiful woman who regularly has guys lean out the windows of passing cars and offer to take a bullet for her, so that probably skews her judgment.

Still, I had lately decided that, against all reason, Traci was probably right. That was bad news, because I rated Vince—a fellow engineer, who loved movies nearly as much as I did—the perfect bud, but nothing more. So even though I was always happy to hang out with him as part of a group, I had to walk a fine line with Vince. Accordingly, when, having opened the envelope, he said, with a sort of goofy romantic smile, "A hundred bucks! How about if I take you out to dinner?"

I answered—

"I'll see you tomorrow night, if you're going with Alicia, Traci, and me to see *Notting Hill.*"

His face fell a bit, but sweet guy that he was, he put another kind of disappointment into his voice when he said, "*Notting Hill?* Uck. Chick flick."

"C'mon! Julia Roberts is a babe. You'll love it."

"Maybe we could have dinner fir—"

"Gotta run," I interrupted hastily. I was halfway out the door when he called, "Hey, Callie?"

Dunderhead that I am, I turned without even raising my pistol. Vince yelled, "Duck!" and then squirted me square in the face with the Super Soaker.

It's not easy managing a genius. Especially since most companies frown on using stun guns.

I went down to the end of the aisle and into the ladies' room, where I wiped my face with a paper towel and then took a deep breath. Jake Miller occupied the last cubicle on my list.

Jake was one of those sun-tanned heroes of the snowy West. If the young Clint Eastwood had been a hell of a computer programmer, he'd have been Jake Miller. Jake wasn't a brilliant mind, like Vince; but he was the high-tech equivalent of the guy you wanted in the bunker beside you when the shooting starts. He didn't exactly solve technical problems. He more like stared at them till they came out with their hands up. When we got a

2 A.M. call from a client in Singapore saying that somebody in Bogotá had figured out how to hack our main product, Jake was the guy who got everybody settled down and focused on the problem.

I'd learned a lot about management from Jake.

I'd learned a lot of other things, too.

When I was twelve, I wanted to be a cowboy. Then I wanted to go to Hollywood and make cowboy movies. Then I met Jake, and I wanted a cowboy to make me. The really embarrassing thing is that about six months earlier, shortly after Jake joined PMT, he and I had, let's say, collaborated on one of my cowboy fantasies. It lasted only a long weekend in the country, but it definitely made an impression on me. Then, Monday morning at the office, Jake had been his usual cool self, as if we'd never taken his pickup into the woods. He treated me like just another boss.

Easy for him to do.

Six months after the fact, I was still in bad shape where Jake was concerned, and I took another deep breath before I went down the aisle to his cubicle. Of course—story of my life—I'd had heart palpitations for nothing. Jake, naturally, was the only person in our group who cut out early. There was probably a damn rodeo in Butte, or something. I pinned his envelope to his corkboard. I considered writing something romantic on it, but came to my senses and settled for printing "Yee-ha" on it in small block letters. Make-a-splash Callie, that's me.

Back in my own cubicle I remembered two Hershey bars were stashed in my bottom drawer. I tried to ignore them, but they kept calling to me. It was like Edgar Allan Poe, with chocolate. Finally I practiced my magic act by making them disappear, then started work on my group's weekly progress report. Next thing I knew, it was seven o'clock and my eyes were still glued to the computer screen.

I realized I was hearing a faint scratching noise every time I blinked.

I was leaning back to put drops in my eyes when a loud bang on my cubicle wall, like somebody hitting it with a baseball bat, made me jump and squeeze almost the entire bottle square onto the bridge of my nose. I swiveled in the chair and called irritably—

*"WHAT?"*

The doorway of my cube was filled with the sort of tall, willowy form that usually fills me with painful envy. But this form belonged to Traci. It wasn't often that Traci snuck up on anyone, since she was generally accompanied by the sound of guys howling like coyotes. Traci's six-feet-one. She has the body of a very athletic professional model, high cheekbones, white-blond hair, and huge, dark blue eyes. She gets more marriage proposals ordering at McDonald's than I've had in my whole life. The fact that she's also a damn good lawyer is pretty much conclusive proof that life isn't fair. When Traci and I were kids, she was the girl my mother cited to shame me into doing better at everything. Then one day I discovered that Traci the wondergirl had become Traci the wonderwoman—and that against all odds, she and I were best friends. Which was strange, since, even after a twelve-hour day, Traci looked drop-dead gorgeous, while I just looked dead.

Traci plopped herself down in my guest chair. She has that gift of very athletic people: even her plopping has style. She studied me, and the eyedrops, briefly. I must have looked as if I'd just finished watching Old Yeller go down on the *Titanic*. I was groping for a Kleenex when she said, "I think they go in your eyes, Callie."

"Yeah, thanks. I suppose it was the gunshot that startled me."

"You thought that bang was exciting? Wait'll you hear what I can't tell you."

My eyes still felt as if I could fry eggs on them, but I managed to say, with polite interest—

"Can't tell me what?"

"Nope, I absolutely can't say a word."

"Okay. Bye."

She stayed seated. "Not a single word."

"Okay. You can't tell me. *What* can't you tell me?"

"Brilliant examining technique." She hesitated—about two seconds. "About the takeover offer from the second-largest media company in the world! Which shall remain nameless."

I sat up straight. "You're kidding."

"Right—I'm kidding. And I'd stay here kidding, except that I'm *not* leaving for New York on a red-eye tonight so tomorrow at 8 A.M. I can start *not* working on the *nonexistent* deal with the *unnamed* company, and I have to go *not* pack. And if you tell a single soul about this, they'll never find your body."

She was excited, and I began getting excited, too.

"And that's all I can say. I'll e-mail you from Manhattan." And she was on her feet and out of the cubicle in one long stride. I called after her—

"Yeah, well, have fun, Miss 'I'm-not-going-to-New-York.'"

Suddenly I felt quite low. Not only did my eyes, wrists, and back hurt, but I was envious. A takeover sounded like very small news for me: I owned a bare handful of PMT shares. Plus, I wasn't even getting a trip out of the deal. I already knew what lay ahead for *my* weekend. Saturday would consist of a meeting of the Larksdale Ladies Investment Club (where I was an honorary member), some errands, and then—with Traci out of town—dinner and a movie with Vince and Alicia Lee. Then around ten o'clock Saturday night I'd convince myself I had some work that desperately needed doing, and I'd return to the office. Yuck.

It turned out I was right about all that.

But what I didn't know was this: that day marked the last boring weekend anybody would have in Larksdale for a very long time.

CHAPTER TWO

# The 20th Century's Last Boring Weekend

Saturday morning, after an early morning half-awake stumble around Lake Larksdale for my weekly exercise, I picked up Aunt Dolly at her home and drove her to the regular meeting of the Larksdale Ladies Investment Club.

Aunt Dolly wasn't supposed to know, but she was the main reason I had returned to Larksdale after getting my MBA. The Ladies had arranged it; they were worried about her health and thought she needed family near her. The job had been a blessing: nobody was hiring aerospace engineers (my undergraduate degree), and I wanted Internet experience (and money!) while I prepared to follow my big dream: moving to Hollywood and becoming a film producer. Plus—not to get corny on you—Aunt Dolly was my only close surviving family, and I had always liked being around her. And it was fun being her secret protector.

Especially since the job consisted mostly of letting her take me out to dinner every Sunday.

Above all, Dolly was a sweetie: For all her problems, she still knew how to laugh at things—including herself.

Now, of all the Ladies in the club, only Martha Crittenden owns a home suitable for someone rich—but then, according to Aunt Dolly, Martha *always* lived that way, even before the Ladies hit it big. Twenty years ago Martha had been the wife of Larksdale's most prominent physician. In fact, it was old Doc Crittenden's running off with a former Miss Lutefisk, aged twenty-four, that had made Martha mad enough to join in the Investment Club.

Martha's housekeeper had Saturdays off. My 10 A.M. sharp knock on her door was answered by Deborah Cohen.

Deborah was the "mostly" in the original Mostly Methodist Club, from which the Larksdale Ladies Investment Club was born. She had lived an interesting life, beginning with joining the Marines long ago, then helping the Ladies to glory, and continuing through five years of the high life in New York. Now divorced and back in Larksdale, she was raising her teenage son alone. Deborah wasn't shy about anything. In fact, she and I had become pretty good friends because we both had a habit of speaking our minds—sometimes a little too hastily.

"Holy Cripes!" she said, pulling Aunt Dolly and me in the door. "The sun's shining, and we're in here?" She was still looking past us, at the hot Midwest day outside. Then she shook her head and said, "Let's go see if anybody still has a pulse."

I followed her past several vases of fresh-cut flowers from Martha's amazing gardens, and lots of museum-grade furniture. The living room was cool and dim, with the curtains drawn. Only four of the original Ladies were present. Martha (who always seemed very daunting to me) gave me a regal nod and beckoned Aunt Dolly to join her and Sophia Green. Sophia, a slender blond woman a little over forty, stepped solicitously close to Aunt Dolly, who, though only ten years older, was badly overweight and moving very slowly. Gladys Vaniman, a tiny creature of about seventy, looked up from a newspaper, gave me a kind smile from behind oversize glasses, and resumed reading. Not wanting to interrupt them, I turned back to Deborah, who asked me what was new.

As had become my habit since moving back to Larksdale, I answered by talking about somebody else's life—

"Well . . . Traci won't be here because she's in New York."

"New York, huh?" She ran a hand through her mane of jet-black curls, which held a few streaks of gray. "New York was always *way* too stressed for me. They climb gym walls for exercise. It's a miracle *everybody* there isn't climbing the walls. Big surprise: Spiderman's the top New York hero. He spends *all day* climbing the walls. In fact . . ."

Martha signaled that the meeting was about to start, so Deborah excused herself and quickly loaded a plate at the buffet table (we both liked food, but she never seemed to show it, confound her). Then she slipped quietly into a chair along with the rest of the Ladies. I sat next to Aunt Dolly.

We began with a rather dull summary of old news.

I won't repeat it here, mostly because I wasn't listening; I was holding on for the new business topic, when I could hit the Ladies with my hot rumor. But no sooner had Martha called for new business than Sophia Green announced, "Friday afternoon our takeover talks with NDN suddenly heated up."

So much for my hot tip.

I was behind the curve and annoyed at having missed the obvious: If Traci, a junior attorney, had known the details, so would Sophia, PMT's general counsel. Sophia gave us the full scoop. NDN—National Digital Network—had first contacted PMT on Monday; but until Friday PMT execs had assumed the high-powered New Yorkers were merely fishing. Only late Friday afternoon had NDN signaled that a bid might be coming. Still, neither Sophia nor Milt, her husband and PMT's CEO, believed there would be an offer. They'd sent our CFO and Traci to field NDN's questions. Only if the deal got real would Milt himself head to New York.

Martha turned to Gladys. "Well? What do we know about this NDN?"

"NDN?" Gladys summarized, in her best former librarian tone, "Price-to-earning ratio pushing 90-to-1. Supposed to be the perfect company for the new digital age. After buying that media conglomerate, Golden West Holdings, they own every kind of content and have pipelines into more homes than any other company in America. They plan to make a fortune sending their own content down their own pipelines." She paused. "So far, though, they're hardly making expenses."

Deborah snorted. "That part, I'll believe."

Gladys shrugged. "Their theory is that, in a few years, your computer and TV will be the same thing, and you'll be able to download anything you want—movies, sports, music, you name it. *If* you're willing to pay a fat fee to companies like NDN."

"Fat fee?" Deborah shook her head. "Fat chance."

Knowing Deborah was attacking the general business idea, and not her personally, Gladys answered placidly, "If it happens, NDN might start minting money. Enough to justify a stock price that may be triple what it is today."

Despite Gladys's quiet tone, she was clearly excited. In fact, all the Ladies were stirring like young plants in a spring breeze. I looked around the room and suddenly wondered: Were the

Ladies *bored* with their quiet, prosperous lives? Some kind of wind was blowing, that was for sure. Then, for the first time in months, Martha actually looked my way and asked, "And, on the hardware side, this would require . . . ?"

I was so startled that she had addressed me, and that she had remembered what it was that I did at PMT, I needed ten seconds to collect my thoughts. I stumbled a little, then said—

"At least three things: that they can drop the cost of a high-def TV from $4,000 to about $600, including a digital tuner; that the average household will pay over $100 a month for content plus some sort of cable or satellite digital high-def signal; and that those high-def signals are available everywhere in the country, not just in New York and L.A. and such."

"And PMT technology could help make it happen?"

"Yep. We're not critical, but we could help."

"So, overall, the chance of that . . . HDTV? . . . happening is?"

"Long-term, nearly certain. In the next few years? Probably zero."

I had just amazed myself, because—despite my tendency to hem and haw—I'd just said exactly what I thought, and in a very few words.

Unfortunately, I'd also squashed the enthusiasm. I knew it because Deborah said, "Oy."

This was Deborah's all-purpose note of rejection and protest, and she managed to get almost any kind of meaning into it, as needed.

"Point taken," Martha told Deborah.

For two people so very different, they seemed to understand each other very well. Martha shifted in her chair and told the room as a whole, "Unless I hear objections, I'll assume we are, for now, opposed to the sale of the company?" Martha rarely heard objections to anything, and the vote was unanimous. We turned quietly to Gladys's report on our week's mail.

Even in the Internet age, the Ladies received quite a few snail-mail business offers and requests for help. Many were flaky, crooked, or both, but the Ladies considered them all. The mail arrived at a downtown office building they owned; once a week Gladys would stop by, sort through the stack, and bring anything that looked like non-junk to the Saturday meeting. The Ladies' mail always meant a twenty-minute discussion. I fidgeted and tried to ignore the homemade sticky buns cooling on the buffet table.

Half an hour later the meeting broke up. Aunt Dolly was staying to chat and would get a ride home from Sophia. I promised I'd see her for Sunday dinner and, sticky bun in hand, sped out the door to make the bargain matinee of *Star Wars: Episode I—The Phantom Menace.*

Not a bad flick, but it reinforced the unfortunate idea that all villains make weird breathing noises through full-face black masks.

If only life were that simple.

# CHAPTER THREE

# My Wild Night Out

About six-thirty I drove downtown to meet Vince and Alicia Lee.

Once a Ph.D. student in Victorian Lit., Alicia had realized that blacksmiths enjoyed better job prospects than aspiring English professors. So she quit the U.M., and used the $6,000 creative writing fellowship she'd won a few years earlier (and tucked away) to buy a bankrupt doughnut shop. She renamed it "Lord of the Rings" and sold the lightest, fluffiest doughnuts anybody had ever tasted. Within a month she was making as much money as the average junior professor, and she kept building from there. She doubled the size of LOTR, then opened an upscale, mostly-vegetarian restaurant called Bread and Roses.

That's where Vince and I were dining.

Bread and Roses was a little too fancy, a little too modern, and a lot too pricey for local tastes. In California it would have triumphed; in Larksdale, it was a struggle. So Vince and I (and

Traci, when she was in town) made a point of dining there whenever we had bonus money to blow.

Alicia wasn't just a great cook with a vast fund of literary lore; she was also the kindest, most forgiving human being I'd ever known. Whenever I needed an impossible standard of kindness to measure myself against, Alicia was perfect.

Good as the food was, Vince and I were two of only six people eating there that night. Alicia was doing a wonderful job of helping guests without smothering them, but, as usual, most appeared mystified by the smallish portions and the Afro-Asian-Caribbean veggies. A little before nine, when the last guests left, we helped her close up shop and then the three of us headed to the movie.

Larksdale has two wonderful classic theaters, the Rialto and the Palace. The Rialto's neon front glows like a giant, glorious Wurlitzer, but the Palace has the better seats and sound. We picked the Rialto, and *Notting Hill*. The movie was fun; but it gave me the gnawing feeling I should have tried harder to live my Hollywood dreams. After my parents died, the neon-bright Rialto had been my weekend refuge; but I studied math and science because that's what my dad would have wanted. That night, in the dark, I told myself I would find a way to make him proud *and* make movies.

By ten-thirty we were back out on the cooling street, walking toward the Larksdale *Herald* building. The really hip couples were lining up for the late show. No; that's not right. The *really* hip couples had gone into the Twin Cities for the evening.

At least we had a plan.

Across the street from the *Herald* stood Dagmar's Danish Scoops ("The *Herald* Gives You the News. We Give You the Scoop!"). I have no idea what ice cream tastes like in Denmark, but I suppose a country where everything's generally frozen all the time would have a fair leg up on the competition. Certainly Dagmar, who'd been at the same spot since 1946, knew his business. Even at 11 P.M. the crowd pushing against his takeout window looked like rush hour at a good-sized commuter train station.

During our ten minutes waiting in line, Vince changed his mind about his order at least seventeen times. I, on the other hand, was constant as the North Star. By the time we finally reached the window, maybe fifty people had already passed us carrying scoops the size of softballs, in handmade waffle cones. A single Dagmar was enough for any sane person. But my theory about ice cream is: Life's short. Order two scoops. I got caramel pecan, and chocolate chocolate chip.

A double Dagmar's is sure to brighten anyone's mood; and I was feeling the boost of my renewed Hollywood promise. As we cleared the crowd I said expansively—

"Look at them." I gestured with my waffle cone. "They're happy just to walk around eating ice cream. Is that the spirit that made America great?"

"Eat your ice cream, Callie."

We slurped on our cones and walked in silence a while. We were just tossing away our napkins when Vince, a goofy romantic gleam in his eye, said to the empty space between Alicia and me, "Take you clubbing in Minneapolis."

Alicia and I exchanged looks, and suddenly were in a race to bow out first.

"*I'd* better get back to the restaurant."

"*I* want to get a jump on Monday."

It was a tie, which took the pressure off, so then of course we both felt instantaneously sorry, and both got super-gracious.

Alicia, the softie, gave in, but said she'd have to get back early. Vince looked at me, then sighed. He told Alicia, "That's okay. I won't keep you from the restaurant. Maybe I'll go home and invent something, instead."

I patted his arm. "The people of PMT thank you. Your country thanks you."

I was betting he'd go home and watch a *Farscape* video. I parted from my friends and headed back to the office. It was my comfortable old pattern, but that night it battered my good mood.

No street in Larksdale seemed to lead to Hollywood.

Which shows what I knew.

# CHAPTER FOUR

## Life Heats Up

Monday morning, Traci sent me an e-mail:

*Having a wonderful time. Wish you were a major share-holder.—T.*

Twenty-four hours later nobody in Larksdale was interested in witty e-mails. They were too busy going bananas—and I was there when the first peel hit the sidewalk.

More precisely, I was sitting in Lord of the Rings at 6:10 A.M. Tuesday morning. At that hour in June in Minnesota, the sun is up and shining, which is more than I could say for myself. As usual at that hour on a workday, I was using both hands and most of my strength to get the coffee cup to my lips. I'd already eaten half of one of Alicia's lighter-than-air glazed doughnuts, but the sugar and caffeine had barely reached my bloodstream when a bloodcurdling "Yee-ha!" from the direction of the glass front door interrupted my sugary serenity. I looked up and in strode Tom Deits.

Tom was about fifty. He was a senior purchasing manager at PMT, a genial man with a beefy frame and a bulldog face who looked a lot gruffer than he was; he always reminded me of a rough forties police detective. Now, however, he was looking far too jolly to be any kind of detective. In fact, he looked almost giddily excited. Larksdale people usually wait until at least seven-thirty or so before yelling yee-ha in public, but Tom yee-ha-ed again, even louder, if possible. He was only halfway to the counter when he called out, "Hey! Did you guys *see* these?"

He was waving overhead the morning editions of the *Herald* (which had just hit the streets), and the *New York Times* (which I doubt he'd ever bought before). He slapped them both down on the long counter, and those of us nearest to him started to crowd around. The *Times* business section had a small article, and the *Herald* a huge special edition, both entitled NDN BIDS TO BUY PMT SOFTWARE. The two headlines were identical except that the *Herald*'s used three exclamation points, while the *Times* wouldn't use three exclamation points if aliens landed and started selling lutefisk on Madison Avenue.

Suddenly, along with the smell of coffee and hot fresh doughnuts, there was plenty of YEE-HA!!! in the air. Guys were exchanging so many palm slaps and high fives it looked like the sidelines of a U.M. football game with us up by twenty-four points. Alicia asked quietly, "What does it mean?" She asked it first generally, and then to me in particular. I didn't answer her until I had a chance to read, over a bunch of other people's shoulders, the basics of the deal. Then I couldn't decide whether I was delighted or miserable.

NDN was paying a *huge* price in stock for PMT—and NDN stock was predicted to triple in the coming year.

I took Alicia aside, and told her—

"As nearly as I can tell, it means anybody who's been at PMT at least ten years, at even a mid-level job, can pretty well count on a million-dollar buyout."

"That's a lot of people," she said slowly, amazed. Alicia, who is, doughnut jokes aside, the sweetest person I know, sounded just a little bit envious. I felt kind of rotten replying—

"I'm guessing, of course, but it looks to me like Larksdale's adding about five hundred millionaires, plus maybe another seven hundred half-a-millionaires."

In a town of under twenty-two thousand people, that was a lot of millionaires. If I had the numbers right, we were about to become the Martha's Vineyard of the Midwest. By the time I finished this explanation, I'd decided on at least part of how I felt. I knew I could drop the idea I was delighted. Not because I was such a spiritual, evolved person that money meant nothing to me. To put it simply, I hadn't been on the job long enough to have any money coming. Oh, my few stock options, plus the shares I'd been buying on the company stock purchase plan, might mean I'd be in line for, say, a $10,000 payday—but that wouldn't even put much of a dent in my student loans.

Let alone get me to Hollywood in style.

The more I thought about it, the lousier I felt.

So maybe it was just me, but it seemed that in the five minutes or so since Tom's announcement, the doughnut shop gang had been divided into winners and losers; broad, genuine grins and tight-lipped little smiles of congratulation. Alicia had gone back behind the counter, to help Luís box up doughnuts for the grinning people who were buying extras to take to the office to celebrate the news. The whole focus of the place had switched to the cash register, and I was left off by myself.

So the Ladies had been wrong on one point: The takeover was for real.

I was wondering if they might have been wrong about something else: how brilliant a business National Digital Network really was. In a few minutes, the people with good news were hurrying for the door with their fat boxes of doughnuts. The sun was now blazing, and you could tell the day was going to be a scorcher.

Alicia walked over to me, refilled my cup, and sighed. She said glumly, "You know what, Callie? This feels like the high school prom all over again."

I knew exactly what she meant.

I hadn't had a date for that party, either.

CHAPTER FIVE

# Like the Doughnut Shop, Only Worse

By the time I got to PMT, the immediate shock was wearing off, and I was starting to feel really anxious. The feeling only worsened as I reached the third floor and saw the social split everywhere. I swung past executive territory and heard, from beyond one open office door, an older guy's voice saying, incredulously, over and over, "Six million dollars . . . six *million* dollars . . . six million *dollars* . . ."

I'd like to think he was talking to someone, but I couldn't guarantee it.

I figured it was time to check in with Floyd and see where we stood. But when I reached him, he wore a stunned expression best suited to a particularly slow-witted steer who'd recently been whacked over the head with a baseball bat. Being Floyd, though, he rallied as I appeared in the doorway and after a moment said, "Don't know how much work we're going to get done today."

I sat across from him. "Not much, I suppose."

Floyd nodded and sat up straighter. "Maybe we should move up salary reviews to this afternoon?"

I didn't think anybody would be terribly interested in whether they were getting six or eight percent raises when some New York company was flying over the building dumping money out of a helicopter, but before I could speak something strange happened: The loudspeakers came on with a godlike electronic click. The loudspeakers were used only to announce things like bomb threats and fires in the building. We'd never had a bomb threat, and the only fire we'd ever had was when a couple of guys in accounting tried to make s'mores over a space heater, and a burning marshmallow dropped onto the package full of other marshmallows. So when the speakers clicked on, the whole floor came alert like prairie dogs at hawk time.

But nothing was on fire except our stock price.

After a second a folksy voice said neatly, "Hey, everybody. This is George Harris, your director of Corporate Communications. We have a message from Milt, who's been in New York since seven this morning. Eh—I guess I'll read it." The disembodied voice cleared its throat, and went on, "At ten forty-five A.M. this morning, National Digital Network Corporation issued a revised offer for the shares of PMT Software. The current offer is for eighty-six dollars a share. The board of directors of PMT Software will meet at seven P.M. Thursday evening and present its recommendations at an employee-shareholder meeting in the PMT Auditorium, eight P.M. next Wednesday, June 12."

Eighty-six dollars was twelve dollars more than what the newspapers quoted.

Floyd, looking startled, asked me, "What the *heck?*"

I hadn't slept through *every* class in biz school. I said—

"There must be another buyer threatening to come after us. It's a takeout bid."

I was thinking people who threw around that kind of dough could take me out anytime, but figured it probably wasn't the sort of crack Floyd would appreciate, especially since nobody in his group, except Floyd himself, had been with PMT long enough for a big payday. So I just rose from my chair and said, in my best Midwest fashion—

"Well, that's all fine, but I still work for a living. I'll be at my desk. Let me know what you want to do about the reviews. And, Floyd—try not to worry, eh?"

Then I went back to my cubicle, to worry.

I took the long way back. The last thing I wanted to hear was some chucklehead saying over and over, "Eight million dollars . . . eight *million* dollars . . . eight million *dol* . . ."

CHAPTER SIX

# Fantasy Island, Minnesota

While Milt and PMT's directors were analyzing NDN's offer, the Ladies were doing the same—and they were ready to discuss it a good five days earlier. I won't recap the whole long, polite, frustrating Saturday morning discussion, but here was the basic issue: Would it be smart to swap ownership of safe, profitable PMT, for a bunch of shares in maybe the world's most glamorous stock? In plain English: Did they want NDN to buy PMT?

At first glance, the question was a no-brainer.

NDN was one of the hottest stocks of the red-hot Internet boom. You might remember the whole business case for the Internet boom was a land-grab in cyberspace: Companies didn't have to make money, they had to grab market share. With twenty million subscribers, NDN was the hands-down winner. Its stock had been doubling, splitting, and doubling again for so many years, analysts never tired of announcing that every dollar invested in the company at startup in 1990 would have grown to $1,400 by the summer of '99.

There was just one catch.

NDN had never made a dime.

All that incredible jump in the stock price was, as Gladys said, investors betting that *some* day NDN's huge subscriber base would lead to huge profits. But so far the profits were just around the corner, and had been, for the last eight years. Sure, the studio side sometimes posted spectacular years; a hit movie, especially with product tie-ins, could bring a couple of hundred million bucks to the bottom line, and videotapes and DVDs had opened up huge new revenue streams. The real problem was the Internet side. It had created most of the stock price—but had always lost money hand-over-fist.

To cynics, NDN was like the old business joke about the two partners who meet on the street: "Joe, I've got a great business idea! We'll sell five-dollar bills for two bucks apiece and we'll build a giant business overnight." "Are you *crazy*? We'll lose three dollars on every sale." "Sure—but we'll make it up on volume!"

So far, NDN was losing money on every subscriber, but the smartest analysts on Wall Street were saying it would soon be making it up in volume and that, accordingly, the stock would keep soaring. And who were the Ladies to contradict the smartest guys on Wall Street?

Well, they were the Ladies.

They contradicted anybody they felt like contradicting.

That Saturday morning was one of those rare summer days that are sunny and warm, but not muggy. The French doors to Martha's garden were all thrown open, and the scent of roses filled the big room. The setting was garden party, but the meeting was pure business. The Ladies were taking this possible buyout very seriously, not only because their own money was on the line, but because after nearly two decades of calling the shots (very genteelly, of course) in Larksdale, they basically assumed that, as they went, so went the town. So they wanted to be very certain they made the right decision—not just for themselves, but for all of Larksdale.

The twenty-minute presentation the Ladies heard, written and delivered by Sophia and Traci, strongly opposed a sale. They admitted to the Ladies that NDN's price was more than generous; it was rich. They also acknowledged that most analysts rated NDN an unstoppable juggernaut, with first-rate management and technology. But Traci, speaking at the very end, fiercely emphasized one point: NDN was offering us *restricted* shares. That meant they could not be resold for eighteen months. That wasn't automatically a fatal flaw: The stock could be used as collateral on loans during that period. But it *did* mean risk: If NDN tanked anytime before the end of the eighteen months, we'd be taking a ride on a plunging elevator.

Naturally, that eighteen-month clinker inspired most of the debate.

To my amazement, my usually easygoing aunt Dolly pushed hardest for a sale.

Red-faced, and sounding so short of breath I began to worry for her, she kept insisting this was too good an opportunity to pass up. The other Ladies were gentle with her, of course; but they clung to the argument, put most forcefully by Deborah, that the Internet boom might go on, or it might collapse—and they couldn't bet everything on a "might."

The usual rule with the Ladies was even the strongest debates ended in consensus.

Their rule was being broken.

At noon—almost exactly two hours after the meeting had started—Martha thanked Dolly for her comments (interrupting her to do so, which was *not* like Martha, at all), and then asked for a motion to vote.

Sophia said, "I think the motion goes as follows: One, that before discussion opens Wednesday night, we ask for ten minutes to present our views to the shareholders. Two: That we use those ten minutes to say we believe Internet and media stocks are near, or at, the peak of a bubble market, and grossly overpriced, and that, accordingly, we oppose a sale of PMT to NDN. Three: That we vote against any resolution urging the sale. And Four: That, if the vote should somehow go against us"—Sophia's tone suggested how unlikely that was—"we meet next Saturday to discuss other forms of opposition, including legal action."

They adopted the motion by show of hands, with only Aunt Dolly opposing. The room's overall tone, formerly of frustration at Aunt Dolly for breaking ranks, lightened the minute they had voted, and they made what I'd call a genteel rush for the snack table.

Aunt Dolly was hastily downing a glass of iced tea; I decided it was better manners to leave her alone awhile. So I caught Traci's arm as she was zipping toward the food and said—

"Hey! I thought you were hot for a sale. What's up with that?"

She didn't smile. "I got caught up in the thrill of deal-making. It could have happened to anyone. Once I got home, I realized we'd be nuts to chase all that fast, risky money. It would be . . . well, it would be wrong."

I thought about citing John Wesley's famous Sermon 50 (where he talks about how you have to *make* money before you can give it away, one of the few sermons I'd studied with interest in my Methodist Youth Group days), but thought the better of it. Traci might look as if she'd just stepped off the runway; but at heart she was 100 percent small-town girl, a real Lady-in-training. Besides, it would have been off-point. She wasn't down for any more of a payday than I was.

Deborah, toting her usual heaping plate of food, approached us. On an impulse I asked—

"What do you think?"

"We've run this town a long time. Maybe too long."

I was getting more confused by the minute. "I thought you were *against* the sale!"

She smiled. "All I mean is, maybe we've forgotten that other people might prefer the idea of *their* being on top."

Knowing how much stock the Ladies controlled—and how much Larksdale owed them—I shook my head. "Who could stand up to you? You're Olympians!"

"Yeah. I just hope we're not the Jamaican bobsled team."

Aunt Dolly joined us. Her color had returned to normal, but I still suggested it might be time to get her home, and she didn't argue.

As we left, the Ladies mostly seemed relaxed. And why not?

Over the last fifteen years their record was about five-thousand-and-oh.

As I drove Aunt Dolly home she was looking much better, but I was still worried. I looked over at her in the passenger seat and asked—

"Are you okay?"

"I'm fine. The heat just got to me."

"I meant . . . well, you weren't pushing for a sale because it would be easier to estate-plan with publicly traded stock, or anything?"

She gave me her old, wide smile. "You kidding, kid? I'm just looking for a quick chance to triple my money. I want to buy a yacht and sail to Tahiti." She wiggled her eyebrows. "Whaddya say? Want to come along and be pirates with me?"

If she was conning me, I decided, she was awfully good at it.

After dropping her off, I returned to a nearly deserted PMT, where I spent the rest of the day writing code and wishing I were writing a screenplay. I didn't give the Ladies a thought, though if there'd been a betting line on them, and I'd been a gambler, I would have bet my shirt they were going to win in a walk.

At eight that night Vince, Traci, and I drove to our customary weekend dinner at Bread and Roses. Traffic on Main Street was heavy, but I put that down to the start of summer weather. Then, a block from the restaurant, I realized *every* parking space was taken. We swung onto a side street and still had to drive a block and a half to find a spot—which was unprecedented. Things got truly bizarre, though, as we walked back to Main. We were still almost a block from the restaurant when Vince pointed and exclaimed, "Hey, look!"

A crowd was spilling out of Bread and Roses and filling the sidewalk.

I didn't quite believe it; seeing it was like hearing scalpers were getting $1,000-a-ticket for the chicken-judging finals at the State Fair.

Soon, though, we were pushing through the masses.

Actually, *pushing* isn't quite the right word. With Traci along, the guys pretty much parted like the Red Sea, except I doubt the Red Sea ever backed over its dates to get out of the way of the advancing Israelites, or stared in rapt delight as they passed. Traci took this as perfectly normal. She wasn't vain—but she *did* have a few unexamined assumptions about how the world worked. Just then, I didn't mind. I was too curious to know what Alicia was giving away to draw this kind of mob.

At the front of the line, behind a maître d's stand I had never seen her use before, stood a very frazzled-looking Alicia, polite as ever. She waited until we were very close, then whispered, "Hi, guys. I tried to save your table, but a couple of people got sort of nasty, so I gave it to them. If I give you cuts, there'll be trouble, but I can seat you in about an hour, or"—her voice dropped even lower—"I can give you the chef's table back in the kitchen. It's noisy and crowded, but the food's the best, and the hottest."

Vince was scratching his head, looking mystified, and I blurted, "What the heck happened? Is the Larksdale Society of Soon-to-Be Millionaires meeting at Bread and Roses?"

"Oh, Callie." Alicia gazed at me with pity. "Where have you been? Everybody thinks they're *already* a millionaire."

The three of us didn't have to consult; we made our apologies and told Alicia we'd see her later. As nonmembers of the Larksdale Zillionaires' Club, we'd spend our now-meager paychecks elsewhere with the rest of the peasants.

I didn't care. I wasn't thinking about food any longer. For me, that multitude of free-spending diners meant one thing.

The Ladies were going to lose the vote.

## CHAPTER SEVEN

# Domestic Issues

The trouble caused by NDN really started precisely ninety minutes after PMT's CEO, Milt Green, who was also Sophia's husband, got off the red-eye from New York. That was the night of the day the deal had been announced; it was also four days before Sophia's presentation to the Ladies.

Milt had gone to the Big Apple (his old hometown) the previous Monday morning with an open mind. He had grilled NDN executives on their plans. Once he saw they were serious, he had negotiated fiercely for a better deal. He used rumors that Microsoft was thinking of bidding for PMT to get NDN to raise its offer to the takeout level. He figured he'd made Larksdale—where he'd gotten married and raised his kids—around $120 million dollars just by playing hardball.

He had come home feeling heroic, and ready to be rewarded. Playing in the big leagues again had rejuvenated him. He'd opened the door bubbling with plans for where he and Sophia, with NDN's resources behind them, could take PMT—and there she stood, like a stone wall.

Sophia, who was usually considerate, started talking even before he'd put down his bags. Even before that, he'd seen the set, slightly flushed look she got before an argument. For a couple married almost twenty years, they fought very little—but still, he knew *that* look. He'd flinched even before she said, "The kids are staying with friends tonight."

"Oh, yes?"

"I think we need to talk about the deal."

Milt had had a long trip and a tough negotiation. He disliked travel, generally, and had missed Sophia very much. His high spirits were fragile. Now, fighting down fatigue, he asked through compressed lips, "Didn't you get my phone message?"

"I got it."

"Weren't you pleased?"

Sophia said nothing.

"I got us another $120 million, all in."

Silence.

"Well?"

"Well. All you really did, Milt, was railroad us into taking an offer nobody could refuse. Without waiting to get any input from your directors, the Ladies, or me."

Milt finally let the bags drop. They hit the ground with an undramatic, leathery squish. "Sophia! It's a fortune for everyone. And we'll be joining an absolute powerhouse company!" Milt took a deep breath. "I checked it out. NDN runs like GE: Operating divisions have to make their numbers, but otherwise they're completely independent. They—"

"Did you happen to *notice*, in your due diligence," Sophia was impatient, and angry because she didn't know where her patience had gone, "that NDN's bought *eight* software companies in the last three years? And that today *none* of them still exists?" She put up a hand for silence. "They've *all* been folded into NDN's ongoing operations, and they've all been *shut down*."

"Those 'companies' were all dinky little start-ups. PMT will be an *operating division*. No way they'll close it down."

"Is that in writing?"

"Well . . . not yet." Milt tried to move closer to her.

She moved away even faster. "That's what I thought."

For a frozen moment they simply stared at each other.

Sophia's anger suddenly turned inward. How on earth could she have let Milt run off to negotiate without input from her and the Ladies? Yes, it had been reasonable to think he would view things exactly as she did, he always had, on everything that mattered. But she'd been a lawyer for twenty years; she was trained to nail down every point to a certainty. It was her mistake not to have gone with him.

It would have been much nicer to believe Milt deserved all the blame.

Milt, meanwhile, had stiffened. He said coldly, "I did what I considered was my duty to the shareholders."

"Remind me what dinner at Lutèce has to do with the future of Larksdale?"

Milt was surprised by this unfairness—especially since his phone message had clearly explained he would accept that invitation in order to bond with PMT's future owners. He returned to the original quarrel. "I can't believe you're bringing this up now. If you had issues, why didn't you raise them when I was in New York, and could do something about them, instead of sandbagging me now?"

"Well, why didn't you treat me with some respect, instead of acting as if you had all the damned answers?"

Alarmed that this was becoming more than a business dispute, Milt tried to rein it in. "I know you've studied the issue. But so have I. If we differ, I guess we just differ."

"Yeah. I guess we do."

It was an awfully cold cease-fire.

Sophia slept little that night. In the early hours she began to see how betrayed Milt felt, but that didn't change how she saw the deal. For the first time in their lives, they were on opposite sides of something crucial, and she could not cross over just to oblige him, or even to admit she was sorry.

She only hoped they would fight fair.

In the morning she tried to apologize for having attacked him on arrival; but when Milt asked if that meant she would support the deal, she shook her head. He responded with wordless fury, storming away, showering and dressing in silence, and leaving by slamming the front door. Now the ground beneath Sophia's feet felt like quicksand. How could one mistake have landed her in such chaos?

Nothing improved over the rest of the week.

On Thursday, Sophia, claiming she didn't want to spread a miserable summer cold she'd caught, moved to the guest bedroom. By Tuesday she'd stopped sneezing, but she did not move back. Lying in bed alone Saturday night, she realized PMT Software was more than a company. For her, and for the Ladies, it had been the focus of their lives for a decade and a half. She'd always read that being defined by your career was primarily a guy problem.

Showed what magazines knew about anything.

CHAPTER EIGHT

# The Ladies Get Swamped

The Wednesday night meeting started promptly at 8 P.M. The presentations ended at 8:45; the discussion at 9:05, and the yelling at 9:20.

It was pretty much the Ladies' Waterloo. I'm not saying it was a "pride goeth before a fall" situation, but they were awfully confident, going in, that they were going to win. Not only did they own the largest block of stock, but since they saved PMT back in the late eighties, they'd been very good to Larksdale. I think they really believed Larksdale was going to return the favor.

Unfortunately, most Larksdaleans thought any deal that put a lot of dough in their own pockets was too good to pass up.

That night I worked at my desk until 7:25, because Traci said she wouldn't save my seat past 7:30. I found her in the front row. She looked surprisingly tense, almost angry. Now, technically, the vote was merely a recommendation. Each shareholder could still vote his or her proxies exactly as he or she saw fit. But for the Ladies, the "recommendation" would be a real test of which way the wind was blowing . . . and would, by default, be proof of their status in Larksdale. The pressure definitely lay heavily upon them as they sat, neatly but not expensively dressed, up on the stage next to Milt and the PMT board of directors. Still, as I said, they appeared cool and confident.

The audience, though, had the vibrant energy of a tough English soccer crowd: They didn't just *smell* victory; they *demanded* it.

Things started slipping out of control shortly after the Ladies' presentation. Stan Farthingale, PMT's hulking, bald-headed COO, gave the board's forceful but fair answer to the Ladies' presentation. That was okay—but as little Gladys opened her mouth to respond, some guy I didn't know stood up in the audience and shouted that the Ladies were a bunch of rich—let's say *biddies*—who didn't want anybody else to have as much money as they did. Gladys stood there looking shocked; then Deborah stepped past her, took the microphone, and made a reply which was, more or less, an invitation to step outside.

That brought a new liveliness to the evening, indeed.

Traci, who'd been sunk in gloom, now seemed within a breath of leaping up onto the stage to join the fray. Deborah was more than capable of holding her own, but the argument quickly became a three, then a four-, five-, and six-way yelling match. People piled into the argument, and they weren't merely opinionated—they were furious.

At its worst, the shouting match involved fewer than a dozen people out of about two thousand in the auditorium. And, to be sure, other people in the audience were shouting for the hecklers to sit down—but, unfortunately, that only boosted the chaos. Yet until the rumpus started, I would have said not a single person in Larksdale disliked the Ladies.

Milt kept trying to restore order. He's a fairly big guy, with a lot of presence, but they simply ignored him. Fortunately, it's pretty hard to win an argument with the guy who controls the technology. He must have hand-signaled the technicians, because after another minute or so of general shouting, his voice boomed over the sound system twice as loudly as before, saying, "I MEAN IT! IF PEOPLE DON'T SETTLE DOWN *RIGHT NOW*, I'M DECLARING THIS MEETING OVER AND HAVING THE ROOM CLEARED."

About the third time he repeated that, the fight began dying out.

Deborah, still looking tough, set the wireless mike down and returned to her seat. The storm was over, and young people from Corporate Services quickly started down the aisles distributing ballots. For a software company, we were awfully low-tech about voting. The ballots had to be hand-counted by volunteers from Accounting, so it was after eleven before Milt stepped back up to the podium.

"The vote on the Advisory Resolution is as follows—" The room fell absolutely silent. "In favor: fifteen hundred, fifty-eight." Huge cheers erupted. I could barely hear him say, "Opposed: three hundred, sixty-six. Marked 'Abstain' or not voting: three hundred, eight." The cheering redoubled. Milt raised his hands and pushed them out for silence. The noise died off some. "The resolution is carried. Within six days the board of directors of PMT Software will notify all shareholders in writing of its recommendation that the NDN offer be accepted. I declare this meeting closed!"

He banged the gavel; the sound system boosted it to the noise of a gunshot.

The cheering and applause exploded again. Some people were dancing in the aisles. Traci used one short, concise, unprintable word, pushed herself out of her chair, and disappeared into the crowd. I dropped the notion of following her, and looked back up to the stage, trying to catch a glimpse of the Ladies.

As a group, they seemed small and shaken—even stunned. I didn't blame them. They'd taken a thorough whupping. I moved close enough to see a few other things. Aunt Dolly did not seem nearly so pleased as I'd expected; Deborah's anger had turned to grim amusement; and Sophia was putting all her energy into glaring at her husband. Most alarmingly of all, the Ladies weren't talking to each other. As I watched, Dolly, looking even worse than she had on Saturday, headed slowly for a back exit. Milt and Sophia fled a few moments later, by opposite stage wings.

And that was it for the vote, except that at the parking lot's edge, I caught up with Deborah. Her fighting demeanor had vanished; she merely looked glum. To cheer her up, I said, "Hey! The Games are just begun!"

Deborah shook her head. "The Games are over. And it's a long walk back to Jamaica."

As last hurrahs go, it wasn't much.

But then, since it involved the Ladies, neither was it the last.

CHAPTER NINE

# Liberation Day

The day after the vote I reached the office at seven, started working, and did not turn my grumpy head from the computer screen until around 9:30, when the revelry from the hallway became impossible to ignore. It was strange: A week earlier, every bit of eccentric office behavior, from water-gun fights to Friday beer busts, had seemed evidence of our great team spirit. Now all the craziness just felt like arrogance.

It amazed me what a ruckus our newly rich colleagues (roughly about half our workforce, eight hundred people) could raise—and that Thursday morning they'd had no practice at it. I didn't want to think what it would be like in another week, when they had gotten really good at it. Actually, I saw two possibilities. If they kept going the way they were headed, the place would become as work-productive as New Orleans at Mardi Gras. If management woke up and cracked down, they'd all take their newly made fortunes and disappear—and those of us left behind would face a doubled workload with no comparable raise in pay.

I was feeling more annoyed and resentful every minute.

But it wasn't the pranks that finally drove me to the edge.

It was two guys from Accounting standing right outside my cubicle holding a loud, bragging argument about whether a BMW or a Mercedes would draw more "chicks." I pounded loudly and grimly at my keyboard until I was interrupted by Traci, minutes before noon, who appeared at my cubicle opening saying, "Get me out of here. I need a drink."

"Are you kidding? It's eleven A.M.!"

"It'll be eleven-fifteen by the time we find a bar. It'll be midnight, if you don't get a move on." Traci could be a force of nature when her blood was up. "Are you coming or not?"

"Drinking before noon? John Wesley will be spinning in his grave."

"If John Wesley isn't buying, I don't care."

"Some Methodist you are."

"In or out, Callie?"

I switched off the computer. "In," I said, picking up my purse. "Let's go."

"Wait here a minute. I'll get Vince."

*"Vince?"*

"Absolutely. I have something to say that concerns him, too."

I should have known. Traci *always* has an agenda.

Ten minutes later we were driving around in my Taurus, with the air-conditioning running full blast, looking for a place to get a midday drink. I pointed out the only two places in town that looked properly divey. I figured if we were going to debauch, we should do it right, at a real forties-film-noir-*ish* kind of bar. I was vetoed. Instead, we got on the road toward the Twin Cities and finally found a place Traci decided would serve. As we stepped inside, I said—

"Cool. A den of sin."

"It's a Hooters, Callie."

I decided not to press it. Traci was acting like a woman on a mission, so I kept quiet until we were seated. The place, for all its apparent frivolity, was efficient; we'd barely ordered when the waitress returned with our drinks. She had hardly set them down when Traci got to the point. "Look. I didn't get you guys here to drink. Or, at least, not *mostly.*" She eyed me shrewdly and demanded, "Now, right or wrong: You're always telling me Vince is a genius."

Vince, who'd been fiddling with the little umbrella in his drink, looked up sharply.

*"Trace!"* I yelped.

"Right or wrong?"

"Well . . . right," I said reluctantly, staring at my margarita. What did she care if she embarrassed me to no end? I could feel Vince staring at me, and thought, *I should have ordered tomato juice. Then it would have matched my cheeks. . . .*

Traci kept talking: "Okay. Once the NDN transition is in full swing, the first big question they'll ask you is, 'Which personnel do we most need to keep?' You tell them the first guy they need to *dump* is Vince, because he's a no-talent *and* a lot of trouble. *But,* you warn them, they should do it carefully because he's just the kind of troublemaker to sue their pants off. Then you mention, casually, that I'm his friend and just the sort to help file the lawsuit. So while they're at it, they'd better fire me."

"So, you want the severance package?" I asked, baffled. This hardly sounded Traci-like. "What for? A year on the Riviera?"

"I want the severance package so we can underwrite Vince until he gets his next genius idea. Then we start our own company and tell the nice folks at NDN to go climb a big, tall tree."

"That's it? That's why you asked us here?"

"You bet." Traci was undauntable. "Whaddya think?"

"What do *I* think? I think NDN's going to look over your record going back to law school and make you a big, fat offer to stay on. Which, frankly, is probably a fairly smart idea."

Traci shook her head energetically. "Even saying you're right, what are they going to offer me to stay on? Go wild, and say a fifty-thousand-a-year raise. Honey, a bunch of suckers just ponied up one *billion* dollars to back a system to let people order groceries over the Internet! You're telling me Vince can't come up with a smarter idea than *that*?"

Now I did the head-shaking. "It takes more than an idea—"

"Oh, don't be a wimp." She slapped the table, and I remembered why she'd been such an unstoppable athlete; Traci had enough self-confidence to power a nuclear submarine. "Bill Gates was nineteen when he dropped out of Harvard after one term and started Microsoft. His favorite sport is bouncing on a trampoline. You think we're not as smart as him? At least I *graduated* from Harvard."

I noticed Vince was suddenly looking at Traci very strangely. He'd finally noticed she was gorgeous. That was classic Vince: spends half his time around one of the most beautiful women on the planet, and only notices her after he finds out she's Ivy League. It was like noticing the Taj Mahal because it had a great snack bar. If she'd said she'd majored in physics, I think he would have proposed on the spot.

Vince aside, Traci certainly had a point. Every ex-used-car

salesman was launching a company and taking it public for, like, $100 million. Who was to say a lawyer, an MBA, and a tech genius couldn't do the same? The world really does break into two basic groups of people: those who explain why something's impossible, and those who go out and do it.

The Ladies, after all, had started with far less than we three brought to the table.

But something was bothering me.

If Traci had a flaw, it was that her enthusiasm—as at the start of her NDN visit—sometimes got the better of her. Mentally, she had what engineers call a "high moment of polar inertia." She was a little too quick to change directions.

I had spent too much of my life as a leaf swept up by Typhoon Traci to go along without some questions—

"Now wait a minute. Until about two minutes ago, you were saying it was immoral to chase the Internet boom. Now we're supposed to jump in with both feet?"

Traci was ready for that one. "You know what John Wesley said in Sermon 50. You have to make money before you can use money to do good."

Well, that figured: the same text I'd been too sporting to use against her a few days earlier. I changed tactics—

"Okay, Trace—talk. What happened in New York?"

"What do you mean?"

"I mean, when you went there, you were so hot for a deal you could hardly stand it, and by the time you got back you were acting like we were about to be overrun by fire ants. So, what happened?"

She looked flustered. "Nothing."

Like I'd believe that. With Traci, something *always* happened. "Somebody hit on you? Who? The CEO?"

Vince was listening with *intense* interest.

"I'll tell you later."

"I want to know!"

"Forget about it. It wasn't important—and it wasn't what started this. Keep your mind on the topic."

"*You're* the topic."

"Starting our own business is the topic." She was getting steamed, so in fine lawyerly fashion, she turned the tables on me. "Oh, for heaven's sake, Callie. If *anybody* should be running her own business, it's *you*. You're the biggest workaholic in Minnesota, and you should at least be reaping the—"

"Whoa! Wait! 'Work*aholic*'?"

"Oh, good Lord. Callie, my biggest fear is one day I'm going to find you living beneath a freeway overpass with mice in your hair and a spreadsheet in either hand."

I turned bright red—looked to Vince for support—and cried out eloquently—

"But . . . but . . ."

"But *nothing*. Callie, if you took one of those 'Are You an Alcoholic?' questionnaires and substituted *work* for *booze*, you'd answer every question *yes*. Try it. Yes or no: You work because it relaxes you? You've tried to stop working, but always restart again within a few days?"

I sputtered.

"When you're going somewhere you don't think work will be available, you work extra before going?"

This was *so* unfair. I stayed silent.

She looked to Vince. "Am I right or wrong?"

Vince, the big rat, said nothing. Traci, going for the kill, turned back and told me, "I know! You're just a 'social' worker. You could quit any time. . . ."

The morning was spinning totally out of control, and I was getting upset. I didn't even like that Vince had joined the local Traci fan club. Traci must have seen it on my face. Abruptly her tone changed, and she said softly, "I talk too much. Sorry." She took her wallet from her purse. "It's been a tough week."

Later that afternoon Traci stopped by my cubicle to apologize. I told her to forget it, because if your friends can't read you the riot act and make you feel like total poop, who can? When she left, we were best buds again and had decided to research starting our own company, but meanwhile to wait and see how the NDN takeover developed.

The third floor's festivities had faded—the winners had presumably sped off to hit the Ferrari dealership before it closed. I felt awfully low, and workaholic or not, I logged out before seven and made my way, solitary and slow, to the elevator.

When I got home to my apartment that evening, I found in my mailbox two bills, a card from an old friend in Virginia—and one amazing letter from ICAAM.

## CHAPTER TEN

# My Hollywood Dream

Clutching what I'd found in my mailbox to my chest, I hurried to let myself into my apartment. Once inside, I dropped everything onto the table by the door except the ICAAM letter.

Then I ripped open the envelope.

About six months earlier, on a whim, I'd sent a short letter about my background and interest in the movies to Hollywood's four biggest talent-and-literary agencies. I'd tried to convince them that (despite having absolutely no film credentials) my technical background made me a natural to help any agency navigate the unknown seas of new media, from HDTV to video games to downloadable software. I hadn't heard back a word, and had since decided that silence is Hollywood's way of saying no.

And now this letter.

True, the most logical thing to expect would have been a rejection note—except that, after six months, why would they bother? My educated fingers—which had handled a lot of envelopes—told me it was too thick to be a rejection. Of course, my educated fingers were also shaking uncontrollably as I pulled the packet from the envelope and unfolded it. Only then did I realize I hadn't turned on the room lights, and that sunset through the curtains wasn't enough light to read by.

Finally, with the lights on, I read—

*Dear Callie,*

*I read with interest your letter of January 5. We are seeking an agent-trainee to serve as assistant director of our New Media Lab (please see enclosed articles), and also to train as an agent representing ICAAM clients interested in new media.*

*I should warn you that the selection process at ICAAM is long and rather arduous: Each agent-trainee accepted must have not only the endorsement of the hiring committee, but the sponsorship of an agent-partner. In addition, our new trainees enter as a group, in the spring of each year.*

*Accordingly, please consider yourself under consideration for hiring as part of the trainee class of 2001, with employment beginning on or about March 5 of that year. As you will see, I have enclosed forms requesting a range of additional information about you, your background, and your achievements. If you choose to, please complete and return them to me as soon as possible. It may be many months before you hear definitely from us, but I promise you your application will be given the fullest possible attention.*

*I look forward to hearing from you. Thank you for your interest in ICAAM.*

*Sincerely,*
*Peter Goldfarb*
*Partner and Head, Hiring Committee*
*International Creative Artists Agency and Management*

*encl.*

The enclosure wasn't too elaborate; they just wanted to know everything that I'd thought, done, or had done to me, beginning roughly with a list of any stars that danced at my birth, and ending, presumably, with any stars I now knew personally.

I finished reading and yelled "WOOO-HA!" at the top of my lungs.

The noise might have bothered my neighbors, but it didn't bother me.

I was getting the heck out of Dodge, where, for all I cared, the world's corporate giants could shoot it out on Main Street.

I was going to Hollywood.

CHAPTER ELEVEN

# The Martha Stewarts of Finance

To say the Ladies' next meeting started out gloomy would be a masterpiece of understatement. I've been to snappier funerals. I knew it was going to be grim when I reached the buffet table and saw nothing but a coffeepot and three packages of store-bought cookies. The Ladies were practically in mourning.

Standing up at the front of the room and adjusting her reading glasses, Sophia could have been any corporate executive giving bad news to any board of directors anywhere. She looked nothing like her usual, humorous self.

"As directed, I've reviewed our options in light of Wednesday's vote. Broadly speaking, we don't have any." She glanced up, but hearing no response, went on. "Technically, we *do* have options: a shareholder's suit, or a simple refusal to tender our shares. But neither is likely to get us what we want." She sighed. "A shareholder's suit would cost us at least a million dollars in legal fees. It *would*, potentially, delay the deal by up to a year—by which time I'm guessing we'd need a police escort to keep our neighbors from stoning us. Shareholder suits do sometimes kill deals, but usually, they just waste money. This deal has a willing buyer, a whole bunch of willing sellers, and a price that everybody calls generous. NDN is Wall Street's fair-haired boy; discrediting it would take something like a miracle.

"Refusing to tender our shares makes even less sense. At the expiration of the offer period, shares not tendered go into a kind of limbo: They have no value because there's no market for them, and no reason for anybody to buy them. We'd be making a very expensive gesture—and for no real purpose."

She set her notes down on Martha's French Empire desk. "Any questions or suggestions?"

A glum silence lay over the room like an unlaundered blanket. Sophia resumed: "If nobody has anything to ask or offer, I guess we should vote?"

It seemed we were hauling down the colors until Deborah called out, "Wait! I want us to go on record as calling this a *stupid* deal. If we really believe it—and we do—then we should stick to our guns."

"People will think it's sour grapes," Aunt Dolly protested.

"Let 'em. If they want a gushy sentiment, let 'em buy a Hallmark card."

"And if they want a happy ending," Gladys joined in, "let 'em rent *It's a Wonderful Life*. This is going to be a disaster, mark my words."

Deborah nodded emphatically. "I say we go on record. If we won't do it as a group, I'll pay for it myself."

They voted 4–3 in favor of a statement.

Two minutes later, after barely a discussion, they voted to tender their shares to NDN.

In the grumpy silence that followed, I noticed Sophia was still on her feet. Once everybody else noticed, she pointed to the far back of the room. "Maybe this isn't the best time, but I'd like to introduce you to a new friend of mine."

Turning, I saw someone had slipped into the room since the meeting had started: a very demure young woman, dressed modestly. She had straight, short black hair, perfect brown skin, and large, quiet eyes. I knew her as a secretary on the executive floor. She was about my age, and we exchanged friendly words whenever our paths crossed, though that wasn't often: She lived with her parents in St. Paul to save money for grad school, and mostly, she kept her head down and her eyes on her work.

Sophia, sitting, said, "Her name's J'Nelle Baker, and, well, she can speak for herself."

Walking to the front of the room, J'Nelle looked nervous—but not *too* nervous.

"I'm here, thanks to Sophia, for investment advice. I started at PMT when I was eighteen. I'm twenty-four now, so I've got six years at the company, and even at my salary level, I'm due for more than a sixty thousand dollar payday when the deal closes. I guess I could buy a new car and go to Europe, but I'd rather do what you all did: invest the money so I end up being really independent." She paused, then concluded, with rising excitement, "In short, I'd like to buy into the Ladies."

Clearly, that last bit had been a sudden brainstorm.

I liked the nerve of it.

But it startled Sophia so much she spun in her chair, and said apologetically, "Unfortunately, the partnership is made of equal shares. Having someone with . . . well, a small stake would cause problems."

Sophia was too polite to mention each share was worth

around $17 million. "But," she quickly continued, "there's nothing in the rules against letting someone sit in on the meetings and invest in tracking fashion . . . buying, on her own, whatever we decide to buy?"

Sophia ended this as a question to the group, and was met with nods of approval. The Ladies usually liked a project—now they were desperate for one. They unanimously approved J'Nelle as the group's third observer, after Traci and me. I gave J'Nelle the thumbs-up and got a brief smile in return, which for her was a wild burst of frivolity.

J'Nelle returned to her seat. I was pleased for her, yet mostly, I felt deflated. What was she going to observe, really? A bunch of rich ladies in retirement? I figured the meeting was winding down, and the Ladies along with it. Then, to my surprise, Aunt Dolly spoke up. "But this raises an interesting point."

We all resumed listening. With Dolly so ill, we were relieved to have her interested in anything, and now she looked almost lively. "J'Nelle can't be the only person interested in old-fashioned financial advice, even with all this Internet junk. Now, we published those business books, years ago . . ."

The Ladies were already ahead of her and shifting in their chairs in anticipation of adding their two cents' worth. But Dolly wrapped it up for them: "So why not get back in the game, with, say, a seminar program? We're a lot more fun than Tony Robbins!"

"And cuter, too!" Gladys shouted.

Aunt Dolly joined the laugh but pressed on, "We could teach investing the Larksdale way: not chasing every hot stock tip from overpaid brokers, but really doing the research. And investing in things you believe in. We could call it . . . maybe, 'Value and Values' investing?"

Many years earlier, after their PMT takeover, the Ladies had enjoyed a nice run of fame as investment gurus. Their books were dated, but surely could be fixed. They even owned a corporate shell for a company which could promote Value & Values investing everywhere.

So Aunt Dolly's idea wasn't only sensible, and ethical in the best Mostly Methodist tradition; it was doable. And it would offer an outlet for their energies while recovering from the sting of NDN.

The Ladies were perking up like morning coffee.

"We'd have to be careful how we do it," Gladys said. "We can't go around promising we'll make people *rich*—"

"Of course not." Dolly was firm. "But nothing's wrong with a little basic common sense and business advice. As far as I can see, they're both in short supply these days."

"It'll be a lot of work," Martha warned, with what sounded suspiciously like enthusiasm.

"It beats sitting around watching our wrinkles spread," Deborah replied.

Martha winced, and Gladys declared, "We'll be the Martha Stewarts of money!"

I was happy for the Ladies, but mostly wondering about my own options. Was it time to mention Traci's plan—to try convincing them to jump in as investors? I was still totally jazzed about ICAAM, and would soon be dashing home to finish my packet for them, but I had to be realistic. If no job resulted, I'd still need to pay my bills until I found some other route to film glory.

My heart was in Hollywood, but my fanny was in Larksdale.

And unless the Ladies were wrong, I'd be silly to trust my fanny, even short-term, to NDN.

I decided to ask Traci about bringing J'Nelle into our cabal.

Heck, she had discipline, gumption—and sixty thousand dollars. We could find way worse partners.

I was still thinking when Martha called for the vote on Aunt Dolly's plan.

It carried unanimously, and that was that.

The Ladies were back in business.

CHAPTER TWELVE

# The Indiscreet Charm of the Suddenly Rich

If you still think the speed of light is the fastest thing in the universe, you haven't seen newly rich Americans spending money. While the Ladies were rediscovering their work ethic, a whole bunch of former PMT employees were making a discovery of their own: Being rich is a hoot. As summer weather came on in earnest, and the roads became suitable for fancy cars, Larksdale's newly rich showed off their wealth in time-honored American fashion: They converted some of it to four wheels and a big, hot engine, and drove it right down Main Street.

The new ethos became clear to me the day I ducked into Madsen's Grocery and saw the old deli counter had been replaced with a newer and fancier one. A sign above it declared, in heavy gold script, GOURMET ITEMS. Behind the counter, Harold Madsen, the owner, was watching me with his pleasant gray eyes. I started toward him and called out—

"Hey, Harold."

"Hey, Callie. Want to try some *carciofi alla romana*?"

"What is it?"

He grinned at me. "Expensive."

I got his point.

In Larksdale expensive was all it took, and the signs of new money flourished. Almost instantly jet-skis were racing across the lake, and Larksdale Audio and Video was back-ordered a month on forty-inch plasma TVs. Even Alicia was swimming for her life against a flood-tide of cash-flashing new customers; we told her she should rename her place "Bread and Ro*ll*ses."

Not until early autumn did our local merchants begin to see the negative side of our golden rush of success, when they had to compete with newly opened shops whose windows read, in small gold letters at the bottom, PALM BEACH-BEVERLY HILLS-LARKSDALE.

Except for Alicia, my friends and I were mostly unaffected by Larksdale's new riches. Mainly we looked on, with some jealousy—and waited anxiously for the first really loony behavior by our new owners. Traci, Vince, and I discussed Traci's idea every day. My proposal about J'Nelle was approved, then delayed when she headed back East to spend a few weeks with relatives. J'Nelle's vacation caused us no real problems, though, because Vince was temporarily short on billion-dollar inventions, and Traci had decided that, if NDN bollixed-up the takeover, our smartest plan might be to keep our jobs as an easy source of cash while our plans developed.

That approach seemed smarter every day in June.

Our new bosses sent a broadcast e-mail from NYC congratulating us on joining "the driving Force of the Internet

Revolution"—but the Force seemed to have driven off into the Distance. With half the workforce off spending money like sailors on shore leave, and the rest of us still waiting for our new bosses to arrive, PMT was running about as smoothly as a speedboat that had just slammed into a sandbar; the slowdown was neck-wrenching. So our time went into plotting ventures and (at Vince's instigation) holding lots of evening picnics at the lake.

The Ladies, meanwhile, were pouring their usual energy and efficiency into their new project. Sophia, Gladys and Aunt Dolly (when she felt up to it) were contacting small-town libraries and clubs for speaking opportunities. But invitations were slow in arriving—even the smallest Midwestern towns had caught hot-shot investing fever. The Ladies persisted, but then a much bigger challenge came unexpectedly and from another direction entirely, just a week or so before the annual fourth of July celebration.

The fourth of July always meant major festivities in Larksdale, thanks largely to underwriting by the Ladies. Now, though, the NDN folks were promising "the last fourth of the millennium" would be the one to remember.

It was the third Saturday of June when the *Herald* detailed the additions to the lakeside celebration. In less than two weeks NDN had assembled a fireworks show three times as big as what had originally been scheduled *and* booked a band people had actually heard of.

For Larksdale, this was equivalent to bringing in all four Beatles.

It was starting to look like a mighty fun weekend. And then . . .

That same Saturday, when Martha, in her light linen dress, rose to address the weekly meeting, a faint tightness about her mouth hinted something was up. Indeed, it was a good thing Martha's stiff upper lip ran all the way down her spine, because the news she brought proved more than slightly humiliating. She pulled a letter from an express envelope. "This arrived early this morning. It won't take a minute to read:"

*Dear Mrs. Crittenden:*

*At the request of the entire committee, I am writing to thank you and your colleagues for their many years of support of the Larksdale Festivities Committee. I must tell you, though, that we have today accepted a new Main Sponsor, the Larksdale Community Fund, headed by a woman I am sure you know, Mrs. Patricia Farthingale. Mrs. Farthingale's personal generosity, her close ties with the LCF, and her excellent working relations with the new ownership of NDN/PMT Software, make her the natural choice to build upon the foundation laid by you and your colleagues.*

*Thanking you for your many years of valuable service, I am,*

*Yours Faithfully,*
*Samuel Mason*
*Chairman, The Larksdale Festivities Committee*

Even I, with my nearly total lack of social subtlety, recognized this for what it was: the surprise opening of a full-scale attack on the Ladies' social dominance of Larksdale. I searched my brain for Patricia Farthingale. *Wasn't she the principal of Horace*

*Biddlesworth Junior High?* Whoever she was, she certainly understood the time-honored military principles of surprise and speed. It might not exactly have been sporting, but then, when the Mongols swept across Europe, they didn't exactly send a telegram ahead to each town they were about to rape, pillage, and burn reading—

*Dear Mayor:*
*Arrive Thursday. Have virgins, gold, and wooden buildings waiting.*

*Love to All,*
*Genghis*

Traci and I had both brightened up immensely. We were expecting action.

Certainly the Ladies seemed ready to rumble. Aunt Dolly, who had been sitting listlessly next to me, now demanded, "What the heck is the 'Larksdale Community Fund,' and who the heck is Patricia Fattingale?"

"Far*th*ingale," Martha corrected gently. "Patricia Farthingale is the wife of Stan Farthingale. You know him, Dolly. He's one of PMT's top managers."

I knew him, too. "Big Stan" was the football lineman-sized, bald-headed, and loudmouthed COO who'd argued against the Ladies the night of the vote. Now, with the deal done, Stan and Patricia Farthingale were among the richest of our newly rich.

"And what the Larksdale Community Fund is," Gladys added, showing more excitement than anything else, "is competition."

"We're not afraid of competition," Deborah said firmly.

"We're not *in* competition," Martha replied, even more

firmly. "If it's about good works, there's plenty of room for all of us. If it's about social standing, well, they are welcome to whatever they think it is they want."

And that was one of the few times I ever saw Deborah silenced. To her credit, she took it gracefully, first thinking, then nodding and saying, "You're right."

Martha relaxed. "Good," she said. "Then I move we all go to the picnic and have a very good time. And if called upon, I very definitely will get up and try to say something gracious about that annoying *bit* . . . about *Patricia* Farthingale."

I felt a secret delight that, for all her pretty summer dresses, elegant gardens, and old-fashioned manners, Martha Crittenden could still get ticked off. I glanced at Traci, who'd watched all this with intense interest. I figured it would be just a matter of time before the Ladies counterattacked.

I didn't realize I'd be the one leading the charge.

## CHAPTER THIRTEEN

# The Rockets' Red Glare

Vince, Traci, and I got to the lake around 6 P.M. We found parking on the grassy side of the road about a half mile from the lake parking lot, which was par for the course in "New" Larksdale.

Vince, like a lot of geeky guys, was a car buff, but Larksdale in years past had been awfully slim pickings for him. As we walked to the lake, though, he had a field day pointing to new Porsches, Beemers, and Mercedes, all still bearing paper tags instead of license plates. He became so engrossed Traci and I joined the game. The walk was pleasant and relaxing; the day was still warm, but no longer sweltering, and the crowd, as we joined it, looked very festive. And sometimes we could travel as much as three whole feet without running into a reminder that our approaching good time was being provided by "NDN and the LCF."

I had to hand it to the Larksdale Community Fund (the

fatheads); when this night was over, Patricia Farthingale and her cronies were going to be at least as well known as the Ladies—and the Ladies had been doing good in Larksdale for many, many years.

But they did it *quietly*.

Even when you're acting virtuously, I guess it pays to advertise.

The evening's program was also plastered everywhere: dinner, 6–9 P.M. (the Ladies had always trusted people to bring their own food, but the "NDN and the LCF" were providing a huge barbecue run by Carl's Country Catering); remarks and patriotic invocation (with musical interludes provided by the Larksdale High School Marching Band), 9–10; then fireworks followed by a country-rock concert, 10–midnight.

When we finally worked our way into—and through—the jammed parking lot, we could see the huge portable stage (at least three times as big as in years past) was covered with patriotic bunting, and stacked along the wings with massive Altec-Lansing speakers. The stage also held a podium with microphones and a row of folding chairs, presumably for visiting NDN executives . . . and the elite of the LCF.

Most riveting of all was the barbecue. Carl must have been taking a Ralph Lauren cowboy course by mail, because his usual gang had been smartened up in blue jeans and red calico shirts and blouses with—I'm not kidding—blue neckerchiefs with little horses on them, and Stetsons. The sweet smell of their cooking, as we neared the lake, was irresistible. It was a torment to wait the forty minutes until we reached the head of the line—but then came the compensation.

They loaded up our plates with barbecued beef and chicken, barbecued beans, corn, coleslaw, and shoestring potatoes. This beat charred burgers and lime Jell-O any day. With both hands full of plates, we made plans to return for the cherry pie and true vanilla ice cream, and brownies and blondies and such.

Unfortunately, even the paper cups had little red-white-and-blue LCF logos.

When we had scrunched into seats on one of the jam-packed green benches, I whispered to Traci—

"You realize this is causing a collision between two of my most cherished beliefs: Never compromise your self-respect, and never pass up a free lunch."

"Traitor. Pass the ketchup."

Once we'd eaten, and gone back for thirds, we headed off to the very edge of the crowd, to an unclaimed grassy spot, where we sprayed on another coating of bug repellent and settled in to wait for the show. As first choice for our new book club of two, Traci and I had both brought *Huckleberry Finn,* which I was wondering about for a movie adaptation.

An hour and a quarter later, with the sun heading for the horizon, and the light getting a little orange for reading, I started growing restless. Did I *really* want to see some upstarts steal the stage and usurp the Ladies? I closed the book and turned to Traci—

"I say we get on the raft and sail on down the Mississippi."

"This is a lake, Callie."

"Well, then, let's sail to the other side. Let's blow this burg."

"We'll miss the show."

"Exactly my point! I mean, fireworks are great—but who wants to see Patricia Farthingale humiliate the Ladies?"

Traci nodded, adding we could still see the fireworks from across the lake, anyway. All we had to do was find Vince, who had wandered off a bit earlier, as he usually did at any outdoor gathering. I looked around at the crowd and saw everyone milling about, enjoying themselves. . . . Philosophically, I was entirely on Martha's side. There was no point in being a sore loser. But there was no good reason to help celebrate social climbing, either. As I was thinking this, Vince, holding a beach bag and working his way through the closely packed blankets all around us, hove into view. I waved to him—

"There you are! Where were you?"

"Oh, wandering around." He was looking pleased with himself.

"Good. Well, we're thinking about paddling over to the North Shore. We'll still have a view of the fireworks. We don't want to listen to Patricia Farthingale."

Vince grinned. "You know, we could arrange it so *nobody* has to listen to her."

I sat up. "You have my attention."

Vince sat beside me. "This is kind of cool, really. I read somewhere that nowadays fireworks are fired electrically, with everything controlled by radio links."

Now I was *really* listening. When it comes to knowing about controlling stuff by radio links, Vince is just a little behind MIT's Lincoln Labs.

"So I kind of wandered over there and got into a conversation with the fireworks guys, and kind of saw what they're using as controllers, and realized they run on the same frequency as the transmitters we tested last year for remote data."

Traci and I were already exchanging intent looks.

"—and where I've been since then is bumming a ride back home to pick up some stuff we could use to, um, move up the launch date, so to speak."

I was loving the idea, but a tightening in my stomach was warning me not to get carried away. "Hold on," I said, almost against my will. "This is how people get hurt, fooling around with—"

Vince, for once, cut me short. "Are you kidding? This is a public service! They need to know it's not a safe frequency for triggering fireworks." He frowned. "Look, Callie, I'm not *that* much of a dope. If we decide to do this, I won't be pushing any buttons unless I can *see* we're clear, that no one is close by to get hurt."

Spiritually I'm all about turning the other cheek. And someday I even hope to *live* that way. Just then, though—well, the game was afoot. I turned to Traci, and asked hopefully—

"What do you think?"

"I thought the Ladies had decided to live and let live."

"The Ladies didn't know about Vince. Come *on!* You know they'd love this."

And of course, Traci, who *did* know the history of the Ladies, knew they would.

She made a brief pretense of being all lawyerly and cautious, but I ignored that, because while doing it, she'd been tucking her legs under her and sitting up straighter. She was *totally* hooked. We took another five minutes to work out the details, which was plenty of time, since there were only about two. Vince was going to leave me one of a pair of Motorola mini-walkie-talkies, which had plenty of range over water. He was going to signal us when he was ready, and I was going to give him the "go" signal when the time looked right to teach Patricia Farthingale a major lesson.

It could not have gone better.

It took about fifteen minutes before Vince signaled he was in position. A minute later Mayor LeBrand introduced Martha, who, gracious as ever, introduced the odious Patricia Farthingale. Patricia was just stepping to the podium when I switched on the walkie-talkie, and whispered into it—

"Vince?"

His voice, also whispering but excited, came back. "Yeah?"

"You may fire when ready, Gridley."

"Cool."

Ten or fifteen seconds passed. Patricia Farthingale had adjusted the microphone; with her smile beaming out over the crowd, she began, "My fellow Larksdaleans! It gives me great pleasure—"

Suddenly, across the lake, there came the yellow tail of a skyrocket climbing into the night sky. The crowd gasped and Patricia Farthingale, thinking they were gasping at her eloquence, looked gratified. Then the skyrocket exploded in a bright pink-red star burst, and a moment later the sharp crack of the explosion reached us, and this time *Patricia* gasped. Having perhaps a slightly tardy premonition, she spun and looked back over the lake.

By then, rockets were going up in profusion. And the crowd—probably about as fond of speeches as any other modern-day crowd, which is to say, not very—burst into wild cheering.

Things turned *perfect* as the Larksdale High Marching Band, taking its cue from the fireworks, broke into its Patriotic Medley, segueing from "The Star-Spangled Banner" to "Louie, Louie." Patricia Farthingale went from surprise to fury to a kind of slumping defeat. Martha, with her patrician smile and grip of steel, crossed to the podium, shook her hand, and led her off the stage. If Martha wasn't looking triumphant, I'm a Spice Girl. Within ten minutes the once-famous country-rock band was fully set, ready to play the moment the fireworks and the marching band quit.

Traci and I were laughing so hard we collapsed. When Vince showed up a minute later, he flopped down on the grass and howled with us.

I'll tell you, Huck: It made you proud to be an American.

CHAPTER FOURTEEN

# The Takeover

At 7:30 A.M. on July 19, an NDN corporate jet touched down on PMT's landing strip. Onboard was the takeover team: a tall, lanky, senior NDN executive of about forty-five named Lamont Patterson; a very severe-looking lawyer named Monica Rathburn; and a handsome, dashingly dressed twenty-eight-year-old named J. Brian Henley.

From the moment they stepped from the plane, the first two of these imported hotshots acted as if they owned Larksdale—and had overpaid for it. While J. Brian Henley did a nice job of being polite to everyone, the other two treated the reception committee like a pack of mangy dogs left on their doorstep.

The takeover team and its greeters had barely reached Milt's office when Lamont Patterson clapped his hand on Milt's shoulder and said jovially, "Milt, I know this is a little unusual, but I'd appreciate it if you'd just turn us loose here for a couple of days to look around on our own."

Milt, who was rarely at a loss for words, stammered, "But—"

Patterson squeezed Milt's shoulder. "Be a lot easier if we had a clear field to form our own impressions. I'm sure you understand."

A suggestion from the headquarters guys is really an order. Milt, seething, nodded and said politely he'd be available if they needed him. Then he told Alice, his secretary, he'd be back Monday morning, and left the building. A few minutes later, Sophia, standing at her own office doorway, got the same treatment from Monica Rathburn.

I heard this story about fifteen minutes after it happened from Janet Carter, who'd heard it in the rest room from J'Nelle. The fact that J'Nelle was passing along gossip was itself proof of how astounding the news was. I was sitting with Floyd Higginsbottom, and Floyd's not stopping Janet—his just slumping in his chair and listening in amazement—was a sign of how shocked *he* was.

Not that stopping Janet would have accomplished much.

The story swept the building in minutes. It was so startling, it even stopped our newly rich from talking about their money. By 9 A.M. the interoffice phone calls were flying, with people venting, and even proposing protests. By 11, loud arguments were breaking out between the haves and have-nots, about whether a management change was good for PMT.

Traci acted more constructively.

At noon she brought J'Nelle to my cubicle, so she, Vince, and I could explain our plan and invite her to join in. To our surprise, she declined. She was very nice about it—and seemed embarrassed. She brushed at her hair and said awkwardly, "I . . . I'd like to, but I can't. My dad's not well and, um, I . . . I can't take the risk. We might need the money to support us until he's better."

And that was that. She stood and left.

Traci, who has a very good heart, went after her, caught her at the elevator, and told her we still wanted her whenever she was ready. Traci said J'Nelle seemed grateful almost to the point of tears and promised to keep it in mind. Vince, showing gumption, said, "Okay—it's a setback, but we can't fall apart. We need to keep working, and to find things to keep our spirits up."

I was feeling stunned and low, and afraid Vince was going to propose something like a Quake-playing club. I asked—

"Such as?"

"A softball team."

This sounded like a Quake-playing club, only with sweating—but Traci, who loves sports, agreed instantly. I went along, vaguely, to be a pal. Mostly, I wanted to leave. I'd just remembered Jake was back, and the news from the executive suite meant I had an excuse to talk with him.

As I left, Vince was saying they should call the team the Do-Loops.

I found Jake in his cubicle. He'd just spent six days at a software developer's conference in Colorado, an assignment he'd grabbed while everyone else was obsessing about NDN. It must have been some tough conference: He looked tanned and fit—and, well, irresistible. A small, fancy radio on his bookshelf was playing Mozart; I forgot what I'd planned to say, and, heart pounding, asked—

"What? No country and western?"

He rose slightly—he had old-fashioned manners—and crinkled the corners of his soft brown eyes. I saw friendship in them, but nothing more—darn it. No bystanders were likely to get trampled in his rush to embrace me.

"I'm taking a vacation." He waved me to a chair, then nodded past me, toward the corridor. "Looks like I might be getting a real long one, any time now." He shook his head and smiled at me like a pal. "Dang—and just about everybody at the conference was hiring, too."

I slipped into the chair beside him. "Pretty strange happenings here, eh?"

"I guess. I'm still glad to be back."

I had just about turned that into a warm personal message, when he picked up the spreadsheet and said, "Way I see it, we're ten days late on version 4.2, but if we . . ."

I sighed inaudibly, then listened to his plan, and okayed it—though I doubted anyone on the team had enough focus to follow through.

Mozart or no Mozart, it just wasn't my day for romance.

Two minutes later I was back in Traci's office, helping to organize the Do-Loops. Even a single day earlier it would have been unthinkable for me to use work time to organize a softball team. But that morning I realized how much of my loyalty had been not to the company, but to the people: my colleagues, the Ladies as a group, and Sophia and Milt.

But Milt and Sophia were no longer PMT.

When NDN took over, they really took over.

In a matter of days it became clear Sophia and Milt would never be allowed back in the center of the action. They were given smaller offices and pushed to the side without ceremony. We all waited to see what direction new management would take, but NDN's hotshots did *nothing* to improve PMT. Rather the opposite, in fact; they seemed to be working to make PMT look *bad*. Lamont Patterson spent most of his time in New York, and the rest of it closeted in Milt's former office examining financial documents. Stan Farthingale became Patterson's right hand man and—I'll say this much for Stan—seemed very uncomfortable with his new job. Stan and Milt had been pals for years, but by the end of July they could barely look each other in the eye; by the middle of August they were barely speaking. Monica Rathburn occupied Sophia's office as if she never intended to leave—but instead of tackling pressing legal issues, she reviewed stacks of old documents and then shipped them off, box by box, to New York.

A tech company works by hotlists, schedules, and drop-dead dates—by bonuses, challenges, and all-nighters. The new NDN team gave us absolutely *nothing*. Since the bid, we'd been drifting forward mostly by momentum, and now we were losing most of that. Those of us who missed the big stock-option payday still burned to be in the thick of the tech boom, not on the sidelines. NDN's mismanagement was blowing our hopes of ever making our bones on a big project, and crushing whatever morale had survived the announcement of the sale.

As the weeks passesd, I didn't exactly despair. I hadn't heard from ICAAM, but they'd said a decision might take a long time, so I kept my hopes. Meanwhile, determined to keep busy, I did whatever real work was offered, threw myself into the softball team, and more or less lived for the Ladies' weekly meetings.

Unfortunately, the people at the top had fewer options. While Milt decided to bide his time, and prove he deserved a chance to run with the big dogs, Sophia's resistance was more active. Traci reported hearing one loud argument after another coming from Monica Rathburn's office.

And on July 30 Sophia ended the arguments.

She quit.

CHAPTER FIFTEEN

# Sophia's Summer . . .

Leaving PMT, Sophia had hoped to find useful work helping the Ladies.

In part, she did.

She now had plenty of time to take leadership of the Value & Values program. But she'd also expected to find some pleasure in helping with the Ladies' charitable activities—and there, she, like all the Ladies, was stymied at every turn. Patricia Farthingale moved fast and spent freely: Sophia and Gladys were actually in the boardroom of the Friends of the Larksdale Library waiting to announce their annual donation when the head of the Friends, Nadine Markham, stood up and said that a new committee headed by Patricia Farthingale had pledged $150,000 for remodeling the Genealogy Room.

The Ladies had been planning to donate $15,000.

The Ladies held an emergency meeting that night and decided not to start a campaign to outspend Patricia Farthingale.

As Martha put it, "Nobody wants a bidding war on good deeds."

It was very sensible, but it made all the Ladies feel even more isolated and unimportant in the town they'd help build.

Even worse, for Sophia, the disappearance of her formerly rich work life gave her too much time to look at her marriage.

And by mid-August her marriage was looking very shaky, indeed.

At least, Sophia thought so.

You might have thought NDN's aggression would have pushed Milt and Sophia together, to forget their grievances and make common cause against the invaders. In fact, it did just the opposite. Sophia had opposed PMT's sale bitterly; but once it was completed and she and Milt were pushed aside, her thinking shifted, and she began to see it as an opportunity. Horizons seemed to be opening before them: Leslie, their daughter, would be entering college in a year, with Will set to follow in another two. Sophia, an optimist at heart, wanted to find the good in this inevitability—to build for whatever would come next.

Wasn't this the time to start planning for life beyond PMT?

She and Milt were still young. They had enough money for several lifetimes, with a lot of the money now in booming NDN stock. As she spent summer days at home alone, with the sun sweeping through parted curtains and falling on the vintage Swedish-modern furniture she adored, she began to plan adventures. She would spend hours on the Internet assembling fantasy vacations. A literary walking tour of England to follow her passion. A tour of rural Japan to indulge Milt's once-passionate interest in martial arts. Inns and hot springs; old country houses and London backstreets.

But her plans almost always turned to arguments.

In younger days Sophia and Milt had often fought like cats

and dogs, true—but back then, the resolution was routinely "fight called on account of laughter."

Now instead of laughter, there came only smoke and fire.

A strange cycle repeated itself through too many days. Sophia would form a plan; Milt would come home, exhausted, and dismiss her idea out of hand. His dismissal would make her angry, and they would fight. She was not used to lacking authority; he was feeling challenged.

The night in mid-August when she proposed the Japan trip marked the peak of her generosity and optimism. She set dinner at the outdoor table between arbor and swimming pool, with lemon-citronella candles and subtle lighting from the pool, and finished the scene with roses and soft jazz. Then, though eager, she waited all through dinner, until Milt's energy seemed to be returning, before she pitched the idea.

Milt, obviously stifling irritation, listened for two minutes, then said, "It's good, but, honey, I can't commit to anything right now."

Sophia fought her own irritation. "All right. Then when?"

"Just let me solve the problems in hand. Then we'll see."

She thought she had an insight. "Do you want to make a run at *NDN*'s top job?" This was an extraordinary longshot, but she didn't underestimate Milt's abilities—or his ambition.

He crumpled his napkin and threw it onto the table, then answered quite sharply, "Yeah, maybe I would, with the right backing. A lot of people I counted on have cut and run." And, moving very quickly, he left the table.

That was the way their summer went: one pointless, unfinished argument after another, separated by long, hot days of silent misunderstanding.

## CHAPTER SIXTEEN

# . . . And Nine

Somewhere around the end of July, or the start of August, I just gave up and quit worrying. While the Ladies were getting pounded by Patricia Farthingale, and PMT was being sabotaged, my friends and I did what any rational young people would have done.

We played a lot of softball.

Vince had gotten us into the LVDSL—which sounds like a new kind of broadband service but actually stands for the Larksdale Very Dismal Softball League. The league's only membership rule read: "Each team shall consist of a minimum of nine living persons." We fit the bill perfectly.

We opened the Do-Loops (it comes from an old programming term) to anybody who worked for PMT, but ultimately only have-nots, including all our friends (even Jake, after the fourth time I asked him) joined.

We had a blast.

Jake and Traci were our standouts, both playing as if they'd come down from a far higher league. Jake making the long peg from the centerfield wall to Traci on the mound, so she could pivot and nail the runner, was a beautiful sight—although, in truth, I didn't always enjoy seeing what a lovely pair they made. Vince never looked very coordinated and wasn't much of a hitter, but on defense he seemed to have an instinct for getting in front of the ball. He claimed it came from playing lots of baseball video games.

With Vince, you never knew.

Even J'Nelle showed up, taking my manager's job for the last half of the season—and leaving me to huff and puff and enjoy myself hugely as backup infielder. Traci's pitching kept us in most games with, usually, an easy dozen strikeouts, plus a nice assortment of pop-ups and weak ground balls. On the hitting side, she always seemed to be rounding second, at least; and often enough, as the sun went down on some close game, you'd see her sliding home with the umpire waving arms to signal her safe.

Between six o'clock, when games began, and around ten-thirty, when we generally said "good night" after nine innings and one or two friendly beers, nothing was allowed but joking and sports talk. No politics—and especially no shoptalk.

It was one of the two best parts of summer.

The other part was, with the help of Traci (and sometimes, J'Nelle), sticking up for the Ladies, and carrying to the enemy the fight for Larksdale's soul—or, in simple English, annoying Patricia Farthingale.

Patricia was advancing on several fronts. Not long after the fireworks, she and two of her friends told the *Herald* they were launching a glossy monthly called *Larksdale Living*, to promote Larksdale's own special brand of "upscale, down-home" style; mostly, though, she moved into politics.

When Bill Parker, owner of Wild Bill Parker's Lincoln-Volvo, announced he was leaving the town council because his dealership had more business than it could handle, Patricia got herself appointed interim council member—and began proposing one overreaching project after another for the greater glory of Larksdale. Her strategy was to let her followers propose extreme notions, so she could weigh in with what sounded like a sensible compromise, but had in fact been her objective from the outset.

The August town council meeting was as good an example as any—and it has the advantage, from my viewpoint, of being the only one I attended.

The meetings were held in the big room on the courthouse's main floor. The interior had been redone in the early sixties—and very nicely, with Swedish-modern furniture and paneling. The sweeping, elevated seating area for the council members and the mayor was especially lovely.

The meeting opened with the usual heated argument about parking conditions on Main Street, which ended when Mayor LeBrand banged the gavel and announced wearily that if anybody knew how to make the blocks on Main longer than they already were, they should call her at home.

After parking came new business.

One of Patricia's cronies—I never caught his name—took the floor on behalf of some new civic improvement group and proposed we spend some of the tax money piling up in the town treasury. "After all, Madam Mayor"—he waved a clipping from the *Herald*—"we are now residents of a town with a higher per-capita income than Martha's Vineyard."

"I'm sure that's very good for all our egos," Mayor LeBrand said, with pleasing levelheadedness, "but I don't see—"

"It's perfectly simple. We need to make some provision for

those unfortunates who weren't part—a significant part—of the recent NDN stock bonanza."

Beside me, Traci started singing, "Brother, Can You Spare a Dime?" very softly.

"And . . .?" Mayor LeBrand demanded. Her Honor was losing Her Temper.

*"And,"* persisted the crony, a short, stout man with remnants of black hair and a scalp badly sunburned by the summer sun, but a remarkably strong voice, "The people of Martha's Vineyard built a tourist business to create jobs for people without money. Tourism is a clean industry; it doesn't take a lot of—well, *skill* to work in it, or a lot of education, and I . . . we . . . think it would be right for Larksdale."

Mayor LeBrand, after drumming her fingers on the fine woodwork, replied, "I'm not sure I see how that's a town issue. I mean, if people want to open a motel or—"

"It's an *issue,*" persisted the crony, who had a real gift for interrupting, "because we need something dramatic to put Larksdale on the map. Something people will automatically associate with Minnesota, and especially, with Larksdale."

This was perfect—because it gave our collective imagination free play.

"How about a sixty-foot blue ox?" somebody called out helpfully.

Several people shouted back, "Brainerd already has one."

"And Bloomington," somebody else added.

"And don't forget Blackduck!" some enthusiast chirped—although, technically, I think Blackduck's statue is of Paul Bunyan's duck.

The crony seemed somewhat taken aback by this flurry of replies; and Traci, no doubt in a spirit of Christian charity, tried to help him out by suggesting, in her best-reasoned lawyer's tones, "Maybe we could *donate* a blue ox statue to Martha's Vineyard. That ought to kick-start *their* tourist industry."

He nodded, but looked uncertain as to whether Traci was for or against him.

Soon everbody was shouting out suggestions, trying to improve on the blue ox idea. Somebody suggested a scale model of the Eiffel Tower. That conjured up the rich idea of a bunch of Larksdaleans strolling down the *Champs D'Mort's Dry Cleaners* singing "Thank Heaven for Little Girls." I missed a few proposals thinking about that, then heard someone suggest, "A Hobbit?"

This one, I admit, appealed to me. But Mayor LeBrand was annoyed.

"May I suggest we confine ourselves to symbols somehow tied to Larksdale, or at least Minnesota, in some way?"

Patricia Farthingale moved in her chair, and then, with a smirking modesty, leaned toward her microphone and said, "Madam Mayor, if I may. Perhaps a giant lark, for *Larks*dale?"

Beside me, Traci, overcome, shouted, "Why not a big cuckoo, for your idea?"

A rush of laughter, followed by a certain chill, settled over the room at that, and Mayor LeBrand said firmly, but without malice, "Oh, hush, Traci."

Traci hushed, but her mission was accomplished. The question of how to spend the town's recent tax bonanza was referred to a committee; the meeting adjourned; and everybody drifted down to Main Street for ice cream at Dagmar's.

We'd foiled Patricia Farthingale once again.

During that long summer, I was taking my amusement where I could find it.

CHAPTER SEVENTEEN

# J. Brian and I

The only thing wrong with having Jake part of my softball life was having Jake part of my life. Now, I'm not naturally obsessive about men. My usual response to being cut loose is to grieve a little, get some distance between me and the cutter, then find the humor in it. In college I invented St. Dumpkin's Day, which marked the sunny June day of freshman year when my boyfriend, saying he was looking forward to a really fun, sexy, adventure-filled summer, announced he was dumping me.

By the second year I celebrated it, it was a running joke.

As the summer of '99 ended, though, I was in a little trouble. Except for Vince, I had no men around who were attracted to me. I also had way too much free time, and way too much of it had to be spent around Jake. I couldn't get out of the corral, and the bull wasn't interested.

An idle Callie is the devil's plaything.

In early September, just as I decided I had to take action, a new wrinkle appeared.

J. Brian Henley, the nicest of the three-person NDN takeover team, was at the far end of the guy-spectrum from Jake. Where Jake was silent and just a little rough, J. Brian was chatty and outgoing. He was always supremely well groomed and dressed as if he'd just stepped out of a J. Crew advertisement. Jake was calves birthing during a summer thunderstorm; J. Brian was sailboats on Nantucket Sound.

During his first two months in Larksdale, J. Brian founded a BMW Club, a Wine Club, and a Gourmets' Society.

I figured he had to be a snob.

But it turned out I was the snob. Even though rumor was he came from a family whose money was so old it was practically mulch, J. Brian showed a gift for getting along with everyone from the janitors on up. And a lot of PMT women found him *very* attractive. So on the day in early September, when I noticed he seemed interested in *me,* I was pretty flattered.

He didn't do anything grand, just paused and smiled as he passed my cubicle.

That was it; he just smiled and moved on.

But the next morning I got an e-mail:

*Dear Ms. Brentland:*

*I understand you're an aerospace engineer by training, and wondered if you'd like to come watch the Balloon Rally next Saturday. I'd be glad to show you around, and if the Rally ends early enough, even take you up for a short ride.*

*J. Brian*

Of all the groups and events Brian had organized, his masterstroke was the PMT Balloonists' Club; by early September its sixteen members could field four balloons. I turned J. Brian down (which I think shocked several of the women in the office), but I did drive to the launching point, about thirty-five miles from Lake Larksdale, so I could watch the rally.

I stayed far from the crowd and got a thrill from the balloons, which were entered from three states. I've been nuts about anything that flies since I was about two and the only thing flying was me, in some adult's arms. Fifteen minutes at the edge of a cornfield watching those colorful balloons sailing through a clear blue sky, and I was hooked.

Which was why I made such a weak reply when, the next Monday morning, J. Brian, wearing a pricey suit that highlighted his pale skin, black hair and *very* blue eyes, stopped by my cubicle and began, "I saw you out at Reiker's Farm Saturday. How'd you like the balloons?"

"You've got good eyesight."

"I've got good binoculars. And I was hoping you'd like to go for a ride with me. You can't appreciate balloons from half a mile away."

Okay, so he knew my price.

That didn't mean I had to take the offer. I absolutely meant to turn him down, but before I could, he added, "After we're off the ground, I'll let you pilot. There's nothing to it, really." And he smiled again—and he had a *very* sincere smile, with perfect teeth. Plus, I wanted to be a balloon pilot like Mark Twain yearned to be a riverboat pilot, so I said—

"*Well . . .*"

"Good! I'll e-mail you the details, but figure we need to make an early start Saturday morning."

I'm a bit ashamed to admit it now, but right then, I was suddenly hit with the force of revelation: *If I go, I can make Jake jealous.* The whole plan arrived in a swift montage of images: the balloon ride (delightful in itself); the landing-site photo of Brian and me, champagne glasses in hand, toasting our big adventure; the snapshot of same, framed on my desk, where it would strike *Jake* with the force of revelation.

All, of course, followed by Jake's coming to his senses.

As soon as I was sure J. Brian had left the area, I headed over to Traci's cubicle and spilled the beans. Or some of them. I presented it as a simple date with J. Brian. She eyed me sharply. "Hold the phone. I know you better than that. This is about Jake, right?"

I shrugged. "Why not? It's a time-honored approach."

"Listen, Callie, I lived in New York. I know that guy's type. All of his charm and flattery, it has its dark side. I don't like the idea of you and J. Brian out in the middle of nowhere together."

"What dark side? We're going for a balloon ride. If Jake's jealous, bingo, true love triumphs. If he's not, and J. Brian and I hit it off, likewise bingo. At the worst, I get to ride in a hot-air balloon, which I've wanted since forever. There's no downside. It's pure, classical game theory."

"Classical game-*playing,* you mean." Traci threw up her hands. "Okay. You're going to do it, I hope it works. We'll miss you at Saturday's meeting."

So I sent J. Brian a cute reply and waited for him to take me flying.

CHAPTER EIGHTEEN

# I Fly Through the Air

Saturday morning dawned clear, bright, and windy. When I say "dawned," I'm not being poetic. I saw it from first light, because I'd already been up for two hours. The prospect of going ballooning had pushed out every other thought, from my frustration with PMT and my career, to the state of Larksdale and the Ladies, to my slight doubts about spending a whole day more or less alone with J. Brian Henley.

By the time Brian and his team—four friends, traveling in the Chevy Suburban balloon transporter/chase vehicle—pulled up in front of my home, I'd been dressed and ready to go for hours.

I rode with Brian in his Land Rover, and between the snazzy vehicles and the prospect of ballooning, I thoroughly enjoyed the ninety-minute drive out to our launch point. Brian's charm was running full speed, and he scored big points by having hot coffee and warm *pain au chocolat* waiting for me. If I had been more alert, I would have worried a little about the new, vaguely wolfish gleam in his eyes, and the fact that he was talking a lot more rapidly than usual.

I thought he just really liked balloons.

I won't say I was being swept off my feet, but I scarcely thought about Jake the whole drive out into the country—and by the time we arrived at the launch site, I was totally caught up in the adventure.

Except for, maybe, a paper airplane, a hot-air balloon is probably the simplest flying machine in the world: There's the balloon itself (usually brightly colored nylon, with a volume of about sixty-five thousand cubic feet), a basket (usually made of wicker, to absorb some of the landing shock), and a system for heating the air inside the balloon (usually a set of liquid-propane-powered burners).

At the very top of the balloon is what's called a parachute valve—basically, an adjustable opening in the nylon fabric for releasing hot air to slow the balloon's rise or start it back to Earth.

The burners—two, in Brian's balloon—have preheat coils, which warm the liquid propane back into a gas, so it will burn hot. It's also possible to bypass the preheaters, in which case the burners run on liquid propane, which burns quietly but inefficiently. The only reason to run liquid is to fly quietly over herds of animals without disturbing them: Balloons burning gas are astoundingly noisy.

But our setting-up, that chilly September morning, was almost silent. To my amazement, Brian's well-drilled support team had the balloon off the support vehicle and ready to fly in under an hour—and their work was quiet enough that I could hear cows in nearby fields.

I waited while the crew placed the basket at the edge of the ground tarp, a huge square of ripstop nylon meant to keep the balloon from tears. They unrolled the balloon fabric until it lay on the tarp like a rainbow-colored drawing of a balloon, lit up the burners, and stabilized the fabric while the balloon inflated. I really wanted to jump in and help, but an ingrained respect for well-drilled teams stopped me. On my own, internal soundtrack, though, the music was really swelling, and my heart was pounding as the balloon inflated, and then, finally, as Brian, standing by the wicker basket, waved for me to join him.

Technically, Brian's balloon had a four-passenger basket, but two of the four would have to have been pygmy hedgehogs. Inside it, taking up a lot of the limited room, were three large cylinders of liquefied propane gas, each wrapped in a thick insulating jacket to keep it cold, plus a jumbo wicker picnic basket. The basket caught my eye despite all my excitement about flying, because it was open and I saw not only champagne on ice, but a variety of food containers with the labels of the Twin Cities' top caterer. This was traveling in style.

Brian helped me aboard like a perfect gentleman; the balloon by now was fully inflated. Two of the ground crew had been holding on to the basket to provide extra ballast, and the whole craft was anchored to the SUV to prevent it from taking off on its own unscheduled flight.

I noticed Brian held what looked like an oversize cigarette lighter. He saw me studying it, and thrust it into my hand, while saying, "The auto-igniter's out. Keep this in case we need to restart manually."

Boy, do I love it when men talk tech. I nodded enthusiastically, while Brian moved the big red overhead handle to full on. The twin propane burners responded with a roar.

I was far too fascinated by the soaring blue flames to care much about problems with auto-igniters. There's a time and a place for engineering questions. Without much thinking, I shoved the lighter into one of the pockets of my puffy jacket. A chilly near-autumn wind was sweeping over us and making the massive balloon tilt off the vertical, like a dog straining at the leash.

It kept getting better.

The two ground crew members—big guys, probably weighing close to five hundred pounds between them—who had been gripping the basket's edge let go at a signal from Brian. The other two crew members now, like Brian, leering with what I took to be sports excitement, unhooked the tether line. The line snaked briefly across the ground, and then we were airborne.

I'll admit it; I was thrilled. I'm so jazzed by anything related to flying, that I can generally cheer myself up just by jumping.

But this not only beat jumping, it beat any flying I'd ever done. We were climbing swiftly, but, even better, the wind was pushing us over the flat terrain at a delightful clip.

Of course, the one thing you don't get from watching ballooning is that those big propane burners really roar. That might have made the whole experience less romantic—but I wasn't there for romance. I was there for flying, and the sensation, with the basket rising, pitching, and sweeping over the prairie, was terrific.

In truth, I couldn't constrain myself. I was leaning over the basket's edge (still gripping the lines, I was excited, not crazy), and yelling—

"Wa-hoo!"

The first crosswind caught us; the balloon bobbed and swerved about forty-five degrees, and headed off on a new course, while the basket swayed dramatically. This was twice as cool. I felt like an eagle.

Unfortunately, my copilot was a weasel.

J. Brian made a move that I don't think is part of the Balloonist's Handbook. How should I say this? He put his arm around my shoulder, only his hand wound up about three feet too low.

Automatically I changed my yell, the minute he grabbed my fanny, to a very worried—

"Uh-Ohh."

I looked over at him, in the vague hope that the balloon had needed some immediate adjustment to, say, a flow-line and his hands had merely missed its mark.

No such luck. He wasn't looking embarrassed; he was positively leering.

Never mind the Mile-High Club; he wanted us to join the 700-Feet Club.

Now, nobody could exactly say I'd just fallen off the turnip truck. I realized that Brian's move was, very possibly, the second ballooning maneuver attempted, after the vertical takeoff, or that at least it likely dated from the first time one of the Montgolfier brothers invited some cute French chick up for a ride.

But the Montgolfier brothers probably had the decency to quit if they found the object of their affections wasn't enthusiastic.

And one party was definitely not enthusiastic. In fact, my feelings were a blend of at least four factors: shock, anger, desperation, and shame.

Given that I now found J. Brian disgusting, and that I was then about two thousand feet in the air, in a fast-moving wicker basket with roughly eighteen inches of maneuvering room in any direction, you've probably figured out the shock, anger and desperation. The shame, though, was what slowed me. I knew perfectly well I'd gotten myself into this fix through my nutty desire to make Jake jealous and my eagerness for free adventure, and that precisely that combination of flaws had made me ignore Traci's advice and my own good sense.

I freely tell you I came within an instant of absolute panic. What saved me was a personal quirk: I would, as the old saying goes, joke at my own hanging. That might sound wacko, but it was also, just then, essential, since it kept me calm.

Not that J. Brian had lost all his East Coast preppie charm, and was falling back on stale material. Leaning close to my ear, he bellowed:

"YOU'RE SO BEAUTIFUL!"

Now, that's not one of the great romantic lines, anyway—but since the propane burners on a hot air balloon have nearly the acoustic output of a small jet engine, old J. Brian was more or less screaming which, combined with his rather high-pitched voice, gave him roughly the volume and intonation of a British cavalry officer ordering a charge during a Crimean War artillery barrage—a sound which might be romantic if you're a horse, but which otherwise will never make moonlight and roses obsolete.

I figured maybe I could embarrass him into giving it up, so I bellowed back—

"WHAT??"

"I said, 'YOU'RE SO BEAUTIFUL!' "

He made another lunge at me. Just as he did, the balloon rose into a conflicting wind and veered, sending the basket in a new, jerking arc. I almost thought Brian had simply fallen into me; but based on where his hand ended up, he was interested in a lot more than regaining his balance. Amelia Earhart never put up with this crap, I'll tell you. In our bright-neon puffy down jackets, we must have looked like a couple of psychedelic wrestling polar bears.

I forgot all about my share of the blame. I thought briefly of whacking J. Brian over the head with the lighter. But while I was plenty angry, I wasn't much inclined to draw blood. Mostly, I just wanted out of the basket.

I adopted a compromise plan.

I threw the lighter overboard.

And then I reached up for the bright red handle, and shut off the propane.

# CHAPTER NINETEEN

## *We Run Out of Gas*

The propane roar ran on for several seconds, weakened sharply, then ended with a *plop* barely audible over the wind noise. Brian, after staring in outraged amazement for about fifteen seconds, reached for the two-way radio, switched it on, and said through clenched teeth, "Rick! You there?"

"Roger that, buddy."

"I need you to deploy for a burner-out landing."

"Uh, Roger. What's your approach vector and E.T.A.?"

Rick obviously dug the whole military angle of the venture. The few, the proud, the full-of-hot-air.

"Just *do* it, damn it!"

The support truck, still a thousand feet or so below, cut sharply left and headed out over the open country.

I, meanwhile, had had plenty of time for some rapid second-thinking. A number of points had already become clear. First, I had absolutely no idea how quickly a balloon descended. I mean,

I knew *generally* that it would go faster or slower depending upon whether we opened the parachute valve; but I also assumed that if we held the parachute valve open too long, we'd start descending like the proverbial ton of bricks.

I began to see certain negative implications to dropping like a ton of bricks. Sure, broadly speaking, the sooner I was out of the basket, the better I'd like it, but there were limits to the principle—mostly because I had no great desire to form a crater on landing.

I mean, the first recorded experiment in modern physics was Galileo's dropping two round objects off the Leaning Tower of Pisa. Far as I know, nobody interviewed the two objects afterward, but it's a safe bet they weren't so round after they hit terra firma.

Brian was now one busy pilot. He had to keep an eye on the parachute valve, on the winds, on the ground and the swerving support SUV, and on his controls and gauges. That left him very little time for giving me dirty looks—but under the circumstances, he did a darn good job. The closer we got to the ground—and we were getting closer by the minute—the worse he was making me feel.

The problem, of course, was that with the gas cooling rapidly, the only way to slow our descent was to throw stuff overboard. Based on the looks Brian kept shooting me, his favorite object to toss would have been me.

"Get ready to dump the picnic basket overboard when I tell you to," he snarled.

The thing was confoundedly heavy, but in my state of adrenaline-enriched alarm, I managed to get it balanced precariously on the lip of the passenger basket. Looking down below, I started considering the terrain before us for a potential landing site, and what had been alarm grew quite close to panic. The chase truck was still sprinting forward, but just ahead of it I saw the road took a wide curve around a small lake. We, of course, couldn't swerve around anything. We had two modes: We could sail over stuff, or we could hit it.

The idea of hitting the water was unpleasant.

But the water seemed almost tempting, because not a quarter of a mile beyond it rose a tall ridge of trees, the beginning of a forest. We might possibly clear the pond—but it would take damned good ballooning to manage that and then not whack into the trees.

Brian had clearly come to the same conclusion, because he was on the walkie-talkie and trying to say calmly, "Rick, man, get this right. You're going to curve around a big pond, just ahead. Once you do, get a wind-line on us and set up as near to midway between pond and woods as you can. And do it fast, man. Okay?"

Rick wasn't sounding like Space Command anymore. He was sounding worried—or at least very focused. "You got it, man. We're haulin' booty."

Brian told me to dump the cooler. I did, and felt the balloon bump upward. I had no way of knowing how much altitude—or time aloft—we had gained, but it didn't feel like a lot. Brian stepped close to me and said angrily, "Help me get this overboard."

Looking down, I saw he was unhooking one of the propane tanks. It took both of us to get it overboard, and this time the gain was noticeable. I'm so much in favor of technical competence I was actually starting to forgive Brian, even though he was giving me a steady, poisonous stare. Then he stopped glaring and started looking worried—and I had sudden doubts about his expertise.

Had we lightened the craft too much?

We were about a mile and a half from the tree line. Based on our drop rate, an eight-mile-per-hour wind would land us safely short of the trees. But figure more like a *ten*-mph wind, and we were going to wind up wearing pine tree overcoats. I look lousy in pine. Suddenly I was scared.

With his eyes fixed narrowly on the distant tree line, J. Brian gave the parachute valve cord one long tug. The chase truck had finally come to a stop about eight hundred yards ahead, and now the crew jumped out and began racing to roll out the pale-blue landing tarp. We were now low enough, thanks to that tug on the valve cord, that I could see everything they were doing clearly.

They were still laying out the last ten feet of the tarp when we slammed down—and we surely hit harder than we would have with full control of the burners—but it was bearable. The basket tipped over, pitching Brian forward onto me, and making me into a kind of human air bag—but I didn't think he'd planned it. Between them, Brian and the ground crew actually did a darned good job of coordinating this rocky touchdown; I doubt we were more than twenty feet off the ideal landing point.

I was so grateful to be safely on the ground, I could have kissed it (easy enough to do, since it was about two inches from my mouth).

I wasn't so grateful I could have kissed J. Brian, but all in all, I was inclined to let bygones be bygones. I figured we were going to keep a stony silence the whole way home, and then never talk to each other again. He'd gotten out of line, and I'd wrecked his balloon. Case closed.

But Brian had other ideas. Breathing like an asthmatic bellows, he scrambled from the basket shouting "YOU'RE DAMN LUCKY I'M GIVING YOU A RIDE BACK HOME!"

"Don't do me any favors, BUSTER!" My fury was back, in spades.

"*Fine!* We're about—" He looked angrily toward Rick.

"Forty-eight miles," Rick said, apparently reading his mind.

Brian turned back to me. "*Forty-eight miles* from Larksdale. HAVE A NICE WALK!"

If there's one kind of scene I absolutely hate in a movie, it's the kind where two people "fight cute"—when we're supposed to believe that after one of them acts like a total jerk, and they fight furiously, they're going to wind up loving each other madly. That stuff may work if you're Spencer Tracy and Katharine Hepburn—but we were a Spencer short.

I told J. Brian what he could do with his ride, turned on my heel, and lit out for open territory.

## CHAPTER TWENTY

# Rescue Party

Fortunately, I'd had just enough presence of mind to get the lay of the land while the balloon's height still gave a broad view. I hadn't spotted anything as handy as, say, a combination gourmet restaurant and Hertz Rent-A-Car location—but I knew the way to the road and to what looked like a reasonably large farmhouse less than a mile distant.

I set out with firm-jawed determination, but I'd gone about, oh, fifty feet, when the reality of the situation began to dawn on me. The air was brisk—and late-September days are short. The land was already turning a pale-honey color as the sun touched the edge of the western woods. Since I'm a firm believer in never letting them see you squirm (unless they're close, personal friends), I strode away forcefully for a good five minutes, until I'd put a decent distance between me and the Balloon Boys, *then* I reached for my cell phone.

Naturally, the phone read "No Service."

I used some suitably choice language and kept walking.

My imagination started kicking in. If there's one thing you *don't* need to do, alone in the Minnesota countryside with the day winding down, it's to start thinking about every horror movie ever set in a corn or wheat field. Thirty nervous minutes later I reached a farmhouse. It sat about fifty feet back from the road, beside a considerable apple orchard and behind a good-sized pumpkin patch, the pumpkins already showing flushes of autumnal orange. A sign over the front porch read THE LINDSTROM FARM STORE and APPLES—PICK 'EM YOURSELF.

I asked the woman behind the counter if I could pay to use their phone for a short long-distance call. And then, like the nervous wreck I apparently was, I started blurting out the whole story of my horrible day. I'd barely gotten to the good part when Mrs. Lindstrom pointed me to the phone and said kindly that when I finished we'd have apple pie and coffee.

I picked up the receiver, then hesitated.

If I sounded *too* fat-and-happy, Traci would tell me to walk down the road until a Greyhound bus appeared. If I sounded shattered, I'd not only be dishonest, I'd upset my best friend for no good reason. I decided to be matter-of-fact, with just a hint of underlying heroic tragedy, and to let her feel I'd suffered enough for ignoring her advice. When she answered (on the first ring, as usual), I said—

"Trace? Me."

"Oh, yeah? So how was the date?"

"Let's just say . . . I let the air out of his balloon. And I guess I need a ride back to Larksdale. Can you maybe come get me?"

"He dumped you in the middle of nowhere? That creep!"

"I'm fine. Really. But I could use a ride, if you can manage it."

"I'm on it. The Volvo's in the shop, but I'll call Vince. Tell me where you are."

I gave her the directions I'd gotten from Hilda Lindstrom, and we hung up. My worries were over, and I put my mind entirely on the apple pie.

About 6 P.M. an old Jeep Cherokee pulled up in front of the store, and I saw, to my shock, Jake at the wheel. Vince and Traci were in the Jeep, too. I figured Traci was going to give me a big lecture about the letches of NDN, but all she gave me was a big hug—which was extraordinarily kind of her. Then came the usual rush of everybody (well, mostly Traci and Vince and I) trying to talk at once. Traci said she invited Jake "in case anybody needed his nose punched in." We decided that J. Brian would catch punishment enough in the next life. Then Vince announced that he had brought along the ReadyPack.

The ReadyPack wasn't one of Vince's million-dollar ideas; it was just a big cooler he'd fitted with some extra compartments holding a portable CD player and a small bundle of fat pine kindling, plus plates, silverware, and condiments—as he said, all you had to add was sandwiches, chips, and drinks, and you had a complete picnic in a box.

It was typical of Vince to see the chance for fun. He had come prepared to help punch J. Brian's nose; but now that I was okay, he happened to know of a great county park . . .

That was where we headed.

The air was chill, but we had jackets. Vince and I spread out the ReadyPack goodies (readied in haste, they included PB & J sandwiches, pretzels, and Cokes) while Jake and Traci, two natural Scouts, built a fire in the fire ring. Jake, bent over the fire till it glowed, definitely had his Gary Cooper thing working—though it felt a bit odd to see Traci working right beside him. Vince had brought a homemade CD of classic fifties songs, from Sinatra to "Earth Angel," and after we ate, Traci got us all dancing. She was so graceful, she made even Vince look good.

By eight o'clock, having traded partners twice, we ended on a Sam Cooke ballad, and a few minutes later we had the Ready-Pack closed up and were starting for the Jeep. I maneuvered it so Jake and I went back to police the site and make sure the fire was out. That last part was probably unnecessary: dark rain clouds were spreading over the countryside. Still, not wanting the trip to end, I made a show of stamping out the last bits of fire. When I looked up, Jake was studying me.

I stopped kicking at the ground.

He said affectionately, "You're a fair amount of trouble, gal."

That was practically the cowboy version of "My love is like a red, red rose."

"It's nice to have someone care," I said.

It was dark, and Vince and Traci were forty yards away; the opportunity for romance looked perfect.

Jake nodded slightly. "You know I'll always be your friend."

He didn't put a lot of emphasis on "friend," but Jake was so careful with his words, I got the message. Any other time it would have crushed me, but just then I had a very high regard for friendship, so I nodded. "Good deal," I said as I stepped up, put my arms around him, and kissed his cheek. Of course, even while hugging him, I was thinking that any deal could be improved.

Before we were halfway back to Larksdale, the storm broke in earnest, with hail the size of peas banging into the SUV.

Summer was clearly over.

## CHAPTER TWENTY-ONE

# Life Intervenes

Aunt Dolly wasn't well. That much had been obvious to the Ladies at least since the time, nearly a year earlier, they recruited me to return to Larksdale to keep an eye on her. And yet, it had not been clear to Aunt Dolly herself until a Tuesday morning in late September, when she sat on the white paper covering her doctor's examining table, looking at the cold white walls and the glass-and-Formica cabinets.

Aunt Dolly was used to Dr. Harris's office, and usually passed the time with his nurses and clerks quite cheerfully. Today, though, nobody was terribly friendly. The new nurse, who had shown her to the examining room and taken her vital signs, had avoided chatting, and that left Aunt Dolly vaguely worried.

Dr. Harris arrived quickly; but instead of his usual plump geniality, he moved with brisk professionalism, and every poke and prod seemed to inspire another entry on her chart. The uncomfortable thought arose that they were treating her so distantly because she was very ill. The small thought grew to giant size when Dr. Harris closed the thick file. "Get dressed, please, and then I'd like to see you in my office."

Aunt Dolly's fingers trembled as she re-dressed, and she had to swallow hard before she was ready to leave the examining room. The short walk to Dr. Harris's office seemed to stretch to a mile, and left her short of breath. Dr. Harris sat at his document-strewn desk reading with fierce attention. He kept reading while Aunt Dolly entered timidly, tried to draw his attention by waving her hand, and then sat humbly in a chair facing him.

This was a war of nerves, and he was winning.

Finally he set down his papers, and said, "Dolly, it's time we had a serious talk. For the last three years I've seen you every ninety days. Every visit I've asked how you felt, you've said, 'Fine,' and I've upped your insulin and added meds and sent you out the door. And in those three years, though you've promised me you've been eating smaller portions, watching your weight, and exercising, we've managed to lose a negative sixty pounds." He leaned forward, so there'd be no misunderstanding, and rephrased it: "Three years of dieting, and you're up by sixty pounds, and your insulin metabolism is steadily worse, and so's your blood pressure."

"I don't feel so very bad."

He shook his head fiercely. "You want to know how many problems your weight is causing? You're at elevated risk for a heart attack or a stroke. Your mobility's restricted and your diabetes is on the verge of getting very serious. You want me to scare you? If you keep going this way—and don't die from a heart attack or a stroke—you can expect to be walking with a cane in less than a year. There's a good chance you'll go blind. Eighteen months or so, and you'll be taking five insulin shots a day, minimum, and probably a dozen different pills."

Aunt Dolly was already preparing to tell him she was actually feeling much better, and besides had decided to try a new diet which had done wonders for the people on the *Today* show. In the past, Dr. Harris had always paused at this point in his lecture to let her talk him out of his stern approach.

This time he did not pause.

When she tried to speak anyway, he held up a hand, palm out like an old-time policeman. "Now, I've spent the last three years letting you talk me out of saying what you need to do, but that stops today."

Dolly sensed a pause. "Yes, but . . ."

The hand went up again. "I want to you think about having a gastric reduction operation. It isn't risk-free, but it may be the only thing that will help. Once it's done, you won't be able to eat more than a couple of ounces at a time, and you really won't want more. You'll start losing weight fast; thirty days after the operation, at most, you'll be on an exercise program, and you'll keep getting lighter and stronger."

Aunt Dolly thought it sounded as if he were describing some new metal alloy.

Dr. Harris finished up, "A year from now, if you do what you're told, you'll be sitting in this office at least a hundred pounds lighter and looking fit to row on the U of M crew."

After a moment, as her heart stopped pounding from fear, she felt oddly relieved. It would be a relief to no longer deny how poorly she felt. This grim diagnosis opened up the possibility—the necessity—of turning to face the beast which had been stalking her. Even better, it had raised the possibility of going after the beast and beating it. She heard herself saying, "When should we do it? And where?"

Dr. Harris had been suffering his own crisis. He was, perhaps, too soft-hearted for his job. Now, still perspiring from the strain of giving Dolly the hard facts, he needed a moment to realize she was agreeing with him. Then, brightening, he answered, "When is as soon as possible; the where is up to you. Of course, the Mayo's the best in the country, but there's a first-rate team in Minneapolis as well. I can contact either facility, if you like. If we move quickly, you can be mostly recovered by the holidays, and then your life can start getting better, instead of worse." His hand reached for the phone. "I know people at both hospitals. Should I make the call now?"

Aunt Dolly rose heavily. At the sight of his hand touching the phone, her courage had faltered a little. "I need to think it over." She reached across the desk and patted Dr. Harris's hand. "You'll hear from me tomorrow morning at the latest. I won't let you down, I promise. And thank you."

From the clinic Aunt Dolly drove straight out to Lake Larksdale. With a little effort, she got herself out of her Lincoln and started down the path around the lake. By the time she reached it, she was winded and her left hip and knee both hurt. She found a bench facing the water and lowered herself carefully, like an old person.

From above came a faint, raucous call she had been hearing all her life. Looking up, she saw the wild geese in their ordered V angling across the blue-gray sky. The autumnal ritual of departure reminded her she missed Harry a lot. Sadness was getting the better of Dolly, when she realized, with a laugh, that her late husband's main interest in ducks was to sneak up and fill them full of birdshot. The ducks, presumably, did not miss old Harry Stensrud at all.

Dolly straightened. For a decade the days had slipped by, and she often resented them because they were without Harry. Over the years her loneliness had weighed her down, especially around midnight. Yet sitting by the lake, thinking about what her doctor had said, Dolly had a revelation: She missed Harry, all right—but she wasn't ready to join him. Dolly was not bookish, but she remembered a line of Deborah's about how if it were done, then it were best done quickly. She fished in her handbag for her phone. She had her second mild laugh of the day thinking it was a sad sign when you knew your doctor's number by heart.

It took less than a minute to reach him.

"Dr. Harris?"

"Yes?" He sounded more tense than hopeful.

"I think the Mayo's too far away."

There was a moment's dead air until he realized what this meant. Then he said eagerly, "Thank you. I'll call Minneapolis right away. You won't regret this, Dolly."

Aunt Dolly, hoping he was right, rang off and returned the phone to her purse. She put both hands on her knees and gazed out at the water. She felt strong enough to walk again, but she simply gazed up at the autumn sky. The birds had reached the horizon, and she had heard no gunfire. She got slowly to her feet. It was going to be a long road back, but at least she was headed in the right direction.

Aunt Dolly was a pretty tough old bird, herself.

## CHAPTER TWENTY-TWO

# Aunt Dolly's Difficult Month

Aunt Dolly had not realized how much bravery would be needed to wait out the weeks between scheduling the surgery and having it. She felt herself on a perpetual shuttle between Larksdale and Minneapolis for physicals, blood tests, meetings with dieticians and even a psychiatrist, to certify she was emotionally ready for the procedure. Then came a visit to donate her own blood for the operation (with her surgeon's gruff assurance it would probably wind up unneeded and donated to another patient).

But she stayed on-plan.

She'd thought briefly of postponing until after Thanksgiving, to allow herself one more spectacular meal, but knew none would match those she'd had with Harry. She took the first available date, 6 A.M. on Monday, November first. Even with four days in the hospital, she'd be home three weeks before the holiday. Enough time, by her calculation, to lose fifteen pounds and grow strong enough to be a surprise guest at one of the other Ladies' turkey dinners. Either that, she told herself when gloomy, or to haunt them as a ghost.

To this point, Aunt Dolly had neglected but one important matter.

She had yet to tell the Ladies what she was planning to do.

By the second week in October, though, she realized not even faithful churchgoing would give her peace of mind if she did not confide in her oldest friends. So on Wednesday of that week, she called me and, sounding very serious, said she would be making an important announcement at Saturday's meeting.

It did not go quite so solemnly as Dolly had intended.

No sooner had she announced she was sick, than Deborah called out, "Oh, *there's* a hot secret."

Dolly looked flustered but nodded. "I suppose not. But maybe this is." And she went on to tell us about her plan. Of course, this was the first any of us had heard of it, and shocked silence was our response. Yet Aunt Dolly made it sound so sensible, safe, and easy, that we relaxed minute-by-minute. When she'd finished explaining, Gladys said, "And of course we'll all be there to support you."

Aunt Dolly shook her head. "I've thought about that. I'd rather just have Callie drop me off the night before, and then be on my own until it's over. I couldn't stand having everybody stuck for hours in one of those horrible waiting rooms." She smiled. "Beside, knowing you, you'll probably start a riot, or pester the male nurses, or something, and it'll all wind up on my bill."

"Well, you've *got* to let us do something," Gladys said in consternation, "or we'll go bonkers."

"Yeah. Maybe I'll give up sweets in sympathy!" Deborah cried.

"Oh, *fat chance*," Dolly said dismissively—and about five seconds later, realizing what she'd said, they all broke into hysterical laughter.

So that part of the meeting ended on a happy note, and Dolly, having asked them not to worry for her, but to say a prayer or two if so inclined, made her quiet way toward the door.

Dolly had scarcely left when Gladys demanded, "Okay, what *are* we going to do to help, really?" Everyone looked at one another. It took about two minutes of thinking for Martha to suggest, "Let's call the others."

In this group, "the others" meant simply, and only, the other Ladies.

The idea was adopted at once.

Of the original Ladies, one, Mary Maitland, had since gone to her reward; but the three others were alive, though no longer investors. Skye Terrell, the youngest and by far the coolest, had cashed in and moved to Silicon Valley many years before. Apparently she'd done brilliantly there. Sophia's mother, Lizzy Peters, was living with Sophia's dad in pleasant retirement in Florida; she had turned over voting control of their PMT stock to Sophia, and now returned to Larksdale only on special occasions.

And Agnes Jane Brinkley, who had been a children's librarian (and Gladys's junior colleague), had learned Spanish and now spent her time helping to build school libraries in Latin America—often, the Ladies assumed, subsidizing the work with money she earned from selling back her LLIC shares.

Anyway, Martha's idea of contacting old colleagues caught fire.

"I'll call my mom as soon as I get home," Sophia promised.

Gladys added, "I'll e-mail Agnes right away."

Then Deborah asked, "What about Skye?"

This, I gathered, was a bit of a sore point—or at least a point of regret. Martha had felt very close to Skye, who had been her personal project. The very conservative Martha and the very pink-haired and sexually adventurous Skye had been the ultimate odd couple, closer than most mothers and daughters, and yet at odds over nearly everything.

But Skye, it seemed, had in good measure dropped from Martha's life.

Martha inhaled deeply, then said, without her usual decisiveness, "I'll see what I can do. . . ."

Martha left several messages for Skye Terrell, who was vacationing in Switzerland, but heard nothing back. However, Lizzy Peters said she would be in Larksdale for Thanksgiving, and meanwhile would send a package. And Agnes replied quickly by e-mail that she could not leave in the middle of the school year, but was sending something, too.

And so October wound on, and the operation grew near.

CHAPTER TWENTY-THREE

# Things Go Wrong

Aunt Dolly knew she wasn't particularly brave, but in the years since Harry's death her loneliness, especially around midnight, had become indistinguishable from fear. Even surgery seemed less frightening than the prospect of a life spent getting ever sicker and lonelier.

As the big day approached, the Ladies did everything they could to encourage Aunt Dolly. They got their first invitations to speak about "Value & Values" investing that October, and though they lost a lot of gigs to local stockbrokers, and to authors pushing books like *Make A Million in Ninety Days of Options Trading,* they persisted. Every time they landed an engagement, they made a point of thanking Aunt Dolly for devising the project in the first place.

They also made her a fake booklet called *Twenty-seven Great Tap Water Recipes.*

My support was less amusing and a lot more self-interested.

Since the end of softball season, I'd had no exercise worth mentioning. I'd also been dealing with severe office boredom, and the frustration of being Jake's "pal." My solution for all these issues had been to eat Ding Dongs. In two months I was suddenly up about fifteen pounds. The trend line was not encouraging.

So a couple of days before Aunt Dolly went into the hospital, I phoned her from work, and told her—

"Listen, I thought about getting you a giant box of Ding Dongs to celebrate your new stomach; but somehow that doesn't seem quite right. So how about I promise to go to the gym with you four days a week, starting a month from the day you're out of the hospital? And we keep it up till you're in shape or I drop dead from exhaustion?"

"Well, Callie . . ." she said, and I could hear the hesitation in her voice.

"Believe me, Aunt Dolly, I'm offering as much for my sake as for yours. What do you say?"

After a pause she said, "That's a deal. Even if we don't do anything but sit at the juice bar . . ."

"Even if. But somehow I think we'll do better. I bet a year from now we'll be in the Ms. Olympia competition, or whatever the heck it's called. We'll look like Arnold Schwarzenegger with boobs. Of course, now that I think about it, *he* looks like Arnold Schwarzenegger with boobs.

She was giggling by the time I got off the phone. For someone pushing sixty and facing major surgery, she sounded absolutely girlish—it was a pleasant sound, and I decided as I put the phone down that everything would be fine.

Which shows what I knew.

* * *

I did not start really worrying about Dolly until the night before her operation.

I left her, looking worried but determined, at the hospital around 5 P.M. and, despite traffic, was back in Larksdale not long after six. It happened to be Halloween night, and while Patricia Farthingale's LCF had (naturally) sponsored both a carnival for young people and a dinner-dance for adults at the Larksdale Marriott, Vince and I had accepted Traci's quieter offer of movies at her house.

Vince had wanted to put on a suit and tie and go as an NDN executive, but I argued there was no point in scaring Traci half to death, so we compromised by investing in a cheap makeup kit and going as the undead. Traci's only comment, on opening her front door to let us in, was that I'd finally gotten my makeup right.

There were only the three of us, but our spirits were high: Traci had rented a double bill of *Young Frankenstein* and *Ghostbusters*, and we were still gloating that NDN stock had dropped a full ten points the previous week. Local experts were calling it a "mere technical correction," but it had cheered us up remarkably. Add in Traci's platters of homemade desserts, and I was ready for four hours of couch potato heaven.

But suddenly, while reaching for my third caramel popcorn ball, I started thinking about Dolly and was hit with an intense wave of loneliness. In most ways Aunt Dolly and I were entirely different: She was relaxed, down-home, and utterly uninterested in science, technology, or rising in the world. But since I'd become an orphan at fifteen, she was the one person who'd always been there for me.

And now maybe she wouldn't be.

So instead of laughing, I spent four hours worrying nonstop.

* * *

The next morning I left work at 10 A.M. to drive with Deborah, Gladys, Martha, and Sophia to visit Dolly. (That was no sacrifice: By now "work" at PMT was pretty much divided between sending out résumés and playing games on the corporate intranet; a building that had once run all night was now almost deserted by 5:05, even on weekdays.)

The operation was scheduled to begin at 6 A.M., and to take five hours. We expected to arrive about when Dolly was being moved into Recovery. Instead, we were delayed when Sophia canceled, then stuck in horrid construction traffic, and finally arrived at the medical center more than an hour late.

And then things went really badly.

We were told to go to the concierge desk. I had no idea there even *were* concierge desks at hospitals, but then Aunt Dolly, to my amazement, was listed as a VIP patient. I guess in hospitals "VIP" stands for "virtually instant payment."

The concierge desk was staffed by uniformed receptionists, not nurses. The young woman I spoke with was charming, until I gave her Dolly's name and asked for her room. She consulted a monitor, and then asked me anxiously, "Are you immediate family?"

Now, I know very little about medicine, but I do know that when you go in for, say, toenail surgery, they don't ask your visitors if they're immediate family. So I was already worried when I answered—

"Yes."

She eyed me narrowly, as if I were part of some weird society of hospital-room gate crashers. After ten or fifteen seconds' scrutiny she finally admitted, "Ms. Stensrud is in the ICU pavilion. Top floor."

My worries weren't vague anymore. Like an idiot, I asked—"ICU? Is it serious?"

We found the elevators and rode silently, exchanging only worried looks, to the fourteenth floor. The glass-walled ICU pavilion looked straight out of *Star Trek*. If you've ever wondered how five days in the hospital can cost $100,000, consider one of these pavilions. NASA needed less technology to land a man on the moon—and I'm not just talking. In a brightly lit octagonal room attendants monitored banks of LCD screens with the patients, awash in very dim greenish light, barely visible beyond the glass walls. The patient spaces looked like the assembly stations of a modern factory: There were no separate rooms, only clusters of high-tech life-support equipment around individual beds, which were spaced about fifteen feet apart. I wondered at the absence of privacy, then realized that for these patients, speed of response mattered more than privacy.

The whole scene belonged in a sci-fi movie—and that was where I was wishing it would have stayed. Unfortunately, it came to life in a most frightening manner. Three different doctors were paged, calmly, to station five, code blue. We watched the doctors converge, and then begin working at one of the most distant patient beds. We had no idea who was in bed five—and with all the control room's personnel so focused on the crisis, we had no chance to ask. Instead, we watched, mesmerized, as the distant doctors fought to save someone's life.

It was all over in less than ten minutes.

The body was covered and removed, personnel all returned to normal.

We, on the other hand, were staring at one another in mutual shock. My heart really was in my throat—or so it felt—and Deborah seemed to be having trouble swallowing. Gladys appeared frozen. Martha, coming to her senses soonest, finally asked which bed was Dolly's.

A young attendant, not looking up from his screen, answered, "Station eight."

With that it became possible to breathe again.

Dolly, who had dozed through all the drama, was a little groggy at first, but explained fairly clearly that she'd been moved to ICU because her blood pressure had spiked during the surgery: It was dangerous at the time, but had no long-term implications. Then she fussed politely but not too alertly over our presence.

I thought we should leave, but Gladys and Deborah kept the chat going, gradually bringing it around to what I might call Hospital Hilarity. Gladys, who had never been in a hospital, contributed stories about her dental phobias, including one very funny adventure when she'd fortified herself with cherry brandy before a filling, and wound up belting out "I Got Rhythm" with a mouth full of cotton balls. She'd gotten so fortified she finally slipped out of the dentist's chair entirely.

Dolly perked up when the jokes started, and soon was taking real notice, especially after Deborah got onto some awfully scandalous reminiscences of her childbirth experiences.

Through the jollity, I tried to act chipper. I thought I was hiding my feelings brilliantly, but Aunt Dolly put her hand on my knee and said, "Listen, you. I'm not here because I'm dying; I'm here because I intend to live, a lot." She took us in generally. "So cheer up, all of you." She eyed me with mock severity. "Unless you were planning to inherit my money?"

At that, Gladys fished in her big handbag. Both hands still inside it, she looked up and surveyed the room sharply. No medical personnel stood within thirty feet, and the dim light helped isolate us. The hands rose from the bag holding a small bottle and a small wrapped box. She said, "Brandy, and a box of Godiva chocolates."

"What? No cigars?"

"What do we look like? Amateurs?" Deborah reached into her purse and brought out a pair of those twist-capped metal cylinders which hold fancy cigars. "Merry Christmas early."

Dolly transferred them—a little weakly, but steadily—to the arm-table beside her. When she looked back up, she was grinning. "Thanks. Even if I can't use them myself, I can bribe a guard and bust out of here tomorrow."

"Fine," Gladys said. "And if that doesn't work, on Wednesday we'll bring you a hacksaw blade and a hundred feet of climbing rope."

Martha shook her head and looked toward the ceiling, but she was smiling.

A few minutes later I thought we were done; but Martha reached into her bag and brought out two more parcels. One was flat; the other thick, like a book. "Oh," she said, "We nearly forgot. Your friends sent these."

Dolly opened the flat one first, studied the contents, and then, grinning with what I took to be pride, passed them around for us to see. There was a stiff, pale-blue piece of notepaper and a photograph. The picture was of a bunch of kids, and one older woman I guessed to be Agnes standing in a small room full of books and a few reading tables. The kids were holding up a pretty hand-lettered sign—BIBLIOTECA SRA. DOLLY STENSRUD—and the card read:

*Dear Dolly,*

*The picture is just for information; the present is I promise not to hit you for a donation for at least a year. Take care of yourself.*

*As Ever,*
*Agnes*

When I looked up, Dolly had unwrapped the package from Sophia's mom, and the note inside had reached me. It read:

*Old Friend,*

*Mack and I are looking forward to seeing you for Thanksgiving, and he promises that if you do the carving, he'll do the eating. Meanwhile, I put together this scrapbook for you. It isn't much, but I hoped it might provide a few pleasant memories, and maybe a few laughs.*

The ladies all crowded around Dolly's bed and were studying the album reverently.

"Were we really that thin?" Martha asked.

"Were we really that young?" Gladys marveled.

"Did they have *cameras* when we were that young?" Deborah asked huskily.

The Ladies were clearly choked up, and I had to look away. In fact, I told them I'd meet them out front, and tried to act as if I was vaguely bored by all the sentiment.

But I'll tell you this: When Thanksgiving dinner came, I shot about three hundred digital snaps.

Aunt Dolly spent two more nights in the hospital, and then, very gratefully, I brought her home.

CHAPTER TWENTY-FOUR

# Thanksgiving, à la Charles Dickens

Dolly bounced back quickly. Three days after I brought her home—and moved in to keep an eye on her—she told me with a grin, "Okay, kid, clear out. This town ain't big enough for the two of us."

No long after that, she and I went to join the gym.

If only we'd made our move a few days sooner.

Only a week earlier the dusty old Main Street Gym had added ten new machines and changed its named to Larksdale Sports Fitness and Spa. It had also raised its rates from $29 to $99 a month. Even at the price, we were assured, it was still a bargain. Prices were soaring all over Larksdale: One afternoon I called a realtor about office rentals in case Traci's stalled business idea ever revived, and found the cost of space had climbed 60 percent since June. Fancy retailers from everywhere were moving into town as the NDN boom continued. Even though we had gloated at Halloween, by the first week in November the stock had regained its lost ground and added another four bucks a share. Analysts were predicting it would double again in the coming twelve months.

Stock-rich Larksdaleans were shopping as if it were two days to Christmas.

Nobody knew then that the four-dollar rise would be NDN's last hurrah.

But at PMT we knew *something* was wrong. A paralysis far worse than the summer slowdown had taken hold. Only the NDN folks were working, and their work had a very sinister cast. That rat J. Brian (who'd spent most of October avoiding me) began making frequent, unnervingly precise inspection tours which had "layoffs" written all over them.

And then good old Floyd walked in and told me he had quit. "I'm starting with a long ice-fishing trip. Just me, a slip bobber rig, and an eight-pound line." He looked away, then added, "All in all, I figure I'll be more useful sitting in an ice shack than taking up space here."

He offered a hand and added, "Well, so long Callie. If you ever launch a venture of your own, and need a gray-haired old project manager, maybe you'll think of me."

Before I could say "good-bye," he was gone.

Nobody took Floyd's place. A company-wide e-mail on the third had announced, "All hirings, promotions, and internal job transfers are now frozen pending completion of staffing review."

To fight depression during that chilly November, when most days were dark and damp, I spent late afternoons exercising with Dolly. I didn't exactly morph into a fashion model, but I did feel stronger and more energetic.

I felt even better when I got an unexpected mid-month phone call: ICAAM wanted an executive summary of the key business challenges new technologies were creating for movie studios. I asked Traci if it was a scam to get me to work for free. She was surprised at my news, then laughed and asked me what else I had to do with my time. "Besides," she added, very sensibly, "they wouldn't *use* the work of anybody in Minnesota. They just want to see if you're smart enough to move to California and learn the stuff for real."

I got real, and started researching it that very afternoon.

It beat the heck out of playing video games or staring out the cafeteria window at the rain.

And it kept me busy and happy until Thanksgiving.

Thanksgiving is always a big deal for the Ladies—and not just because they have so much to be thankful for. Christmases they usually devote to good deeds, so Thanksgiving has become, over the years, their big, lush, at-home holiday. If Charles Dickens had been American, he would have thrown dinners like theirs.

That year, though, as Turkey Day approached, the Ladies were feeling uneasy.

Their innate fiscal conservatism had them increasingly convinced a huge Internet crash was coming. They were also annoyed that Patricia Farthingale had finessed them (again!) by announcing a "Larksdale of Lights" Christmas parade, and they were upset that KLARK-TV was running a four-part series on growing drug and alcohol consumption among Larksdale's newly rich high school students.

But worry did not stop them from planning a heck of a Thanksgiving.

Martha was one of those secret cooks who once a year slips into the kitchen and whips up a nine-course extravaganza that shines like Wolfgang Puck on his best day. Thanksgiving was *her* day, and on it, her kitchen became as accessible to others as Hogwarts school is for a Muggle. I, for one, was willing to step back and let her work her magic.

David, Deborah's son, and Sophia's children, Will and Leslie, had declared their independence by arranging to spend the day with friends, so Traci, Vince, and I (with Jake's subdued cooperation) declared ourselves our own "kids' table"—just to keep the family spirit alive. We all showed up around noon, and, since we were banned from helping in the kitchen, Traci dragged us outside to toss around a football (which for me meant mostly chasing the ball down the drizzle-soaked street after it bounced out of my hands). Pretty quickly, to my disappointment, it became a long-range game of catch between Jake and Traci. Vince and I eventually went inside and had some fun hooking up Martha's snazzy new DVD player and Dolby surround sound. I'm not sure why she'd bought it, but when we were done, anytime she watched *Pride and Prejudice* on A&E, she'd really hear those witticisms whizzing past her ears.

Around three, Martha sent us on a emergency errand to the grocery. When we returned just before 4 P.M., it was all I could do to resist yelling, "Mom! We're home!" as Vince and I came in the door. By that time the fragrances coming from the kitchen were enough to drive me half-bonkers. We handed over the goods—extra lemons—and Martha let us help with setting the table (which she oversaw with the easygoing carelessness of a Marine drill instructor).

The doorbell rang, and Vince opened the door to Sophia's parents, Liz and Mack. They came in to much fanfare, hugs, and "It's been too long's." Mack was a big guy, athletic-looking even in his late sixties; Liz resembled Sophia, only a bit softer and with a lot of gray in her blond hair. They wished aloud that the grandchildren were there, then Traci piped up that we would do our best to roll our eyes and ask to be excused early. That got everyone laughing. Milt had gone into the office early that morning, but was due to reach Martha's no later than five. We all chatted and snacked on Deborah and Gladys's hors d'oeuvres as we waited.

At twenty after he had neither arrived nor called.

Martha invited everyone to the table.

When we were all seated except for Martha and Mack, the Ladies executed a gag nobody had warned me about. With considerable ceremony Martha entered the dining room holding an immense dome-covered silver platter. Setting it before us, she said, straight-faced, "I know we're all watching our diets, but after all, this is Thanksgiving. Let's splurge." She lifted the dome with a flourish.

On the platter were a dozen neatly arrayed grapes, some lettuce leaves, and a few dates.

Dolly gaped in amazement.

"No, really," Deborah protested, "I couldn't eat another bite. "I already had *half* a macaroon in the living room."

"Somebody want to split this grape with me?" Gladys asked, poker-faced.

Dolly, getting it, threw a roll at her. A moment later the kitchen door swung open again, and Mack entered carrying a magnificent turkey.

Milt arrived as we were all laughing and clapping at the joke. He sat down with apologies, praised the aromas and the food while his plate was being filled, and passed a few cheery words with his in-laws before taking up knife and fork. We'd all gathered hints (or more) of the trouble between Milt and Sophia, and I, at least, breathed a secret sigh of relief that the meal now looked likely to go smoothly.

Indeed, we sailed through many splendid courses and dessert was in sight when Gladys innocently asked Milt how work was. Before anyone could intervene, his reply escalated into an argument with Sophia, and he was insisting, "Hey! We built PMT!"

"We, and about *two thousand* other people!"

"But now it's up to *us* to save it. I can do this, *if*—"

"Do we have to discuss this *now?*"

"I'm making the case to New York Monday morning, so I kind of think we do. Are you with me, or not?"

Sophia pushed back her chair and stood, then said to the rest of us—not Milt—"Excuse us."

Milt followed her through the swinging kitchen door. For a moment we heard nothing, then their voices got louder.

"I mean it! I've got them, Sophia. We're four weeks late on the new database."

"We've run late before."

"Yeah, but I just pried loose the 2000 budget estimates. They're way underfunding everything! In six months we'll be dead, and I CAN PROVE IT."

"Oh, honey, take a deep breath. Look at you, you're—"

"I'M NOT LETTING THOSE CLOWNS SINK PMT!"

"Keep. Your. Voice. Down. The people of PMT decided in June what they wanted, which, by the way, was exactly what *you* wanted. Are you sure this is about them, or is it about *you?*"

A pause, then, "Look, maybe my ego's in this, but it's also the right thing to do. And I'm not acting behind anybody's back! I *told* Lamont Patterson I was taking my case to New York, and he told me to take my best shot. Well, so be it. The pompous son of a bitch has no one to blame. So are you with me?"

"I can't decide right now."

"I think you just did."

It took a surprisingly long time for Sophia to return. She looked chalky. "Milt's leaving."

"If he went to get some air," Sophia's mom began gently, "that might not be so bad—"

"No, I mean he's moving out of the house."

My friends and I, after a whispered conference, suggested we might take our dessert out to the greenhouses, and none of the Ladies objected. As we filed out with our coffee and pecan pie, we overheard the Ladies trying to cheer Sophia up. They reassured her that, whether he won or lost in New York, Milt would soon cool off. And that the whole thing would shortly blow over, of that they had no doubt.

Sophia listened to them politely.

And didn't believe a word.

## CHAPTER TWENTY-FIVE

# Milt Versus the Hotshots

Milt, alas, was as good as his word. By Saturday afternoon he was living in a pair of rooms in a downtown Minneapolis men's club. The following Monday, hours before dawn, he rose from his new bed, slipped quietly into the bathroom, and showered and dressed rapidly and almost silently, with the habitual quiet of a good spouse leaving on early business. The cab was on time, and the driver kept a grim silence very reasonable for 5:15 in the morning. Milt felt personally responsible for what was happening to PMT; during the silent ride to the airport he felt equally confident he could set things right. It wasn't until he was waiting to board the plane that he realized how much he had bet on this trip.

Now, Milt—whatever the New York hotshots might think—was no rube.

In the first place he was actually a New Yorker himself, by birth; and in the second, after stellar years at the University of Chicago

Law School and Wharton, he'd gone straight to McKinsey & Co., the country's top consulting firm, and hadn't come across anybody there brighter than he was. He had put everything he had into the analysis he was taking to New York: He would use all of his skill to convince the board that Lamont Patterson was a disaster for PMT and NDN, and needed to be replaced. And yet . . .

Stepping aboard the plane, Milt felt more than anything a hollowness.

He'd never imagined he would carry any fight, anywhere, without Sophia.

He certainly wasn't out of love with her. He'd fallen hard for her about five minutes after they met at law school orientation, and had stayed that way for the past twenty-two years. She'd barely noticed him in school, except as a study mate, but beginning with graduation he launched a four-year campaign to win her attentions. With straightened teeth, contact lenses, and a fitness program that would have crumpled a Green Bay rookie (plus sharp clothes and still sharper haircuts), he had turned himself from the bookish kid she'd known to the business star who reentered her life four years later.

Of course, he thought ruefully while buckling his seat belt, it hadn't been easy to stay in shape while raising a family and running a business. When this business was settled, it might be wise to rejoin a gym. . . .

When they were airborne, the first-class flight attendant brought him a lavish breakfast, but he left the eggs Benedict and potatoes, and settled for coffee and juice, and focused his mind solely on the business ahead. He had come to believe that if Larksdale and PMT were okay, he and Sophia would be okay. After all, it was PMT that brought them together. . . . So if he could set things to rights, he would be what he was before this deal: a forty-something businessman, with a wife and two great kids, from Larksdale, Minnesota.

Which, he realized with a sudden shock, was everything he really wanted to be.

His appointment was for 11 A.M.

At 10:35, slender attaché case in hand, Milt stepped out of a cab in front of Rockefeller Center, and five minutes later he was taking an express elevator to the executive suite. He stepped out of the elevator into late-autumn light, shining clear and hopeful through the floor-to-ceiling windows and glancing off framed posters from some of the biggest hit films of NDN's recently acquired movie studio. Milt was glad for his scheduled time alone with the CEO, Martin Davis, before he had to address the whole board.

He was also glad to have a few minutes' wait to steady his nerves.

He spent the time studying the movie posters, and then passing a few friendly words with the CEO's secretary. When he was told he could go in, Milt felt his heart leap as it had not since his first date with Sophia.

Martin Davis was early middle age, oldish for a high-tech chieftain.

He wore a black business suit with an expensive dark tie. His dark hair had receded halfway across his scalp, but was cut so as to be fairly hip. Rising to shake Milt's hand, he stood perhaps five ten and had a serious-but-pleasant expression.

Milt, taking the chair he was offered, started to relax.

Davis began, "I'm glad we have this time to chat, Milt. It's a lot friendlier than a board meeting."

Milt, startled, said carefully, "I still appreciate the chance to address the board. I have some strong ideas for—"

"Sure, sure. But why put so much pressure on your first visit here?"

Milt, who was anything but a fool, already saw what was coming.

"In fact, why not treat this trip as a chance to get the flavor of New York? Try some good restaurants, take in a Broadway play—"

"Mr. Davis." Milt decided to be blunt. "I may have spent the last ten years in Larksdale, but I made my bones at McKinsey, right here in New York. I'm not some farm boy gawking at the bright lights. I'd appreciate the chance to address the board."

"You think I didn't do my homework?" Davis replied, taking it well. "Milt, I know everything about you, from the grade you got in your Corporations course in law school—congratulations on that, by the way"—he gave Milt a friendly grin—"to what you earned last year at PMT. As for that last number, I think we can raise it a lot—maybe triple it, maybe more."

Milt said nothing.

"Our execution wasn't one hundred percent on this one, Milt. But I assure you, we definitely want you on our corporate team. Here in New York for a year or two, and after that either D.C. or the coast, as you prefer. And we've got a compensation package going forward that I think will get your attention." Davis spread his hands, in an admission of error. "It was wrong of us, maybe, to spring this on you. But you're no fool, and you probably know what's coming. We don't need to review next year's plans for PMT, because PMT is going out of business."

Milt opened his mouth to protest, but Davis went on smoothly and quickly, "We're closing down Larksdale operations and transferring software development to Maryland, and existing-product sales and service to Arizona. Everything's being rebranded as NDN product." Davis leaned back in his chair. "There it is. But I think you know it's good news for you. One big reason we bought PMT was to get you, and bring you onboard here at corporate."

"With all due respect, Martin," Milt said, without a blink, "I think that's a big mistake." He paused. "I think we can make PMT more than viable. I think we can make it a big success."

"As a technology, yes. As a company, not a chance." Davis shook his head. "Maryland gives us economies of scale, and a depth of programming talent, that Barksdale—"

"*Larks*dale."

"—that *Larks*dale couldn't match in a hundred years. Besides, we've already got critical mass in Maryland; it's second only to right here as a center."

Milt persisted. "Martin, NDN liked our products well enough to buy the company. But it took a team of *two thousand* people to get those products to market—"

"*Abso*lutely. But how many of those people were really core? A hundred programmers? Two hundred? You pick them, we'll offer them jobs in Maryland. We'd be fools not to."

Milt barely stopped himself from saying, "You're fools, period." He counted to five, mentally, then said, "I'm sorry, Martin. I know you're doing what you think is best for your shareholders. But I'm not in agreement, and if you insist, then I'm afraid I'll have to exercise the amicable separation buyout clause in my cont—"

"Now, *wait* a minute." Martin Davis was leaning forward, and looking a good deal less genial. "Your contract has a few conditions in it, including something about 'facilitating the complete integration of PMT Software into NDN.' Those aren't the exact words; I'm not a lawyer, I'm just a simple MBA. But I'm sure we wouldn't have agreed to pay you what we did if you refused to help shut down Larksdale and get things running down in Maryland."

It wouldn't be fair to say Milt's whole life flashed in front of him. Just the evening he forgot to review the employment contract because he was so busy arguing with his wife. Luckily, he was leaning back in his chair. That made it impossible for him to act on his impulse to kick himself. Instead, he bluffed firmly, "I *am* a lawyer. And as *I* read the contract—"

Davis raised his hand. "And the courts may well agree with you—in five or six years." He turned his chair away in one of those patented CEO gestures which are somewhere between a reaching-for-the-phone and a plain old dismissal. On a generous impulse, though, he halted himself, turned back slightly, and told Milt, "Why don't you take a couple of days to think it over? You're loyal to the town, that's natural. But believe me, even with PMT ending, this deal has been great for them."

Milt had reached New York under probably the worst pressure of his life, and now the temptation either to explode or to implode was immense. But ever the pro, trained to negotiate by some of the best in the business, he bought himself a few moments by nodding, holding up a hand, and then fishing in his pocket for a handkerchief. He fake-coughed into it while struggling to control his temper.

He was angrier with himself than with anyone else.

At McKinsey he had seen uncountable shutdowns, and he should have seen this one coming. But while he had been bristling at being sidelined, and planning to return as a hero, Lamont Patterson and NDN had been intentionally and intelligently dismantling his life's work. He wanted revenge. He wanted justice. But for now he'd run out of room. Without more planning, he couldn't save PMT. The business case against it was too strong, and people like Martin Davis never saw beyond the business case.

The smart move was to make a quiet retreat, but Milt was too upset for that.

So, for once in his life, he indulged himself in speaking his mind.

He popped to his feet, grabbed his attaché case, and said with a smile, "I'm just a small-town boy at heart, so maybe I *am* missing the big picture. And maybe I *will* go see a play. Is there anything on Broadway about a bunch of crooked businessmen who go to jail? Sounds like just the story I'm in the mood for."

He turned and left, but he didn't feel clever.

By the time he reached the elevators, he just felt lost.

CHAPTER TWENTY-SIX

# Sophia Hits the Road

The Ladies did not let Sophia mope. They were good listeners, true, available to sympathize over her troubles day or night, but they always—above all else—believed in action. And they found an action for her almost at once.

Their first speaking engagement, in the tiny town of Dogg, just across the North Dakota border, was booked for the first weekend of December. Deborah had been scheduled to take it; but now the Ladies pressed Sophia to go instead, since, in Deborah's blunt phrase, "You can't just sit home and rot."

After discussing it with Will and Leslie, Sophia agreed. She was startled by how nonchalant her children were, how quickly they seemed to be adapting to life without Milt in the house. As for herself, she realized she was glad to go somewhere—anywhere—where his absence wouldn't be so painful.

Sophia dropped Will and Leslie off at Deborah's the evening

before she left. She suffered pangs watching them pull their suitcases from the back of the Explorer, and Deborah, no fool, saw she needed comforting. After Will and Leslie headed upstairs with David, she served Sophia coffee in the kitchen and asked, "So, how are you holding up?"

Sophia added milk to the coffee, which Deborah always made at roughly the strength of condensed espresso. "I was trying to figure out how many business trips I took without Milt over the years. I quit at thirty, including four to Europe."

"We don't *need* them, maybe, but it's nice to know they're around."

Sophia felt her throat tightening as she started to answer, so she said nothing.

She lifted her mug to her lips and drank; one sip, and she felt as if her tongue had been boarded by pirates. She noticed that Deborah was eyeing her own cup dubiously.

"Is this coffee kind of *weak?*" she asked.

"It's perfect." Sophia rose slowly. "I'd better be going. I leave at dawn."

As they reached the foyer, Deborah cupped her hands around her mouth and called loudly, "Will! Leslie! Your mom's leaving!" She had to call their names twice more before Leslie, coming from one room, and the boys, coming from another and looking very put-upon, appeared at the top of the stairs.

"Don't you want to come down and kiss me good-bye?" Sophia asked.

"We're playing *Diablo* on David's computer!" Will sounded deeply offended.

"And I was afraid I wouldn't raise an intellectual," Deborah muttered.

Leslie came halfway down the stairs and told Sophia, "See you Monday night."

It was a distressing farewell.

The night was cold and dry as Deborah walked Sophia to her car. "Listen, kid," Deborah said, putting a kindly hand on her shoulder, "all my life, I've had a . . . a reverence for people who fought on when the odds were against them: The Spartans at Thermopylae . . . the Corps at Guadalcanal . . . most women through most of history. It's going to work out, you and Milt. Meanwhile, have an adventure. That's an order."

The early morning air was chill, and the leaves were changing. Before she reluctantly turned toward the interstate, Sophia spent a pleasant hour driving past the muted reds and yellows of birch and aspen stands. Along one lakefront stretch the trees shimmered in blued reflections and made her think of *Hiawatha*. It took about five hours to hit the North Dakota border, and by the time she stopped for lunch, the sun was high and, to her amazement, she was eager for whatever the road might offer.

She reached Dogg at two in the afternoon. On the drive she'd suffered a bout of performance nerves—but she found something so comforting in the scattered farmhouses and autumn fields in this little town that she couldn't stay worried. If this was what running away felt like, she was entirely in favor of it.

Jolly as Sophia was feeling, the quaint town didn't seem to promise much adventure, except maybe the thrill of chasing her hat down the street. She hadn't really felt the wind driving west—it rarely hit her SUV broadside—but as she parked in front of the Dogg House Hotel, it began rocking the vehicle side to side. She was making her careful way onto the street when a cheery voice boomed out, "Don't tell me! Sophia Peters?"

Turning her head, she saw a beaming young man about the size of an oak tree extending an immense hand toward her. He helped her out of her car, while adding, in slightly softer tones, "I'm Mayor Hackett, but everyone calls me Tiny. Which ought to give you an idea of what passes for comedy around here, but it's better than Hacksaw, which was my nickname when I played college ball. Come on with me, and I'll get you oriented."

He led her down the street to the City Hall, a single-story concrete building, and kept talking the whole way. He was a mobile windbreak, which Sophia appreciated; he was also an amusing talker and a relentless town booster. Stepping in out of the icy wind, they were met by a plump redheaded woman wearing half glasses. "This is my assistant mayor, Loretta Parely. Ignore her, Sophia; she's smart, but she has a negative outlook."

"This town needs one realist. Has he told you about his plan to have movie stars live here?" Loretta asked placidly. But she wasn't moving placidly; she was shepherding them very efficiently through the low, swinging gate, to the space behind the counter and then toward the door marked MAYOR.

Mayor Hackett was hammering his point. "Look at all the Hollywood people moving to Montana! What's Montana got that we don't?"

"Cowboys," Loretta said decisively.

"North Dakota's got cowboys."

"Jesse James, maybe." She turned her plain, friendly face to Sophia. "Don't take Hizzoner's boosterism too seriously. The last big news for this state was Lewis and Clark in 1805." She smiled slyly. "People are still talking about it."

Sophia said cheerfully that Larksdale was pretty much like Dogg *without* Lewis and Clark. They waved her into the mayor's office, where for thirty minutes Mayor Hacksaw turned off the booming charm and spoke very sensibly about the economic problems of small towns in the Dakotas. When she left, Sophia was more convinced than ever that Value & Values was a legitimate cause.

It felt good to have a purpose.

At eight that evening, waiting to address a full room at the Dogg Regional Library, her nerves kicked in again in full force, and she felt her heart begin to sink. Could she really help these people? The Ladies, at least at the outset, hadn't been clever investors. They'd simply caught an astounding break when their pink-haired young ward, Skye Terrell, turned out to understand technologies almost nobody had heard of in 1983. Even when they bought PMT, they'd been lucky: Mary's husband had come to them with news of the hot Internet technology buried within the stodgy company. *Will these people think I have nothing to offer but luck . . . ?*

As Sophia stepped to the podium, an immensely fat man of perhaps fifty called out, "So? Are you going to tell us all how to get rich?"

And Sophia, just as cheerfully, called back, "No, but maybe I can tell you how to keep from going broke. Will that help any?"

The crowd laughed, and the ice was broken.

After that, it went well. She was a little stunned to hear that even in rural North Dakota people were day-trading stocks on their computers. But she was prepared for most of the questions and answered them with straightforward good humor. She spoke for forty minutes and took questions for over an hour.

She told herself she was probably the cheapest entertainment in a not-very-entertaining town, but she didn't mind. She was having fun, and not thinking about Milt.

A few minutes before ten, Mayor Hackett stepped to the mike and suggested everyone give Sophia a nice round of applause. They did, and then the crowd divided. Most of them stampeded for the snack tables set up in the Children's Lit section, but about half a dozen, the shyest and the ones most convinced they had a million-dollar idea, stepped up to the podium to chat. Sophia spent another half an hour with them and answered all their questions.

Only as she was slipping her papers back into a manila folder did Sophia notice the two small women at the very back of the auditorium. With the room empty they finally came forward. "We'd like to introduce ourselves. We're the Hagenbloom sisters. I'm Muriel, and this is Emma."

Sophia said she was pleased to meet them, and when nothing followed, invited them to coffee at her hotel. Silence prevailed on the walk; but when they were in the coffee shop and had ordered, and Sophia asked how she could help, the sisters exchanged looks. Then Muriel said, "Why, we've got wind."

Sophia thought of one or two mildly scandalous jokes but, with a very straight face, answered simply, "You do?" She began wondering how soon she'd be able to return to her room.

Muriel, apparently not so dull as she seemed, blushed faintly, smiled less faintly, and corrected herself, "I put that badly. I'd better start again." From a neat yellow folder she extracted a photocopied newspaper piece. "We clipped this out of the *Bismarck Times* a few months ago."

From the size of the type, Sophia guessed the story had run on the second or third page. Taking it, she read MIDWEST WIND

POWER TO DOUBLE IN EIGHTEEN MONTHS, STUDY SAYS. She scanned the first few paragraphs, about wind power projects being considered around the Dakotas, then handed back the paper. "That's very interesting. And . . . ?"

The two sisters exchanged another glance, a kind of silent consultation, then Muriel said, "The thing is, we own a farm in a place called Quiet Valley."

"Quiet Valley?" Sophia would have been more interested in a wind farm called "Wild Storms" or "Hurricane Gulf." "That sounds very . . . peaceful."

The two sisters smiled politely. Muriel said, "That was Great-grandfather's joke. After listening to the wind howl nonstop his entire first winter there, he said he'd swap the whole valley for ten minutes' quiet, so that's what he named it."

At this point Emma, who had not spoken, seemed to lose patience with the leisurely pace of the conversation. "What Muriel's trying to say is that we think Quiet Valley would be a natural place for a wind farm. And a wind farm could be a good business, and it would also help a little to clean up pollution and make the country more independent, since power plants that don't burn coal usually burn oil. So we thought that might fit with your whole idea of 'Value and Values' investing. Were we right?"

Having said so much so concisely, Emma returned to stirring sugar into her coffee.

Sophia was no energy expert, but as an educated Minnesotan, she knew wind power plants, "wind farms," were rising in many places on the prairie. But she *also* knew why North Dakota—often called "The Saudi Arabia of Wind Power" because of the high-velocity winds that sweep much of its northern half—hadn't yet broken into the market. As gently as she could, she said, "I thought nobody could afford to build a two-hundred-mile transmission line to get the power from where the wind blows to where the people live?"

Muriel Hagenbloom positively grinned. "We don't have to send power two hundred miles, because Quiet Valley *isn't* in North-Central. It's a geological freak, made by glaciers, and it's on the Minnesota border. It's only seventeen miles from Quiet Valley to a tie-in to the WMRPG—the Western Minnesota Regional Power Grid. The power lines come that close because they're running to a huge coal power plant at Little Twig."

Sophia had listened to a lot of pitches in her life. The Hagenbloom sisters weren't much on delivery, but they seemed to have the facts. To hold down her rising excitement, she asked coolly, "Why didn't the people from the energy companies figure this out?"

"They made a mistake," Emma said. "Important people—experts—make mistakes, don't they? Just like other people?"

"It's been known to happen." Sophia was starting to like these two. "Go on."

"Well," Muriel said, with a prim glance at Emma, "first of all, we should say, in fairness to the energy folks, that maybe we disappeared off their maps because, by Dakota standards, our place isn't all that big."

Sophia felt a strange mixture of relief and disappointment: She'd been *sure* there was a flaw in the plan. Nobody would run even seventeen miles' worth of power lines to some micro-farm, however windy.

Still, to be polite, she asked, "How big, roughly, is it?"

"Well, even counting the surrounding hills, which aren't as windy, it's only fourteen thousand acres."

Sophia, in a notable breach of manners, spat coffee halfway across the table.

* * *

Tucking herself into bed, Sophia felt strongly she was already dreaming.

It wasn't just that the Hagenbloom sisters—unless they were total loons, who'd invented everything—seemed to have a real business proposition. It was the fierce sense of *déjà vu*. She hadn't felt so much faith in life's goofy possibilities since the day, two decades earlier, her mother had told her she and her Mostly Methodist Club friends had accumulated over $300,000 in stock.

Then she'd been a newly minted lawyer; everything was a potential adventure.

Now she had a large assortment of battle scars.

Yet, on the corner of her hotel room dresser, she also had the Hagenbloom sisters' neat yellow folder. Inside was the Dakota Territories Land Office title description for Quiet Valley, and a brief letter from a man named Dale Harper on stationery from West Texas Consolidated Energy. He wanted to discuss buying wind rights.

That letter, of course, had been the reason the Hagenbloom sisters waylaid Sophia. They wanted her to represent them in negotiations with Mr. Harper. She had warned them there was much to be proven—from the wind's strength, to their undisputed ownership of it—before anybody would be making any deals. She'd also added, very insistently, that many *other* attorneys would be better qualified to help. They, in turn, insisted that they liked the way the Ladies did business, and that she would suit them to a *T*.

And that was how Sophia, lying in bed at 3 A.M., and contemplating taking on her first private clients in more than fifteen years, found herself smiling.

CHAPTER TWENTY-SEVEN

# The Wind Business

Three days later Sophia was sitting at an aged wooden desk in the main branch of the Bismarck Public Library reviewing the Quiet Valley land title report. She was bringing herself up to speed, having already read a stack of articles on wind power, and conducted two long phone interviews: one with the Hagenbloom sisters, and one with a top wind licensing attorney. From the lawyer she had learned everything she could about wind royalties paid to landowners. Now just two tasks remained: She needed a professional opinion on the land title, and she wanted to see one of these windmills that were creating all the excitement.

She had also done some hasty cramming on North Dakota history.

She stretched and rested her eyes for a moment, and thought of what she'd learned.

Lars Hagenbloom had been a hell of a fellow. In 1863, one

year after the act creating the Dakota Territories, he set out from New York for the unknown. In 1865 he spent virtually his whole stake, plus every penny he could borrow, for the vast stretch of land which included Quiet Valley. Then he dug in and held on through Indian Wars and predatory Eastern investors.

And he struck red gold.

The cattle-raising Badlands of western Dakota are better known in history, but in the 1870s the rich land of eastern Dakota Territory produced wheat crops so profitable, properties there became known as Bounty Farms. Vast fortunes were made (and usually squandered) by the lucky farmers. Lars Hagenbloom made his fortune (saved it), and in 1905 he bequeathed his only son, Eric, 18,000 acres and $470,000 in gold-backed securities, with strict instructions never to mortgage an acre of land. The Depression battered Hagenbloom's carefully designed system, but did not wreck it, though Lilly Hagenbloom, Eric's widow, saw all the cash and securities eaten up, and in 1939 sold 4,000 acres to save the rest of the farm. World War II and the following boom saved her, but just barely: The farm she passed on to her daughters, Muriel and Emma, had never again known prosperity. By 1999 it was only a small working area, plus a lot of fallow land.

That was where wind came in.

Sophia opened her eyes and scanned the title report one last time.

A little before noon, her cramming session through, Sophia dropped off the title report at the offices of Hanlon Packard, Esq., a highly recommended land attorney. Mr. Packard's offices occupied a restored Victorian home, and the furnishings appeared to date from an earlier century, as, in a way, did Mr. Packard himself, with his round face and smallish gold-rimmed glasses, and black suit with somber bow tie. Only the laptop computer, with the ethernet cable connected neatly to its back port, seemed to speak of the present age. That reassured Sophia, and so did his crisp geniality. He was a good listener, and a concise talker, and they covered the key issues and the need for a rush opinion very smoothly.

Half an hour later Sophia was driving west, to see a big wind farm Mr. Packard had recommended.

Sophia fell in love with the wind turbines. They were so graceful, their arms constantly sweeping long arcs across blue sky and white clouds, and the noise they made reminded her of the hand-powered lawn mowers of her childhood. Of course, there were also the grander issues to love: clean air, a safer environment, and energy independence, all of which she was patriotic enough to value. In any case, Sophia knew one thing as she drove back to Bismarck:

Don Quixote wanted to fight windmills. She wanted to spread them everywhere.

The Hagenblooms had found the right attorney.

"Well? Is their title clear?" Sophia asked the following morning.

Mr. Packard was handing the packet back to her, and he smiled. "Clear as a country stream. I'd invest in it myself, only I worry whether a place named Quiet Valley has much hope as a wind farm."

As Sophia neared the end of the long drive to the Hagenblooms', she worried over what Mr. Packard had said. *Did the place have sufficient air velocity?* She also wondered whether this Mr. Harper she would be dealing with was an honest man.

The first worry was settled about fifteen seconds later.

As she came around a rocky bluff, what felt like a sonic *BOOM* hit her Explorer. The little SUV bucked sideways to the limit of its springs, and swerved across the dotted line as if a soft-nosed truck had hit it with a *WHAM!* like an explosion.

That was one problem solved.

The Hagenbloom sisters *definitely* had wind.

And Dale Harper, who had arrived at the farm ahead of her, seemed a nice young man. His smooth face was windburned; the hand he offered was calloused; and his manner was neatly split between businesslike and friendly. Sophia, who knew liking isn't a big part of negotiating, still decided she liked him; and for a kid, he showed a lot of poise. After they were welcomed into the farmhouse by the Hagenbloom sisters, and were seated, he began. "Ms. Peters, I know from checking that you're good at your job, so I'll just give you the contracts and wait for your questions."

Then he handed over the papers and shut up.

Sophia read, and she needed all her years of experience to keep a bland expression. Based on what she'd learned during her marathon phone discussion with one of the country's top wind licensing attorneys, she could see that what Dale Harper was offering was an absolute sweetheart deal. When she finished reading, calmly as she could, she looked up and asked, "I assume we can have time?"

"I'm afraid not."

When Sophia looked startled, Harper blushed. "I mean, of

course *you* can have more time, the company will still be here, only I won't. I'm leaving Monday for a job with GE. This is my farewell deal, and I want it to be a good one, for everybody." He leaned forward, with his hands on his knees. Sophia figured if he intended to slip one over on them, this was where it would happen. But what he said was, "Let me explain. The New York bankers and the Texas oilmen behind this company couldn't care less about North Dakota. But I grew up here, and I'm no hustler, and I'm telling you this is the best deal you're going to get, anywhere, by a wide margin. It's no gift—you've got a prime property—but other people will still offer you less, because that's how the business is."

Sophia knew most deals are dragged out so the people involved can feel they're earning their money. Moreover, the best negotiator she'd ever known once told her, "Negotiating has only two stages: *Know* what you want, and *get* it. Problem is, most people never get past stage one." She felt an almost physical jolt as she remembered the negotiator who had told her that was *Milt*.

Sophia signaled the sisters to join her in the other room; while they walked, she thought fast and carefully. By the time they reached the kitchen, she felt ready. "As far as I can tell, the deal's as good as they come. But remember: I'm a one-day expert. I *still* think you should get yourselves an attorney—or a whole firm—that knows power deals."

"In the first place, you're not our attorney; you're our friend. And in the second, we believe in you."

"Believing's fine, but I'm a lawyer. My job's to make it *safe* for you to believe."

"You already have," Emma said. "And we're taking the deal."

From then to signing took less than half an hour.

Fifteen minutes after that, Dale Harper's truck—with Dale's hand waving slowly out the driver's window—disappeared down the road. Sophia, in high spirits, was taking leave of the Hagenblooms as well. "I'll be heading out now, ladies."

Technically speaking, of course, Sophia was entirely off the hook. She had admitted her limitations and advised the Hagenblooms to get better counsel. But her sheer happiness came from more than that. Deborah was right: Whatever happened with Milt, she would be fine.

Over the howling wind Muriel said, "You've done a great job; we want to pay you for it."

Sophia shook her head like the fun-loving young woman she'd been twenty years earlier. "You've done me more good than you know. If you insist, and the deal pays off, send a check to some good cause. Anything you like."

They seemed inclined to argue—very politely, of course.

But Sophia merely shook her head again and grinned. Feeling like the Lone Ranger riding out of town, she said, "My work's done here. Happy to have met you."

And she started the long drive home.

CHAPTER TWENTY-EIGHT

# The Run-up to Christmas

Sophia's adventures in Dogg made a good story for the Ladies' next Saturday meeting but led to no further speaking invitations. Value & Values were not in fashion: NDN hit an all-time high that early December, and Twin Cities TV stations ran evening news features on what one called "The Gold Coast of the Midwest."

To be sure, critics were warning that Internet stocks were poised to collapse. They weren't quite voices crying in the wilderness—more like voices crying on the *Today* show—but nobody took them very seriously. The people with money were just having too much fun. I suspect some folks onboard the *Titanic,* seeing the iceberg looming, wondered how much champagne it could chill.

The Ladies had worries of their own, most definitely including Sophia. When she asked, shortly after finishing her amusing account of Dogg and the windmills, whether anybody had seen Milt lately, an awkward silence fell, until Deborah cleared her throat and changed the topic by saying, "At least he hasn't signed on as grand marshall of Farthingale's Folly."

The irritating-but-energetic Patricia Farthingale had outflanked the Ladies yet again, this time by going on *Good Morning, Larksdale* to promote her Larksdale of Lights holiday celebration (which Deborah had started calling "Farthingale's Folly") as "something the entire community can—or at least *should*—support." She'd gone on to explain that *some* rich people in Larksdale had become so exclusive they were invisible to "the regular folks of this town." When Deborah and the other Ladies heard about it, steam had practically shot from their ears.

Deborah's tactic worked. Sophia snapped out of her gloomy moment to say firmly, "That woman would try the patience of a saint, so you can figure how ticked-off *I* am!"

"We need to go on TV, ourselves, and straighten out the record," Gladys said.

"We need a press agent," Dolly added, not sounding entirely serious.

"What we need," Martha said decisively, "is to be good sports."

The Ladies gaped at her, then Deborah said with some amusement, "You are so *irritating* when you're right."

And that was how they agreed to take part in Larksdale of Lights.

The Ladies were doing a lot better job of getting into the holiday mood than I was. I started December feeling grumpy, and seemed to feel grumpier every day. The PMT Christmas party was moved up super-early, to the twelfth, because so many people (but not me) planned to be in New York for the *real* party at

NDN. *That* party would be filled with stars from NDN's studio side, and bands from its recording label. Then, of course, many newly rich Larksdaleans would be leaving town later in the month, to ring in the new millennium in exotic vacation spots. The rest of us, with nothing to do in the office, and nowhere exotic to go, might as well have raised a giant banner over ourselves reading LOSERS.

On top of that, on the seventh Jake announced he was spending Christmas in Colorado; and on the eighth Milt, looking just a bit desperate, stopped by my cubicle to ask whether the hardware group had any killer projects that happened not to have reached the executive suite yet. I liked Milt—I'd met him socially, through the Ladies, and he always treated me kindly—so I felt extra bad having to tell him the truth: Not only were we fresh out of killer ideas, but our morale basically made *Das Boot* look like a cruise ship.

I did my best to get over my grump by hitting the gym daily and helping Aunt Dolly with her craftsy presents (she really was gifted at anything from macramé to pottery); but by around the ninth I was ready to play the first female Ebeneezer Scrooge.

My absolute low came the morning of the tenth, when the intra-office mail cart brought me almost a dozen Christmas cards. Now, I *love* getting cards, but most of these were from people I barely knew. When I opened them, five showed families I didn't know *at all,* standing in front of fancy new cars, fancy new houses, or both. I was just glowering at the last of these when Traci stuck her head into my cubicle.

"What're you doing?"

"Oh"—I threw a card down in disgust—"just reading about my dear friends, the IownaFerraris."

"You, too, huh?"

I straightened in my chair. Real complaining takes focus and discipline. "I don't know why I still show up here. I have absolutely *nothing* to do."

"You're telling me. Monica Rathburn isn't even submitting Legal's budget until next month. She told us to "act as if it's approved," but except for routine junk, all the legal work's been shifted to New York. If I had a conscience, I'd be feeling guilty about taking a paycheck. Luckily," she ended, slipping into my guest chair, "I have no conscience."

There's no telling how gloomy this might have grown, but just then Vince ambled into my cubicle carrying a shoe box lined with wax paper. He lifted the lid, and out drifted the aroma of warm chocolate. It smelled heavenly. "From Alicia," he said.

I was on my feet. "Put your hands on your head and step away from the brownies."

A moment later, with chocolate melting in my mouth (and around it, and all over my hands), I asked, "What's everybody doing for Christmas?" I asked it reluctantly, because, much as I wanted company, I feared Traci and Vince would, like normal people, have plans. I needn't have worried.

"Me?" Traci said, with a snort. "Staying right here. Last Christmas my father read about chimney fires in *Consumer Reports,* and ten minutes later he had me out on the roof trying to scrape soot out of the chimney pot with a screwdriver." She shuddered. "I love my parents, but since they've moved to Alaska . . ." She shuddered again and fell silent.

This gave me hope I might actually not spend Christmas alone. I even fantasized briefly about Vince's helping us modify my Taurus so it looked like a spaceship for the Larksdale of Lights parade. With sparks flying out the tailpipe . . .

But Vince surprised me. "I was thinking this might be a good

Christmas to do something for somebody else. I'm signed up to serve dinner down at FM. You both could do it, too."

"FM" was Vince-speak for First Methodist, a place I knew all too well. I looked to Traci to frame an excuse for us both, but she, being at heart very spiritual and old-fashioned, said, "Well, we could either do that, or stay home and wait for three ghosts to visit." Then, perhaps thinking she'd been too grim, she slapped me lightly on the arm and added, "It'll be fun!"

So I dialed a number Vince gave me, and heard a voice I hadn't heard in over a decade. It had no sooner said, "First Methodist Outreach," than I blurted, "Mrs. Lamarcka? It's Callie Brentland." To my own ears, I sounded about eleven years old and up to no good.

Apparently I sounded the same way to her. She answered, in a tone most people would use to say root canal, "*Callie?* What a surprise."

My early life of crime had just caught up with me. If you've ever seen the movie *Lilo and Stitch,* you've got a good idea of my Sunday School behavior. I think Stitch is described as "an evil koala." I wasn't that cute. So I skipped the pleasantries and asked if the church still needed volunteers for Christmas dinner. After a long silence, as if weighing the moral cost of fibbing, Mrs. Lamarcka admitted they did.

Alas, once committed, I tried to be sociable. "Think we'll have enough people to feed?"

"Well, it's odd, Callie. Poor people aren't taking off for the Bahamas this year like they usually do."

Good old Mrs. Lamarcka. Eleven years since she'd last taken a shot at me, and her aim was as good as ever. "I get you, Mrs. Lamarcka. So you can put me down, and also Traci. You remember Traci Morrison?"

"Of course. Now, *there* was a—"

"Absolutely!" The last thing I needed was to hear how Traci had outvirtued me since forever, so I stepped on Mrs. Lamarcka's line. "Count her in, too."

"With *pleasure*. Our next CDC prep meeting is 8 A.M. tomorrow. Try not to oversleep, Callie."

It's so great to be home.

## CHAPTER TWENTY-NINE

# I Get with the Program

Over the next two weeks, bossy Mrs. Lamarcka notwithstanding, I became totally wrapped up in the Christmas Dinner Committee.

We were short-staffed: Beyond Traci, Vince, and me, we had only Mrs. Lamarcka and her best friend, the equally bossy Betsy Rawlings and an almost silent assistant pastor named Dr. Kim. The Larksdale Ladies were funding the dinner, as always, but this year were taking little active part because of their decision to support Larksdale of Lights. All the other CDC regulars had Christmas travel plans. With only six of us, it took a lot of hustle and hurry (which I love and wasn't getting at PMT) to cover all the bases, and a slew of meetings to make sure things would run smoothly. All in all, I was so happy to be busy again I wasn't even worried that I hadn't heard back from ICAAM: I figured if they were as busy as I was, they wouldn't be in touch until after the new millennium.

Which explains why we were all alarmed when, the Wednesday before Christmas, Mrs. Lamarcka told us not to worry.

"I don't want to alarm anyone," she began, chilling our blood, "but the Salvation Army in Minneapolis just called. There's a rumor that, with Larksdale so rich, our free Christmas dinner is definitely the place to be." She then assured us the church basement's commercial-grade kitchen could handle all the needed extra side dishes—the yams, mashed potatoes, and vegetables—just by starting early.

"What about staff?" Betsy Rawlings demanded.

This had been a sore point since the first CDC meeting: They were worried that our newly rich youth would decide charity began at home, and spend their holidays buying themselves fancy gifts, rather than helping dole out mashed potatoes and gravy.

"I think we're fine, with the six of us, plus eighteen volunteer servers from the Larksdale High senior class." Mrs. Lamarcka brimmed with irony. "Young people always need a community-service line for their college applications." Her tart little smile vanishing, she went on, "Unfortunately, the kitchen can't handle the extra six turkeys and two dozen extra pies I'm afraid we'll need." She fixed Traci and me with a cold eye and asked, "Could anybody *volunteer* to do some cooking at home?"

I volunteered to make a turkey, and Traci, who could (of course) bake like a pro, put herself down for four pies. We agreed between us to try to persuade J'Nelle to contribute, too.

Dr. Kim shot us a beatific smile and commended us for our charity.

I suddenly felt quite virtuous.

## CHAPTER THIRTY

# Milt Tries New York Again

All that December of 1999, New York was like a wonderland, in both senses of "wonder": both "wonderful," and you had to "wonder" what the heck was going on. That place, that month, was about as wildly rich as any place had been since the Conquistadors rolled back into Madrid around 1550. The car showrooms featured Bentleys and Land Rovers tied up with red bows; the Porsche Boxsters and the BMWs were for the ordinary workers of the stock-market boom.

On a snowy Friday, the day before Christmas, Milt was in a cab, pulling up in front of the NDN Tower lobby. He was tired but excited: tired, because he had been up most of the night in his Plaza room rehearsing the pitch he was about to make to Martin Davis, and excited because he had with him a realistic plan to save PMT.

The plan was 20 percent guesswork, 20 percent hard-nosed

job cuts, and 60 percent brilliant strategy that would lead PMT into strong new markets. Knowing he had at most one last shot at saving PMT, Milt had created the plan over several days and nights of nonstop work. Then he had spent ten long days seeking a second appointment with Davis. To get it he had to eat a lot of crow—but that did not matter to him. He felt responsible for the fourteen hundred employees who were *not* stock-rich.

To save PMT, Milt would have gone on the Dr. Atkins All-Crow diet.

Finally, on Thursday morning, Davis agreed to give him fifteen minutes at 9 A.M. Friday to make his case.

And now Milt was there, and he was ready.

At 9 A.M. on a normal business day, the NDN Tower lobby would have been too crowded to allow visibility for more than a few yards ahead. But this morning, with much of New York already closed for the holiday, Milt could easily see, across the lobby, Martin Davis leaving an elevator and starting toward him—that is, toward the exit. Davis was moving fast, and when he saw Milt, he did not look happy.

One absolute requirement for business success is an efficient reset button.

Milt instantly forgot his planned presentation—and his right to his scheduled meeting—and prepared a six-sentence pitch that would get him back in the game.

He expected Davis to stop when he reached him, but Davis merely grunted something vaguely friendly and kept striding for the glass doors. Milt was a good four inches taller than Martin Davis and, while a little out of shape, still held a black belt in Tae Kwon Do. It crossed his mind to slam the little rat up against one of the lobby's marble walls. Instead, he swung around to keep pace with him and called, "I'd like to talk with you about my propos—"

Davis, accelerating, shot Milt an annoyed glance, shook his head, and said bluntly, "PMT's dead, end of next month. Board confirmed it yesterday. Done deal. It's over."

A black stretch Mercedes 600 limo had just docked curbside, and the thick-necked bodyguard/chauffeur—in charcoal gray, a ship's crew of one—was hauling open the passenger door. Davis hurried toward it. Milt got in front of him, but Davis, now with backup, snapped, "Don't go ape on me. You lost. It happens. The board still wants you, and I'll overlook this, if it ends right now. And I mean *right* now."

"But—"

Davis threw up his hands. "Call me after the first—or don't. Your career." He stepped around Milt and dived inside the limo. The door shut behind him with a luxurious *thunk*.

Milt, stunned, turned up his jacket collar and started walking. He burned with the absolutely humiliating sense that if he didn't move, and move fast, he would start crying right there on the street.

Either that or chase down Martin Davis and beat him to a bloody pulp.

The city was still beautiful, but Milt saw none of it on his long, cold walk.

The next thing he knew, he was at the desk in his hotel suite—the Plaza plushness all about him. He opened his laptop, but the notion of anything electronic repelled him. He'd used a manual typewriter in college, and for his one (quite bad) undergraduate novel, a fountain pen had served. He could still remember every detail of those handwritten days: the coffee shops (when he could afford them) but more precisely, the warm air and fresh-mown grass of the spring term he tried his novel. Did anyone ever remember what the air was like when they wrote an e-mail?

Even before he had the stationery out of the drawer, Milt knew what he needed to say. He would type it into an e-mail later; for now, he unscrewed the cap of the fountain pen which had for so long been a fashion accessory and wrote:

*Effective January 31, 2000, PMT Software will cease to exist as an independent unit of NDN, Inc. Ongoing operations will be transferred to, and incorporated into, NDN Software Development operations in Phoenix, Arizona, and Baltimore, Maryland.*

*It is anticipated that only selected PMT Software products and projects will be carried forward, and that only a small number of present employees will be offered jobs in Baltimore and Arizona. All others will be provided termination compensation according to the terms of their employment contracts.*

That much of the memo was easy, but now Milt hesitated. He spent minutes searching for some legal leverage that would let him challenge NDN's decision, but found nothing. Restless, he jumped to his feet and crossed to the windows overlooking Central Park. As a Brooklyn boy, thirty years ago, he had dreamed of success—in a way, of staying at the Plaza. Well, he had made it.

Finally he returned to his chair and, with bitter heart and slightly shaky hands, continued:

*I disagree with this course of action, and accordingly I will be leaving NDN as soon as can be conveniently arranged, but in no circumstances before I have done whatever I can to manage the shutdown of PMT in a manner causing as little harm as possible to our workforce.*

*I have had the honor and pleasure of serving as CEO of PMT Software for its entire existence. I thank each of you for your loyalty, hard work, creativity, and good spirits. Good-bye, and God bless you.*

He read it over twice. The "God bless you" sounded like General MacArthur bidding farewell to the troops, but it was how he felt, so he let it stand. He capped his pen but resisted starting his laptop. It was the day before Christmas, and he had just written a memo telling two thousand people they were about to lose their jobs. Was it a form of grandstanding—a way of venting his rage?

Early notice was sound business practice: The sooner the notice, the sooner people could start hunting new jobs. And who would thank him for letting them run up huge Christmas bills when their jobs were already as good as gone? Yet he looked at his watch and sighed. PMT was closed for the holiday. If he sent this memo, and even a handful of people happened to check their e-mail, the result would be a panic of rumors. Nothing serious could be done until after the New Year—by which time he could have a decent shutdown plan in place.

Facing Larksdale would be tough, but he was no coward. He decided what he would do. He owed Larksdale the truth—but he owed it in person. He turned the written pages facedown and closed the computer.

He was a thousand miles from home on Christmas Eve, with no place to go.

In six weeks he might well be leaving Larksdale for some new career, perhaps even a whole new life. Without Sophia, he realized with a sharp pang, it would not make a huge difference where he wound up.

CHAPTER THIRTY-ONE

# Dinner Is Served

We in Larksdale, of course, knew nothing about the unsent e-mail, or PMT's approaching ruin. At noon on Christmas Eve day, with PMT closed for the holidays, Vince, Traci, and I spent a fun afternoon grocery shopping for the big church dinner, and generally amused ourselves with errands until we parted as the stores were closing, around 6 P.M.

Next morning I was up way before dawn to cook. The less said about my cooking, the better. Let's just leave it that I managed to get my turkey stuffed and cooked without the fire department having to be called—though there was a minor incident near the end, when I needed a pair of needle-nosed pliers to help the pop-up timer see reason. The fact that my tiny kitchen wound up looking like a war zone is, of course, another matter.

Now, a turkey takes a long time to cook.

By the break of dawn I'd already opened all my presents. Traci got me a great coffee table book on the Westerns of John Ford. Vince got me expensive perfume—a little too romantic, but *very* fragrant—and two *Star Trek* DVDs. Jake, from Montana, had sent me a card with a timber wolf on it.

To kill time, I read the paper.

Then I read the last four chapters of *Treasure Island.*

With all that done, and the turkey still cooking, I was about to start tormenting myself with fantasies about Jake's Christmas, when, about 9 A.M., my own personal Festival of Phone Calls began.

The first two were Traci and Vince, checking in. Traci merely said she was on schedule, but Vince, well, the first thing I heard as I put the receiver to my ear was him yelling, "Oh, the smoke! There's turkey smoke *everywhere!* I . . . Ack!" Actually, it turned out he was done with one turkey and starting a second: good old Vince was lately showing an organizational flair I'd never before noticed.

Then the Ladies started calling. They wanted to wish me Merry Christmas, and offer cooking tips, and reminders to take a sweater because the FM basement was cold, and all of that. Martha called only once, but each of the others called several times—each claiming they'd forgotten some important detail. It got so funny, I started answering the phone, "North Pole. Please hold."

Mostly, perhaps, they wanted me to feel I had family.

But partly, I suspect, they were feeling guilty: They had agreed to take part in both Patricia's Parade of Lights, and her early-evening Larksdale of Lights Fund-raising Buffet at the Marriott. That struck me as being very much in the spirit of the season, but they were upset at missing the FM Christmas dinner, which they had participated in faithfully for a decade.

Aunt Dolly's fifth call warned me to pack food, because "the dinner always runs short and the servers always go without." I dismissed that nonchalantly. I'd lately lost the fifteen pounds I'd gained since October and—if I exhaled vigorously while standing on the scale—another one or two pounds besides. I was an iron woman.

Finally J'Nelle called, which was sweet, and made me particularly happy, simply because it was so unexpected. There's often a moment when you realize you've become friends with someone: That was my moment with J'Nelle.

A little after eleven I had the turkey loaded in the car, and I hit the road.

An awful lot of granite went into the construction of Larksdale First Methodist Church in 1893; also into its expansions in 1912 and 1940. It's one of those substantial old buildings that inspire reverence purely by size and solidity. Christmas morning, with still-fresh snow sprinkled all about it, First Methodist looked postcard pretty, in a blue-sky'd, broad-shouldered, quiet way.

The Reverend John Wesley—yes, he'd heard all the jokes—was out front shaking hands. He was a tall, white-haired, athletic man of maybe sixty-five, and just then, bare-headed in the wind, he had the relieved look of a coach whose team had just pulled out the big football game. I considered getting out to wish him Merry Christmas, but thought the better of it, seeing as I was *slightly* late, and drove around to the parking lot instead. I entered through the back pathway.

Now, fond as I was of First Methodist in the abstract, one part of it always drove me slightly nuts even back in my churchgoing days—and actually worried me a bit that Christmas morning.

Beautiful as it is, not much of First Methodist has been modernized since the Great Remodeling of 1940. The wiring and heating were both notoriously unreliable, and the stairway down to the basement, though patched enough to be reasonably safe, was extremely narrow. I went down the steps very slowly, worrying about safety and struggling to balance the turkey.

I forgot my worries, and nearly dropped the bird in amazement, after I crossed the basement floor and stepped into the kitchen.

There stood Vince, busily handing out radio headsets and wireless ordering terminals to half a dozen eager-but-slightly-confused older volunteers, including bossy Mrs. Lamarcka, Betsy Rawlings, and two of Mrs. Lamarcka's other old friends.

"What the heck are you doing?" I asked.

"Winging it." Vince gave me his usual goofy grin. "There's been a big change of plans."

It turned out things had gotten notably more complicated since Wednesday's final prep meeting. About ten Thursday night Mrs. Lamarcka had begun fielding phone calls from our high-school volunteers. Some of them sounded quite normal, some as wheezy as the death scene from *La Boheme*—but they all made the same point: They were far too sick to serve turkey to anyone on Christmas Day.

An absolute epidemic of flu had apparently struck teenage Larksdale, and by bad luck of positively biblical proportions, all eighteen of our student servers had been struck down.

So instead of twenty-four volunteers, we had six.

Vince, hearing the news at eight that morning, had decided a dose of technology was in order. He'd immediately raced to PMT to pick up an assortment of the wireless restaurant gear we kept around for benchmarking competitors, and now was running a brief introductory course—which, in true Vince fashion, was shaping up to be incomprehensible for anybody without a Ph.D. in electrical engineering.

"First, remember that these are partial-duplexing trans—"

I let him get almost halfway through the sentence, before stepping in front of him and announcing—

"They're sort of like cell phones you wear, only you can't talk and listen at the same time. So when you want to talk, start by giving your name, and when you're done, say 'Over.' Okay?"

Everybody nodded, and I was moving on to explain the terminals when Traci stepped up to me and whispered, "I'll explain it to them. You go help set tables. And put that silly turkey down!"

We were scheduled to start serving at 1 P.M.; by noon it was clear the Salvation Army's warning was accurate. By a quarter to one we had over a hundred people in line. Now, your average Burger King can easily serve a hundred people with a crew of six—but fast-food restaurants are carefully engineered and packed with gadgets to through-put a lot of work. We were dealing with gear Laura Ingalls would have put out in the bin behind the Little House on the Prairie.

I was waiting for the whole system to collapse in a heap.

For the last hour Mrs. Lamarcka had been carefully drilling her crew—and I had to say she was doing it with a patience and courtesy that surprised me.

About ten to one she called me over. "It would help if you could go outside and find someone to wear one of these headsets and let people into the building as we have table space opening up."

I was taking a newfangled liking to Mrs. Lamarcka. I wasn't

quite noble enough, or filled enough with Christmas spirit, to tell her so, but I gave her my best smile and nod, and started for the stairs.

When I got outside, plenty of families, neatly dressed and almost embarrassingly patient, were waiting in a line that snaked well out into the parking lot. There was a sprinkling of old guys with wide toothless smiles, but I had the strange feeling that any of them—homeless guys included—could have been my own family.

I didn't need long to pick my candidate: He was about ten places back in line, and everybody nearby was giving him a wide berth. This guy was about six-feet-three, and nothing but muscle. With his massive, overhanging brow you could have typecast him as a Cro-Magnon man, and from the scars on his face, sometime in the near past he must have lost a fifteen-round decision to a threshing machine. I was a little nervous—okay, on the verge of panic—as I approached him. But I'd already decided, so I stepped up and asked if I could talk with him outside the line. He nodded, but was scowling, so once we were aside, I said quickly—

"We're shorthanded and need somebody to watch the door and let people in slowly." I held up the headset. "We'll let you know how many at a time. It'll mean waiting for your dinner, but it would be a huge help."

He brightened immediately. "You got it. Let's go."

His voice sounded like a beer truck backing over gravel, but to my surprise, he also had quite a likable smile. As we reached the door, I told him—

"I really appreciate this."

He stuck out a huge hand. "I'm Buster."

I told him my name. We shook hands, and I started to relax.

One thing was certain: *Nobody* would be taking any cuts in our line.

I trotted back down the basement stairs as quickly as I could safely manage. Vince had repositioned the big Klipschorn speakers the church used at dances. Traci's Christmas CDs (Aretha Franklin and Ella Fitzgerald) played softly in the background. Against all odds, the heat was actually working, and with the Christmas trees and fragrant cooking, and plenty of running around and organizing to keep me busy—well, I wasn't ready to yell, "God bless us, every one," but I was actually feeling in the holiday spirit.

Of course, this being Larksdale, it was goofy to hope the remains of the day would cruise along so smoothly.

We had planned to serve from noon until four, but the basement's warm cheer had guests lingering too long. By midafternoon the line had stopped moving completely, and except for Vince's notion that we substitute Sousa marches for "Silent Night," we had no idea how to restart it.

About 3:45, as the crush was heaviest, Mrs. Lamarcka began worrying that we were dangerously behind schedule and asked me to check on the line; given the time, she reminded me, the temperature outside would soon start dropping sharply.

I went back outside and it didn't look good; almost fifty people were still waiting. I won't say they were about to start Larksdale's first Christmas food riot—in fact, most were showing remarkable patience in that icy gloom. It seemed more likely that we'd hit the papers as a bunch of well-meaning folks who froze good people to death by making them wait too long for turkey.

Moreover, four tough young men near the head of the line started to make loud remarks about rotten service. Traci was trying to get me over my headset, but the signal kept breaking up, and I couldn't tell what she wanted, and I was getting frustrated.

I was explaining the delay to Buster, and saying that, with any luck, the line would start moving again in another ten minutes. I was raising my voice, to be heard over the men who were complaining, when suddenly Buster whipped around and yelled at them in that beer-truck voice, "Hey! *YO!* Cut me some frickin' slack. THE GODDAM *NETWORK'S* DOWN!" That was when Buster became my hero.

My whole career I'd been wanting to yell that at somebody.

It was better than Sylvester Stallone playing Hamlet. And I'll tell you—that line got quiet, and stayed quiet.

I hurried back inside and the scene that greeted me was even more festive. The basement was warm and cheery: The two flanking Christmas trees were lit up, and I noticed for the first time that they were lovely. Not only had I gotten a big kick out of Buster's system status update, but the air was full of the smell of turkey and dressing and pumpkin pie. I glanced around the entire room: The kids looked happy, the parents looked happy, even the older people who had come by themselves looked happy. True, no one was making a move to get up and leave, despite the fact that many plates were empty, and the diners in front of them, sated. But I felt so cozy myself I figured we would find a solution.

Just then, Betsy, looking worried, tapped my shoulder and said I was wanted up in the vestry.

When I got upstairs, Vince had been transformed. He was dressed in a certain sort of red suit that wasn't exactly Giorgio Armani but had proved popular for a long, long time.

The only problem was Vince weighed about 125 pounds

soaking wet, and this particular outfit was definitely made for someone who stood about six-two and had been living the last few years on Hungry Man TV dinners.

Vince looked like the Grinch's dog in a Santa suit.

"What the heck?" I asked, always being willing to raise the tough issues.

Traci was shaking her head. "Santa's sick. Santa's very, very sick."

Mrs. Lamarcka appeared and, as usual, went to the heart of the issue. "The kids are waiting, Reverend Wesley is with an elderly parishoner, and giving out the gifts will get the folks *moving*."

We rumpled up a bunch of plastic grocery bags and stuffed them inside the red coat. It didn't help.

"He looks like a pregnant spaghetti strand," Betsy said, with great directness.

Suddenly I noticed they were all staring at me, in that highly-interested way a bunch of hunters eye a turkey in mid-November. I looked behind me, vaguely hoping I'd find a tall chocolate snowman or something equally arresting. When I turned back to them, all I could manage was a squeaky—

"What?"

"You've got to do it," Traci said with grim finality. "You're the only one of . . . of *sufficient stature* to carry it off." She snatched the oversize red hat off Vince's head and started toward me.

"You're not serious," I told her firmly, but I was already being outflanked.

"You'll be glad you did." Vince was slipping off the costume, not a very difficult task, since he was too small for it by about nine sizes. "It'll be the sort of thing you'll tell your kids about proudly someday."

"Yeah, except for the part about making a big scarlet fool of myself . . ."

"There's always something with you," Traci said indulgently.

I was already seated, with Vince and Betsy cinching the Santa suit pants around my hips. In short, I'd surrendered. The girl can flee the church, but you can't take the church . . . well, you get the idea. Traci was pulling on the black boots, which wobbled widely on my rather undersized feet.

"How about some bullfighting music?" I pleaded, while they helped me get my bovine self to a sort of upright position.

"Honey, this is a no-bull moment," Traci whispered in my ear. She, or somebody, was pasting an immense white beard onto my face. It blocked almost all my vision. I probably looked like Sasquatch in a red tux; a moment later nearly all the rest of my vision disappeared under the big pointy red hat, which went on right after the wireless headset.

I was already feeling like Franken Claus when, through the cottony haze, I saw Betsy hurrying toward me holding a pair of fat sofa cushions she must have removed from Reverend Wesley's office.

Before I could flee, or at least waddle off, Betsy was pushing the cushions inside the red jacket, and then recinching the wide black belt. Story of my life: Two months of exercising like a madwoman, and I'm being fitted with prosthetic fat.

"What's my motivation in this scene?" I asked Traci, trying to take my mind off my shame.

"Peace on earth, and good will to men. Start walking."

"Which way? I can't see!"

She adjusted the beard, and the view improved notably.

Actually, I was starting to get into this . . . after all, it was Christmas, eh?

I straightened my feet and reeled toward the door. It looked like Santa had been chugging the eggnog.

"Fat man walking!" Traci called to no one in particular.

Even without a mirror I knew I didn't look like Santa; I looked like an overinflated tire in a red suit. Over the headset I heard Vince asking, "Who's your elf?" like he was saying, "Who's your daddy?" Christmas was definitely influencing him strangely.

As we started down the stairs, I couldn't help saying under my breath—

"This is will be a disaster."

Generally speaking, I'm stinky as a prognosticator, but just then, and for the first time in my life, I absolutely nailed a prediction. I was about three steps from the bottom of the rickety stairs, when right on cue, from below, the chorus started singing, "Santa Claus Is Coming to Town," and somebody switched on the glorious colored bulbs of the big central tree.

Instantly, with a faint, distant *pop,* all the lights in the room blew out.

I'd thought I couldn't see with the fool beard hiking up over my nose. Now I *really* couldn't see, so I did the only rational thing: I immediately froze. And Vince, right behind me, did a very Vince-like thing; namely, he kept walking. Until he was slowed down by a Santa-like-object. The slowdown was only momentary, because the Santa-like-object responded by yelping, and then plunging more or less headfirst down the last three stairs.

Now, in case you're wondering, this isn't a ghost story, written by one of the departed—mostly, I think, because I was too surprised to do anything to break my fall, and so I landed right on my Santa pillows. There was a loud "oof" in the darkness, which came from me, and then a much louder, double "oof" as Vince landed on top of me.

Among her other attributes, Traci must have eyes like a cat, because while Vince and I flopped around atop each other like a couple of landed trout in what felt to me like absolute pitch blackness, I heard her voice over the headphones saying with tense, controlled excitement, "Santa's down! Santa's down!"

Perfect. Now my life had become *Miracle on 34th Street* meets *In the Line of Fire*. They got Santa, the rat bastards.

Vince, though, is actually pretty agile. After one very awkward moment, which felt as if he were trying to do a handstand on my backside, he was off me. I figured the only hope of salvaging my reputation was to crawl unnoticed out the door and freeze to death in the snow. I threw my arm out weakly and discovered that, thanks to my tummy cushions, I had the swift mobility of a turtle flipped onto its back. Jimmy Stewart's life started flashing in front of my eyes.

Alas, it was then that I began to hear the clicking of an assortment of cigarette lighters, and in a minute the room was aglow in the light of a wide circle of tiny yellow flames.

It looked like a late-sixties folk-rock concert.

I half expected the diners to start swaying back and forth while singing Joan Baez songs. Except of course that those who were closest were staring at me in vague horror.

I'd been struggling, like some half-squashed bug, to rise, but now I gave up and dropped back down, my head dangling but not touching the ground because of the pillows. Vince, the rat, was nowhere to be seen. It took me a long moment of dangling to regain my senses and energy, and by then Traci was helping me to my feet.

The kids started clapping.

That was more like it.

I made a slow, fairly shaky pilgrimage down one of the two long aisles between rows of tables.

Vince's voice came over the headset. "No worries; I stuck a penny in the fuse slot."

Now, fitting a copper penny into the slot of a burned-out old-fashioned fuse box will certainly get the current flowing again. It just has a few occasional side effects. You know: like electrical fires that sweep through overcrowded church basements and leave dozens dead.

Santa used a word Santas aren't supposed to use, and while a bunch of diners looked on in mild shock, or at least confusion, she went on, "Are you *nuts?*" I was already moving to unplug the central tree. "Kill the power, then call the church maintenance man and find out where the spare fuses are!"

Over the headset Vince answered, "Okay," and a moment later the lights quit again. It all happened so quickly, most of the lighters were still lit.

"Everybody with lighters gather round," Traci said. "We're going to have an old-fashioned candlelight Christmas." To my amazement, I saw Betsy working her way through the crowd distributing white candles from a large box. When it comes to organization in an emergency, the Red Cross could learn a lot from any five randomly chosen Methodist ladies.

So, for the next twenty minutes I handed out presents to a bunch of delighted munchkins. The Ladies had done themselves proud, and there were several gifts—especially, a set of Lego pirates—which I had to resist yanking back while yelling, "That one's for Santa, little boy!"

Ten minutes later the lights flickered back on. Vince, with his usual blend of goofiness and efficiency, had shut off all the kitchen appliances (which were on the same circuit), giving us a safety margin to keep the trees lit, and had found the extra fuses.

Mrs. Lamarcka and Betsy got permission to clear the places of the people whose children were waiting for Santa, and brought in the last families from outdoors, even including Buster. I felt guilty when I saw him: He'd been stoic, brave, and efficient—and he practically had ice hanging from his sideburns. My first choice in good deeds would have been to serve him personally, and to thank him for all his help. For a minute or so, he watched me being swarmed by kids; he didn't smile, but I kind of think he briefly considered it. Something sort of flickered at the corners of his mouth. I figure that, from him, that was practically a standing ovation.

But of course my job was to hand out presents—and with the help of the kind of Bluetooth LAN that Dickens could only dream of, and a lot of coaching from Mrs. Lamarcka, I got through it.

And so, to make the story short, we handed out all the presents, and fed everyone. And by five-thirty—admittedly an hour late and completely after nightfall—we had bid good-bye to the last guests.

That left us with one gigantic cleanup job.

It was daunting, and I was feeling so hungry I was almost faint; but we were still on a sort of Christmas high. Maybe it was the aftershock of my death-defying leap, but I actually stepped up to Mrs. Lamarcka, threw my arms around her, and hugged her. She in turn got the strangest expression on her face, a kind of suppresssed affection. I had a feeling she was going to say "thanks," but she settled for hugging me back and saying "Merry Christmas," as if the whole holiday were my fault.

It's amazing how tired a person can get in just six hours. Ever-energetic Vince started toward the kitchen to tackle the dishes straight away, but I was slumping—and kicking myself for having rejected Aunt Dolly's advice about bringing food. Visions of sugarplums were driving me bonkers. Still, I looked at Traci, she looked at me, and then we followed Vince into the kitchen.

The place looked like a relief map of the Himalayas constructed entirely from dirty dishes.

Just as I felt my knees buckling at the sight of it, a clattering on the steps—like a lot of very large mice or the hooves of tiny reindeer—sent us all hurrying back out into the main room, in time to see the Ladies, in a line, stepping down onto the basement floor.

*They* didn't look tired; they looked fresh as daisies—or maybe poinsettias.

"We're here to do our bit!" Sophia called cheerfully as we approached them.

I perked up immediately. Aunt Dolly and Martha were holding bunches of beautifully wrapped small packages. That was delightful enough, but, hungry as I was, I was even more excited to notice Sophia and Gladys were each carrying two large grocery bags. A new and wonderful aroma was swirling about us. Stepping to Gladys, I asked—

"Is that what I think it is?"

"Well, Patricia Farthingale rather overbought for the big reception," Gladys said, "So when we were leaving, we asked for doggie bags."

"That's some doggie bag."

"I told them I had three Saint Bernards."

Traci, stepping forward to help her with the bags, said cheerfully, "Close enough, we'll certainly eat like them!"

Vince and I were already carrying the other bags toward the nearest table, while Martha seconded Aunt Dolly: In nine years serving FM Christmas dinners, she'd never once seen enough food left to feed the volunteers. So we stuffed ourselves while the Ladies (bless them!) tackled the dishes. We ate quickly and finished in time to pitch in with the last of the cleanup, and then Dolly, with a little embarrassment and a lot of ceremony, handed out our presents. Thoughtful—and well-informed—as ever, she had presents for each of us, even Mrs. Lamarcka and Betsy.

I tore into the wrapping of mine, and in a moment had uncovered . . . a beautiful knitted cap, red with white trim, and one of those flop-over tops with a bell at its peak. I was delighted—but of course I saw Vince and, especially, Traci already starting to crack up.

"I thought you might like it," Aunt Dolly said. "Red's your favorite color, and besides, it kind of makes you look like Santa Claus."

A half hour later Traci, Vince, and I were still laughing.

It was my best Christmas in a long, long time.

## CHAPTER THIRTY-TWO

# The Millennium Ends with a Whimper, a Bang—and a Bit of Hope

I spent the day after Christmas, which was a Sunday, in a warm glow composed of fond memories and a bag of excellent leftovers from the Ladies' generous culinary donation. On Monday, though, life looked a lot less cozy. My big plan for the day was to help J'Nelle hunt for a Larksdale apartment after work (her dad had recovered, and she was moving out); and my big plan for the approaching New Year's Eve was—nothing.

Lacking a date for New Year's Eve is bad; lacking one for the millennium's end is really foul. Traci and I (two of only a dozen people working at PMT during the inter-holidays) were sitting in my cubicle when an e-mail from Alicia raised the sore subject by reminding us she was hosting a Millennium Dinner at Bread and Roses and asking how many of us she should expect.

I read the note to Traci and asked—

"Should I tell her me, Vince, you, and your six dates?"

She snorted. "Please. The male millionaires of PMT are now neatly divided into two groups: those who haven't asked me out for New Year's, and those who are walking around the place referring to me as 'that frigid bitch.' "

"Being a little picky, are we?"

"Not really. I just want a guy who can talk about something other than how much money he makes." She flicked imaginary lint from her skirt. "I'm making up the Date Traci Elimination Quiz. I'll date any guy as long as he can . . . let's see . . . first, name at least three of Napoleon's greatest generals; second—"

"Soult, Ney, and Davout," a voice said.

"—explain in fifty words or less—*what*?"

The "*what*?" was accompanied by a swiveling of heads, as we both, realizing what we'd heard, turned and saw Vince standing in the cubicle entrance.

"Soult, Ney, and Davout," he repeated. "Three of Napoleon's generals. Why were you asking?"

Personally, I figured Vince was making some kind of weird joke, especially since I heard it as, "Salt, neigh, and taboo"—but I saw that Traci, who'd majored in French history, was eyeing him curiously. In her best cross-examining manner she asked, "How did you know that?"

Vince helped himself to a chair and faced Traci, not me. "I used to play sim games in high school, and one was called *Europe: 1800*. Besides, one day I tried to figure out what I'd do if I got stuck back in that era. You could get in a lot of trouble if you annoyed one of Napoleon's generals."

He said this with only the slightest hint that he was joking. Indeed, by Vince's standards, this was a highly rational answer.

Certainly Traci was taking it that way. She said, "Interesting," and shot me a very curious sort of look.

I suddenly had a very uncomfortable sensation. I don't mean physically, like sitting on a tack; this was purely an emotion.

It took me a while to realize it was jealousy.

Three hours later I had something a lot more dramatic than minor jealousy to contemplate. Sophia called to say the Ladies were holding an emergency meeting that night. Her tone of voice made it clear we wouldn't be discussing after-Christmas sales. I told her I'd be there, and that I'd get word to Traci and J'Nelle.

J'Nelle, who spent all her time in executive territory, had warned us to be discreet about passing her messages. It took me about ten minutes to wander near enough to her desk to catch her eye and flash the hand signal we'd worked out. She joined me shortly at a little-visited Coke machine. I told her—

"Never mind apartments. The Ladies have a rush meeting on—tonight, five-thirty, Martha's."

She was no more talkative than usual, but her eyes were bright as she nodded and said, "See you there." Then she started away, leaving me with the pleasant sense that we were playing secret agents. And so, about five-thirty—an hour after dark—we had all assembled. Sophia started the meeting off with five blunt words:

"NDN is closing down PMT."

*I knew it!* was my first thought. Of course I hadn't, really, but it now made perfect sense. J'Nelle, Traci, and I exchanged swift, excited glances; Sophia went on to explain that Milt, after a miserable weekend alone in Minneapolis, had decided to confide in her—but when she in turn insisted upon informing the Ladies, he treated it as treachery, and instantly broke off the discussion.

"So, in case you want to know, I may be wrecking my marriage once-and-for-all by telling you this. I had to do it, but *please* keep it to yourselves. It'll be public news in under a week, anyway."

Gladys raised her hand. "We'll keep it quiet. But what are we going to *do* about it?"

The Ladies were straining at the leash. One thing they'd already kept quiet (for the sake of Christmas harmony) was that they'd been badly snubbed by Patricia Farthingale at the fund-raising dinner. That, perhaps, magnified their sense of fury at this latest news. In any case, the Christmas truce was over, and now they were clearing the decks. Unfortunately they could take no important action, short-term. Not merely because they'd promised silence: Sophia also told them a lawsuit was *still* no more sensible than it had been in June, and any kind of public protest against NDN would need a long stretch of consensus-building, and would depend upon what compensation NDN would offer Larksdale and its employees.

The news and its implications brought a gloomy silence, until Dolly asked grumpily, "I wonder how all the folks who ate NDN's crab cocktails at the big party last week are going to feel?"

"Stuffed," Gladys answered, then giggled as she realized the double meaning.

"They've still got their stock," Deborah said.

"The top five hundred or so do," Sophia clarified. "The rest are sunk. And I'm not betting the stock will be worth much in another six months," she went on, hammering the point. "Never mind any market collapse: If NDN makes bonehead moves like this, I say it's going down even if the Dow hits eighteen thousand."

This, of course, was a key point. The Ladies were hugely invested in the very company that was sinking Larksdale. The room grew even gloomier.

"We've got to pick up the pace on V and V," Martha said, finally, turning us, as usual, to practicalities.

"I'm ready," Deborah declared. She was scheduled to take on the only speaking engagement left on the list.

"But we can't fight NDN with *that,*" Aunt Dolly lamented. Then she turned to me hopefully. "What about Vince's great idea?"

"Nothing yet," I admitted, feeling somewhat defensive about it. I'd pitched Traci's idea to them months ago, but since had scarcely mentioned it. "Vince is a genius, but he's not a genius-on-demand." Secretly, I was wondering whether I'd oversold his abilities. I decided I hadn't. Still . . . I was getting impatient. We all were.

But the Ladies, who'd been around a long time, knew how to deal with setbacks. They decided to seek a PR person to help push V & V, and to stay calm until NDN's plan became clearer. The meeting ended with them urging Traci, J'Nelle, and me to keep our jobs as long as possible, and to stay alert for anything we could use in a campaign against NDN.

It wasn't quite the epic response I had expected—but I figured it was good enough for Round One.

You might not believe this, but it wasn't until I got home that I realized one of the soon-to-be unemployed was . . . me. I was checking my mailbox, as usual, for news from ICAAM (there was none), when reality finally hit. *Keep our jobs as long as possible* . . . I mean, even if a few people got offered jobs elsewhere, I could safely assume my dear friend J. Brian Henley would see I wouldn't make the survivors' list.

That should have been a bleak realization.

So why was my heart beating with excitement?

I suddenly understood that, while the past six months had certainly held their bright and shining moments, I couldn't make a life out of days moping over Jake and nights checking for a letter from Hollywood. I had badly needed a kick in the fanny, and now life was booting me halfway across the room. True, there was going to be a bruise: The immediate future suddenly looked most uncertain.

But at least the boring days were over.

The coming year looked to be awfully exciting, one way or another. Meanwhile, the end of the millennium was four days off—and even I realized it was more of an event than the end of my job.

On the big night Bread and Roses was jammed with a well-dressed, very jovial crowd, many wearing brightly colored foil party hats, and a few blowing noisemakers. Alicia had the place running on autopilot and slipped from table to table looking cool and gracious. In fact, everything about her looked great except, I was surprised to notice, she didn't look happy.

The plan was for her to join us from eleven until just before midnight, when the whole restaurant would make a toast, sing *Auld Lang Syne,* and then sprint outdoors to watch fireworks. At 11:30, when she finally did sit down at our table, Traci, varying a game she, Alicia, and I had often played, asked, "Well, does everybody have their theme song for the new millennium?"

"Theme song?" Vince was perplexed.

Traci leaned toward him and brushed his arm. "You know: You pick a song that'll represent your hopes, your goals, your style for the coming year. It's just for fun."

I was shocked to see her coming on to him—subtly, of course, but unmistakably. Then I figured she'd decided to get into a holiday mood. Besides, they all joined the game. Traci picked "You Can't Hurry Love." Vince, naturally, chose the theme from *Star Wars*; and Alicia went for a Brandenburg Concerto. Those last two struck me as barely meeting the definition of theme *song*, but it would have been small to complain.

When they pressed me, I rejected "My Heroes Have Always Been Cowboys," then said aloud I'd take Cole Porter's "Use Your Imagination."

The way my future was looking, I was going to *need* imagination—big time.

A little before midnight Alicia led the whole restaurant in a toast to the new millennium, then cued the music to *Auld Lang Syne*. We finished singing, and then dashed outside into a cold, snowy night. Bang on midnight, as we all stood out on the street in front of the courthouse, the fireworks began. By Larksdale standards, it was very romantic, even though all I got was a hug from Alicia. I was just turning to my pals to tell them so, when I saw Traci kiss a startled Vince.

And I mean really kiss him.

And two days later PMT got Milt's e-mail.

CHAPTER THIRTY-THREE

# The News Hits Larksdale

Milt's e-mail reached our computers at 9 A.M. on Monday, the third of January, 2000. If I'd ever doubted cyber-warfare would work, my doubts ended that morning.

Two minutes later a stunned silence fell over PMT. Milt had modified what he'd composed in his hotel room; the "God bless" had been removed, and he announced an open company meeting on January 10 to answer questions.

Suddenly we weren't two groups of people: one with lots of money, the other with good, old-fashioned jobs. Now we were people with a lot of money, at bitter odds with people about to be jobless. And Larksdale wasn't exactly Silicon Valley. They said in the Valley if you wanted a new job, you just drove into another parking lot. With PMT shutting down, it was going to be an awfully long drive to the next parking lot, *especially* since the first sounds of the Big Tech Crash were rumbling through the Midwest.

The meeting on the tenth was short and grim, and when it was over, people left the auditorium without meeting each other's eyes, except occasionally to glare. I half expected fist-fights in the parking lot.

It sure as heck wasn't the Minnesota way.

The third week in January the 100 people offered jobs in Phoenix and Baltimore were announced. I was not (big surprise) on the list. I didn't panic. I had enough money to carry myself a good while, and Aunt Dolly had offered me a loan if needed. And I did get a consolation prize, of sorts. I was on the "lights-out team," the gang of sixty or so who were staying on till the very end to oversee the shutdown and the transfer of everything essential to new locations.

Just as I was gritting my teeth and wondering what exactly a "lights-out team" did, the other shoe dropped, right on my head. Jake walked into my cubicle and said he was taking a job in Arizona. I was too numb to say anything but "Good luck."

After he left, I spent half an hour staring blankly at my screen-saver. Then I found Vince and apologized for not having let him in on the secret. He told me to forget it, and not to worry, because he was going to get serious about the whole invention idea. To my surprise, he seemed not at all like the old Vince, but very serious indeed. His confidence was contagious; returning to my cube, I felt much better. I figured sooner or later the Ladies—or my brilliant friends—would pull a rabbit out of a hat.

Even if I had to help them yank.

CHAPTER THIRTY-FOUR

# Deborah Tries the North

All through January, the Ladies noticed something very interesting: when the stock market sank, interest in Value & Values climbed—and vice versa. As the Internet boom grew wobbly, queries and hits to their V & V Web site rose steadily. Gladys had taken to hooting, each time she reported on their Web counter, "We're not just a bunch of old broads, we're a major economic counter-indicator!"

At the Ladies' second meeting in January, the discussion ran along two lines: What could they do to save PMT, and what were their prospects for turning Value & Values into a real business?

For the first issue, they assigned Sophia and Traci to search every NDN/PMT contract for loopholes or escape clauses. They knew that would take time, but no one had a better idea. As for Value & Values, the ladies agreed to put their minds to creating some real plans to take it to the masses. Meanwhile, all they had in hand was a lone invitation to address the library users of Cold Butte, North Dakota—a name Deborah, who drew the assignment, insisted on pronouncing as if it had no *e* at the end of it.

Cold Butte, North Dakota, was just about as appealing as its name.

When Deborah set off, the place was a blizzard waiting to happen. She drove with the radio tuned to the weather channel and pushed hard to beat a forecasted storm. Early in the drive's last hour, the blizzard caught her: a near whiteout reduced her speed to a bare crawl along the soft shoulder. She considered turning back, but the route ahead was shorter, so she pressed on. Luckily, she hit only an edge of the front, and an hour later the snow merely flurried. Still, she reached Cold Butte so late, she had just enough time to check into her hotel before dashing off to the public library.

The crowd, given the weather, was large and cheerful, and Deborah enjoyed the time, until the questions began.

At the back of the room sat a man who resembled a scrawny old chicken. Bald except for a fringe of white hair, he had watery blue eyes and a notable cough. He asked four sharp questions in a row, pressing them until Deborah, never overly sensitive, got the impression he intended merely to insult her. He kept at it while Deborah's patience frayed, until simultaneously she reddened, and a placid-looking man in the front row twisted in his seat and said loudly but without apparent anger, "Oh, *shut up,* Silas."

Silas—Deborah had tagged him "the old geezer"—looked daggers back at the man, but shut up. The rest of the questions, probably out of sympathy, were all cream puffs, and she ended a few minutes later, staying briefly to chat and answer questions from people too shy to talk before the group. Silas remained standing against a back wall, glaring at her in angry isolation.

When the last friendly questioner had gone, Deborah, though nervous, took the initiative. She had to pass the geezer to leave. Pausing before him, she asked, "Can I help you?"

"What kind of name is Cohen?"

Deborah reddened. "It's Swedish." She'd already started around him, to head for the door. "It used to be Lingonberry, but I shortened it."

He blocked her path. "I'm trying to do you a favor."

"Really? Why don't you go jump in a lake? That would do nicely."

"Look, let me make this clear. I know people like you expect to get paid—"

"*People like me?* Let me make *this* clear. In the Marines I learned five ways to break your arm. I'm a little rusty, but keep talking and everything will come back to me. And don't worry about paying me. It'll be my treat."

She was rough because she was frightened. He jumped back in surprise—seemed to consider her for the first time—and said, uneasily, "You *wouldn't*."

"I'd *love* to." She was pushing past him. "Only, based on what I've seen, your neighbors would insist on giving me a parade and the key to the city, and I'd be late getting back to Minnesota. Now, if you'll excuse me . . ."

He caught her arm. "I need you."

Deborah pulled loose angrily and was moving away.

"I don't have anyone else," he said quietly.

The voice held so much grudging defeat Deborah turned back, and he added, "Which shows what a rotten deal you get when you're old."

Against her better instincts, Deborah stayed put. She wasn't particularly touched by his self-pity, and hadn't suddenly decided he was a sweet old man who deserved attention. In fact, she still rated him an unpleasant son of a bitch. But she had no evening prospects beyond dinner in some coffee shop and reading in bed in her hotel room. Besides, she told herself, this was supposed to be a goodwill tour for Value & Values.

So, reluctantly, Deborah waved the old geezer to a chair.

Taking a seat herself, she said, "You've got two minutes."

That was how Deborah became the temporary business consultant to that total coot, Silas Butteroot. She never could resist a good story. Silas Butteroot, she learned, had been born in a Badlands cabin in the middle of the blizzard of 1910—and a cold world had produced a cold but very determined boy and man. Starting as a worker in a lignite field, he had scrimped and saved (and probably, Deborah guessed, bullied and threatened) until he bought rights to his own small lignite mine, and then built from there. To hear Silas tell it, World War II had been a minor sideline event compared with his battle to hold on to his claims against a succession of double-dealing partners, crooked land agents, and unbearably greedy IRS investigators. And now, with his health fading, he was up against his last battle: A greedy son and his greedier wife wanted to have him locked up as senile so they could grab his money.

When Deborah told him his only play was to hire a bunch of top-notch lawyers and fight back, Silas took deep offense. But then, after looking angry, he suddenly looked canny, and said lawyers cost money, and all he had was tied-up property—he had almost no cash.

Deborah wasn't buying that. "Don't con me. A guy like you has money stashed in tin cans from here to the Canadian border.

If you won't spend it now, you don't deserve to keep it. You don't even deserve to walk around free."

"And I suppose you just *happen* to know a good attorney?"

This guy could make "good morning" sound like a deadly insult, but Deborah was over being annoyed. She was starting to enjoy him. His surliness gave free play to her own rhetorical passions. She leaned forward confidentially and said, "As it happens, I do. Only thing is, he's Irish-American, and you know the Irish. Now, his partner's from Scotland, but then, you know the Scots. In fact, the whole damn Minnesota bar's made up of nothing but people, and, well, hell, you know *people*. So here's the plan, you suspicious old bastard. I'll get you the phone number for Harvard Law admissions, and you can go get your own goddam degree. 'Course, you'll probably drop dead before graduation, but who cares? At least then you'll be their problem and not mine."

Silas Butteroot drummed his fingers on the chair arm, then, gradually, a look of something like amusement came into his eyes. "That's one approach," he admitted. "What else have you got?"

So they came to terms.

Deborah agreed to stay on for forty-eight hours to help Silas Butteroot respond to his son's legal threats. The job took no special skills—which, Deborah told herself with some amusement, she certainly had. Silas, in turn, would make a "generous" donation to some charitable cause.

The next morning was spent trying to get Silas to agree to mediation with his son. Silas, clearly enjoying bantering with Deborah, made no concessions—and around noon, complaining he had a sore throat and felt feverish, he called off the session.

By late afternoon his cold had turned nasty; by sundown he

was flat on his back and hacking like a seal with whooping cough. It gave Deborah the creeps to hear it, when she visited him the next morning at the Regional Medical Center. In fact, she was so upset that (while cursing herself for a meddling fool) she went to the nurses' station and asked to see his doctor.

The doctor, whose name was Hanford, was youngish, but seemed wise for his age, and willingly sat down to discuss Butteroot's case. He'd already figured out that Silas was not overburdened with caring friends. Dr. Hanford said the pneumonia, as bad as it sounded, was unlikely to be life-threatening. The infection was already responding to antibiotics. He'd put Silas in the hospital partly as a precaution, and "strictly off the record, to try scaring him into not being so mean to everyone. In fact, if I may ask, why are *you* so concerned?"

Deborah had barely begun explaining when Dr. Hanford interrupted, "You risked a blizzard just to give a talk? Wasn't that sort of foolish?"

Deborah grinned. "You got that right. About ten minutes into the storm I started hearing a heavenly choir singing, 'Steal Away to Jesus,' and I figured, given my background, that *couldn't* be a good sign."

Dr. Hanford laughed; and it was just then that Deborah had her inspiration. When so inclined, Deborah could sell bear traps to the Humane Society. She put a hand on Dr. Hanford's shoulder and said, "Listen, Doc. Suppose we took this whole near-death experience thing, oh, a notch or two higher?"

Dr. Hanford gazed back pleasantly. An uninformed observer would have thought him clueless. But Deborah had lived in the Midwest all her life and knew he was missing nothing.

"You've got the situation," she went on. "Old Silas thinks the whole world's no damn good, most definitely his son included.

And the son's so angry with him, he might just prove old Silas right. But what if the son thinks his dad's *really* dying? Won't it bring out his long-lost devotion? If it doesn't, to hell with him. If it does, and Silas doesn't respond, then to hell with *him*. Either way, we're helping clarify the situation, eh?"

"Are you asking me to lie?" Dr. Hanford now looked positively interested.

"Hell, no! I'm just asking you to choose your language like a . . . like a presidential spokesman. You know: 'Is my father dying?' 'Well, infections are tricky things, and he's an old, old man.' " Inspiration mounting, Deborah jumped to her her feet. "Heck, you might not have to say anything! We'll stage it with . . . with, um, an unsigned death certificate the only thing on your desk, and . . ." She glanced around, saw a small music system on a side shelf. ". . . and 'Steal Away' playing softly on the stereo. All you'll have to do is look sad, sigh, and pat the poor sucker sympathetically on the shoulder. We'll be golden!" She squeezed his arm. "It's for a good cause. What do you say?"

Dr. Hanford gave the smallest nod and smiled.

So that was how they played it.

Deborah wheedled John Butteroot's phone number from Silas, and made the call. It took five minutes of fast talking to get past Helen Butteroot, who seemed to speak in snarls, and another five minutes to persuade John Butteroot, whose manner convinced Deborah that suspicion was a genetic disease. But finally John Butteroot said, "Okay. I'll be there tomorrow."

As Deborah had predicted, the battle was mostly won in Dr. Hanford's office.

She'd spent the previous afternoon searching record stores.

Just before John and Helen Butteroot were shown into the room, she cued-up a Smithsonian recording of a gospel choir singing—yep—"Steal Away."

John and Helen Butteroot were much older than Deborah had expected. For her, "son" and "boy" were almost synonymous terms. But the fifty-year-old man who entered had a face already hardening into the same harsh lines as his father's. For a long moment he said nothing, and even watched, with only a slight jerk of surprise, as Deborah casually straightened the death certificate on Dr. Hanford's desk. She began to worry she'd set the stereo volume too low. But finally John Butteroot asked, "How's my father?"

"The old bastard," Helen Butteroot muttered.

*"My Lord, He calls me from the thunder,"* sang the chorus, ever so faintly.

Dr. Hanford glanced at Deborah, then nailed his line like a pro: "Well, pneumonia's rough on the elderly, and of course he's not a young man."

*"I ain't got long to be here,"* the tenor added plaintively, and even Deborah started to get choked up.

"I . . . I'd like to see him," John Butteroot said finally. His wife shot him a disgusted look, but he ignored her, and Deborah said quickly, "I'll show you," and waved them through the door.

Just before pulling the door shut behind her, Deborah turned back and told Dr. Hanford softly, "You missed a great career in the movies, Doc."

Now, Deborah couldn't rig Silas's room, but any hospital room carries its own drama. And even though she'd been warned it might be another twelve hours before Silas looked better, Deborah was still startled when she entered his room with the others. Propped on pillows, the blankets pulled up around his scrawny neck, Silas looked a frail, wheezing figure. It crossed Deborah's mind the old geezer was playing for sympathy. The notion vanished, however, the moment he wriggled himself higher on the pillows and told his son, "Well, your timing *stinks*. You're too late to suck up, and too early for the funeral."

Helen Butteroot grabbed her husband's arm. "I *told* you this was a stupid idea." She turned to Deborah. "I don't know who you are, you cow, but—"

Her husband cut her off. "Don't blame her. My father can get people to do anything he wants."

Deborah, though not terribly happy with this defense of her innocence, remembered her main objective. Assuming the sympathy angle was played out, she asked generally, "Never mind who got me here. . . . Anybody interested in the opinion of somebody who's *not* totally crazy?"

Helen Butteroot, still desperate to blast somebody, answered sharply, "Okay, fine. What *do* you think?"

"What do *I* think? I think old Silas is half right: You two should be ashamed of yourselves for waiting this long to show up. The frickin' *Menendez brothers* would have shown more family feeling." Faintly, Deborah's ears caught a sound like a rat drowning. She looked over and saw Silas Butteroot chuckling. "And *you,* you old coot, should stop thinking everybody's the same as you. Just 'cause *you're* a crook at heart doesn't make everybody else Jesse James. *Jeez.*" She threw up her hands. "Fifty dollars says neither of you can remember what started this feud, anyway. Fifty more says if you *can* figure it out, you'll laugh at it."

About two minutes later Deborah slipped from the room.

She'd served her role as a lightning rod.

The two male Butteroots had started arguing over who had started their feud, and were slowly, against their wills, coming to admit the whole issue was now pointless. Deborah wasn't misty-eyed, but she *did* have a certain kindly feeling for old Silas Butteroot. If he had a lovable, or even a likable, side, it was like the dark side of the moon, forever hidden.

But she admired toughness.

The following morning, a little before six-thirty, Silas phoned Deborah's room. After she'd thrown herself over the nightstand in a desperate attempt to find the phone in the pitch-blackness, and somehow gotten the proper end of the receiver positioned somewhere between her right ear and her half-shut eyes, she had the pleasure of hearing Silas Butteroot ask what the hell took her so long to answer. She was still asking God to grant her His choice of infinite patience, or a loaded shotgun, when Silas went on: "Johnnie's dropping the lawsuit."

"You must be very proud." She gave it all the irony she had, which in Deborah's case was quite a lot.

But Silas, still sounding cheerful, answered simply, "I'm buying you breakfast. Get your lazy carcass out of bed and meet me at the Happy Waffle in thirty minutes."

This was just too sweet, and Deborah wouldn't have missed it for the world.

By now fully awake, she mumbled, "Okay," picked herself up, and in twenty minutes was showered and dressed and on her way out the door. The snow was fluttering as she walked to the Happy Waffle, but the restaurant was one of those rickety clapboard roadside spots which now-and-then prove to have absolutely glorious food. Silas sat at the back booth and had already ordered and started eating. In fact, as Deborah slipped onto the patched brown Naugahyde of the seat facing him, he appeared to be finishing the last of his coffee.

"Okay, so I'm here. Start gloating. I'll give you five minutes."

Silas set down the cup, then pulled himself up with surprising dignity and said, "You kept your part of the bargain." He managed to make this sound like the biggest miracle since the parting of the Red Sea, but Deborah let it go. When she said nothing, he added, "I ordered for you."

Deborah pretty much expected this meant a glass of water and a napkin, but just then, the waitress arrived with hot coffee, plates of waffles and bacon and eggs and hash browns. For once, Silas hadn't stinted.

"I haven't picked a charity yet." He paused dramatically. "But I'll do it today, and send the check before sundown."

Deborah, not willing to admit she was pleased, started on the food, and only between bites answered, "Take your time. Pick one you believe in."

He shook his head. "We had a deal. I'll have them send you a letter saying I kept my word."

"You old bastard." Deborah sipped her coffee, made a face at its weakness, and shook her head. "In the last four days I've heard you called everything under the sun, except a liar. Besides, I know where you live."

She would have sworn, just then, a bit of a smile formed on the thin, hard face. It fell away, but a certain brightness remained in his eyes, and stayed there as he edged out of the booth and stood. He made sure she wasn't eating, then said, "If I was twenty years younger, I'd marry you.' "

"Lucky me."

This time he really did smile. "Yeah. Lucky you. That's how I see it, too."

And then he was gone.

A full minute passed before Deborah realized he'd left her with the bill for breakfast. She didn't much mind; she was too busy amusing herself trying to guess where he'd send the check for her fee. She thought perhaps a strong sense of family feeling would lead him to endow a home for old buzzards.

It would be a long time before she knew it, but Deborah had done herself, and the Ladies, a most remarkable amount of good.

CHAPTER THIRTY-FIVE

# I Get the Shock of My Life

By February, Larksdale had two thousand unemployed people, and NDN, which had always been an Internet leader, kept its lead by becoming one of the first tech stocks to collapse.

The Internet bubble had popped. The party was finally over.

Now Larksdale's supermarket bulletin boards, which six months earlier had sought nannies (preferably, those speaking two or more European languages), were full of "Take Over Payment" ads for people's fancy European cars. The first week in February, Harold Madsen, my friend with the grocery store, replaced his gourmet counter with a nice display of luncheon meats.

Expensive had gone out of fashion.

The one good thing to come about was that much of the budding hostility between Larksdale's stock-rich and non-stock-rich began to dissolve. With NDN losing maybe 5 percent of its value every week, being a big shareholder was looking a lot less enviable—especially since many shareholders had borrowed against their shares and now faced margin calls. In a shaky world, people began rediscovering their neighbors.

The Ladies thought this revived spirit would give V & V a big boost, and likely it would have, except most small investors lacked the free time to attend lectures.

They were too busy panicking.

A few people did benefit from the collapse. Aunt Dolly started a Larksdale High night class to show folks how crafts could cut their expenses. In February alone, as her assistant and model, I accumulated two sweaters, four hats, and a neat assortment of pot holders. And J'Nelle, after putting off her apartment hunt for sixty days, found a place for about half of what she'd expected to pay.

As Milt and the other PMT old-timers departed, though, I began to realize just how much I'd wanted to lead at least one successful project. It was a big self-esteem issue for me: How could I keep alive my dream of producing $150 million blockbusters if I couldn't even take a ten-person tech team to success?

I just hated going out a loser.

In short, with Jake packing to leave, and ICAAM giving me the silent treatment, I headed into late winter just a little short on joy.

Then came the morning in March that changed everything.

"That Morning" began as one of the lowest of my life. Not only did the NASDAQ drop another fifty points during my ten-minute drive into the office, but I felt so generally depressed I was (in a perverse way) enjoying the bad financial news. There's a scene in *King Lear* where Lear, overwhelmed by his endless bad luck and caught in a sudden, horrific storm, finally reaches his limit. He stands out on the open heath, shakes his fist at heaven, and urges the gods to just go ahead and pile it on, shouting, "Blow, winds, and crack your cheeks!"

I was feeling like that.

Only twenty-six, and living in Minnesota, of course.

To top it all off, the icy rainstorm blowing around me—while maybe not quite Shakespearean—was nasty, dark, and cold, and I was dreading work. I already knew the group would be mostly absent. Even Vince, claiming he was close to inventing something, had lately taken to staying home. I was more than half convinced he had really abandoned hope and taken to spending his days in slippers watching sci-fi videos and playing with his Lego pirates.

For about fifteen cents I would have gone to his house and joined him.

I'd been raised to always be ready to nail the flag to the mast, and to stay with the ship till she sank. But U.S.S. *PMT Software* wasn't sinking; she was just being shipped to Baltimore, and that wasn't nearly as heroic. I'd look pretty stupid standing on top of a Mayflower van heading down the freeway shouting that I had not yet begun to fight.

Fighting certainly wasn't an issue as I parked in PMT's nearly empty lot and trudged into the building.

The lobby had the barren feeling of a bankrupt amusement park, a once-jolly place now dead but not yet gone to ruin. The security guard (we were down to one) didn't even look up as I ran my badge through the reader. The wide stairway to the second floor was empty, and when I reached the bullpen, it was so quiet you could hear the sleety rain pounding the windows. That meant not simply an absence of people, but that nearly all the computers, printers, and such in that whole vast field of cubicles were shut down.

I was so deep in my own gloom I spent a solid hour sorting documents without lifting my head or hearing a single person. So when my computer beeped, and its incoming call symbol flashed, I nearly jumped out of my chair. Every PMT computer had simple video-conferencing software; but even with broadband connections, the pictures were so jittery and small that we almost never used it.

And yet here I was getting an incoming call.

I clicked the Answer button, and a small window opened onscreen. It was Vince, and even in that tiny window he looked excited as he asked, "Callie?"

"Vince? What are you—?"

"Wait."

It was about this time I noticed a faint whirring. It sounded almost as if one of the air-conditioning vents were somehow airborne, and getting closer. I turned, then yelled—

"JESUS!"

Now, I don't use that as a social exclamation, except when taken entirely off guard. And I *was* taken entirely off guard when I saw what was making the whirring noise. It was a remote-controlled mini-blimp, about five or six feet long, the kind you see flying around indoor stadia and trade shows. Only this one was about six feet away, and coming straight at me.

I felt like one of the model buildings in *Black Sunday* or *Hindenburg*.

"Vince, you . . . What the . . . ?" I demanded, from the floor, where I'd taken cover. I was becoming the queen of the two-word sentence fragment. The blimp was directly overhead, and I was yelling into the headset like some forward air support spotter in a really bloody battle. "Get in here RIGHT NOW, and GET THAT THING."

"I can't. I'm home!"

Now, broadly speaking, I'm fond of practical jokes, and don't mind having my chain jerked. But my chain had been pulled too tight for too long, and I'd been feeling choked for days. I was starting to wig out, and I knew perfectly well Vince had to be in the building to control the blimp.

"Okay, don't mess around. This is *really* creeping me out. Are you in the building?"

"I'm not! You saw the video window. I'm at my desk—at home!"

"Yeah, right. And nobody ever digitally composited a scene."

"I'm *home,* Callie."

"Then how . . . ?"

"The Airport."

Oddly enough, I knew instantly what he meant. "Airport" is Apple's trade name for its particular brand of IEEE 802.11b. wireless communication; everybody else just calls it "wi-fi," and I don't even know why I'm telling you this except in my panic I was calming myself by running through the technical details. Anyway, a few seconds of thinking—and the stupid blimp's backing off a few yards—had more or less restored me to sanity. In fact, rising cautiously to my feet, I was feeling something I hadn't felt for a long time.

Excitement.

And suddenly I was a lot more excited than I was creeped-out.

Somehow Vince had realized you could use the extra bandwidth hanging around a wi-fi data broadcast to run gadgets by remote-control. At the very least, he had invented a very cool idea for toys . . . but it wasn't hard to see about a zillion other, more businesslike applications.

I still made myself ask him calmly whether I'd gotten the basic idea right.

Practically dancing around the video window, he answered, "*Absolutely!* Plus, of course, I'm using the video camera on top of your computer, plus one I mounted down at the far end of Aisle C, for guidance. Am I clever?"

"Yes, Vince, you're clever. Now, you give me your word that's *really* what you're doing? You're not here in the building and scamming me?"

"Yeah, sure. Absolutely. This one's pretty clunky, but I've got the basic idea for a general controller that would let people do almost anything by remote. . . ."

He kept talking, but I kind of stopped listening. I'd caught up, and then switched over to a vision of my own. It didn't exactly take a genius to see that a cheap little wi-fi receiver attached to an assortment of gadgets could mean a world of possibilities. . . . Consider the home: You're just leaving the office, so you pull out your cell phone, dial into your computer, turn up the heat, start the microwave, and tell the TV to switch on to the ball game in ten minutes? Then you drive home and step into a warm house with dinner waiting and the ball game on? That wouldn't interest you?

Call me Jane Jetson.

Oh, yeah. There just might be a business in providing that.

I knew something else.

In a year or two wi-fi was going in everywhere. Companies like Starbucks were already arranging to install it in their shops; in cutting-edge places like Berkeley, people were offering free wi-fi access so anybody walking through the neighborhood holding a PDA with a wi-fi transponder could log on to the Internet for free.

There was a lovely new fragrance in the air.

It smelled like money.

"Vince," I said, as sweetly as I could, "turn that silly thing off and get your butt over here."

## CHAPTER THIRTY-SIX

# I Pitch a Crazy Idea

Too wired to sit still, I carried the mini-blimp to the auditorium, our biggest internal space. I figured that would give me at least a sense of the range of Vince's invention. In theory, a digital signal would carry data till it dropped out completely, but given what the economy was doing, I doubted anyone would be interested in buying *theory*.

I was awfully fond of that little blimp.

In fact, it was all I could do not to plant a big, fat smooch on its shiny skin. I resisted the urge to laugh out loud. If Vince was telling the truth, well, then, the nice folks from NDN were about to get blimped—but good.

Twenty minutes later Vince arrived to show me exactly what he'd done.

We brought up the code on his laptop—I was just barely

smart enough not to tell him to load it onto the PMT network, so it would run faster—and it had the kind of elegance only the best programmers can manage. He offered to swear on a Bible he hadn't borrowed any part of the work from anyone else. Then we flew it around the auditorium and, like a couple of eight-year-olds, wound up in a fight over who got to run the joystick.

It was an absolute blast.

Finally, reluctantly, I gave up the controls and let Vince play while I phoned Sophia and told her to rush over to PMT, and that I'd explain when she got there. I knew we needed a legal opinion before getting serious and pitching to the Ladies. Then I went back to the controls. (And just so you'll know, I was a *way* better blimp pilot than Vince.)

Sophia, when she finally arrived, was disappointingly adult and lawyer-like. But she was taken with Vince's wonderful toy and needed barely two minutes to understand the underlying business potential, which she agreed was huge. After my assuring her the whole idea of remote control over the Internet was, so far as I knew, completely new, our entire conversation took about fifteen seconds:

I said, "Can we patent it?"

She said, "I'm not a patent attorney."

I said, "How long will it take to find out?"

She said, "If I can find the right attorney, and we're willing to pay rush search fees, about five days and $5,000."

I said, "What are you standing here for?"

She opened her mouth, closed it, nodded, turned, and left.

Boy, was I getting bossy.

* * *

It actually took Sophia six days to find the right attorney and have the preliminary patent search done. I had planned to pass the time until we heard by giving up breathing; when that proved too difficult, I settled for giving up sleeping.

I'd started working on the business case right after that first conversation with Sophia. They teach you to write cases in business school; as an engineer, I hated all the estimates, guesswork, and plain fakery involved, but I got it done. And I knew the gadget, which Vince had dubbed "RadioRemote," was so appealing my guesswork didn't really matter: Even if some of my proposals didn't work out, others would.

Lacking sleep, I was pretty groggy by the time the lawyer called, but the news was exactly what we'd wanted: While nothing is ever guaranteed in patent law, it looked as if RadioRemote could claim enough territory to protect any business we wanted to build.

After the call, I slept for twelve straight hours.

The following Saturday morning I stood (still bonkers with excitement) in Sophia's living room rehearsing last-minute plans with Sophia and her son, Will. The room was large enough for our Big Plan, but we needed to move furniture to make it work. Milt had a fancy stereo with the electronics in custom cabinets just off the room's main entrance. Huge speakers were set against the opposite wall, and the chairs and sofa had been grouped to face that end of the room. Sophia's light, elegant correspondence desk was set against the first wall, near the entrance and the electronics. We turned the chairs and sofa to face the correspondence desk, which we moved away from the wall and swung to face back at the rearranged furniture.

In sum, the Ladies would be facing the desk where I'd set up my computer.

The stereo speakers would be behind them, and facing them and to their left would be the room's main entrance. We had stashed the blimp in the room that had been Milt's den in happier days, and made Will's first job opening its door once the Ladies were assembled. We practiced our act three times, very smoothly, but still had ten minutes' anxious waiting before Deborah, the first of the Ladies, arrived.

That was unlucky: Deborah, observant and persistent, wanted to know why everything had been moved around. I gave her some baloney answer, to which she replied, "Yeah, but—"

"The food's on the kitchen table. If you have other questions, I'd love to help you, but"—I adopted a fake, Barry Fitzgerald–type Irish accent, and a hoarse whisper—"me throat, it's *that* dry, I can't . . ."

Deborah made a derisive noise, turned on her heel, and started for the kitchen.

Half an hour passed before all the Ladies were assembled. Deborah, though a little annoyed, had resisted the temptation to grill me again. Finally, when everyone was comfortably seated, I stood from the desk and waited a moment until Will manned his station. Then I urged them to set down their cups and plates, and said—

"Ladies, to paraphrase a great philosopher: A blimp is worth a thousand words."

I flashed a hand signal to Will, who, with coordination born of a thousand video games, hit the button on the CD player and artfully brought up the volume on the theme music from *2001: A Space Odyssey*. While the Ladies all swung in their chairs to look at the stereo, I pulled the laptop toward me and started working the joystick.

The music masked the whir of the tiny electric motors, so the Ladies' eyes stayed on the speakers. That made it a slam-dunk to fly the blimp unnoticed through the living room's entrance. I wasn't watching the blimp; I was watching the picture from its tiny nose camera displayed on the laptop. Only when it had closed to about three feet aft of poor Gladys's neatly coiffed gray hair did she apparently hear enough to make her swivel back around. By then it was too late.

I always wanted to be a bird of prey, and just then, I got my chance.

Unfortunately, Gladys was the only one who hadn't heeded my suggestion to put down cups and plates. As the Larksdale Bomber swooped over her head, her teacup went flying. There was payload separation (narrowly missing the blimp itself) about three feet over her head: The cup continued most of the way across the room, while the tea splashed down on Martha's lovely woolen dress.

Martha jumped to her feet, exclaiming a very un-Martha-like word.

It was all I could do to keep from yelling, "*Tora, Tora, Tora!*"

Instead, I had the blimp circle the room, then turn to face the Ladies.

By this time they all stood, some in alarm and others in excitement. For an instant I feared the first words heard over the music would be "Somebody get a rope!" But we were golden. True, Aunt Dolly was shooting me an accusing look for not having let her in on the secret, but Deborah was practically dancing with enthusiasm. J'Nelle had stepped up to examine the blimp more closely, and even Martha was over her snit and eyeing it attentively. Across the room Will was grinning and Traci was shaking her head and laughing.

Finally Gladys, stepping closer to the hovering craft, asked, "Is that what I think it is?"

I said it was—and spoke for two minutes on the basic technology.

The Ladies might not have cared much about the technical side, but they swiftly realized Vince's invention offered a way for them to respond to NDN and the PMT disaster.

They asked all the right questions, and Sophia and I had enough of the right answers; after forty minutes, the Ladies decided. They wanted a better study of RadioRemote's legal status and a careful search for news of other, similar products that big companies might be developing. And they wanted a real, detailed business plan showing the exact path from cool idea to salable product.

But the bottom line was they would spend *serious* money to make RadioRemote a real business.

And they wanted me to run it.

Short of going to Hollywood, it was the next best thing to a dream come true.

## CHAPTER THIRTY-SEVEN

# I Take Charge—and Get into Trouble

In business, everything changes when you start putting the dollar signs in front of the dreams.

I turned in my proposed budget two weeks after the Ladies' blimp demonstration. Three days later, Sophia handed it back to me and said, "It's perfect. Now just cut it by thirty-five percent and we'll fund it."

I went home with a stomachache, cut every penny I could, and reached a grim conclusion: We could offer our hires about seventy percent of what they'd been earning at PMT. It was hard to see any but the most desperate jumping at that.

Welcome to the real world, Callie.

I made the changes, the Ladies agreed, and we started calling people we wanted.

Even with confidentiality agreements, we didn't want anyone to know what we were building until they'd agreed to take the job. I thought that might be a problem, but actually, nearly everyone we contacted *liked* the element of mystery. That still didn't make hiring easy, though. Some top people—not just Jake—had grabbed NDN's offers of work at other sites and were already planning to move. A few had actually found jobs in Silicon Valley. Others, mostly senior level folk, had simply decided to retire for good. Of course, we couldn't afford most senior level folk, anyway.

Even J'Nelle, though devoted to the idea of RadioRemote, had to stay at PMT as long as they would pay her. That ultimately proved to be much longer than any of us had imagined, since, many months after PMT technically shut down, NDN's "transition team" kept working there, even though nobody, J'Nelle included, was ever quite sure what NDN's people were actually doing still in Larksdale.

And there were other glitches.

Old Floyd, my first choice for a hire, had slipped on ice in late February and still wasn't ready to work. But he proposed something nearly as good: For a very modest monthly retainer he'd serve as a consultant and I could call him as often as I wanted. Later, if his back improved and we still needed him, he'd consider a real job. With his invaluable help, we found our team. Except for a consumer products specialist (which PMT had never needed), we filled every slot on our staffing chart. That Jake wasn't on the team was a downer, but I knew better than to start moping about it.

And so, as the stormy weather softened into a bright, drizzly spring, Traci, Vince, and I began preparing for RadioRemote's startup.

Those four weeks were great fun, but also the hardest I've ever worked. Finding a location was easy: Vacancies were popping up all over Larksdale. We took one about two blocks from Bread and Roses (which Alicia was closing after months of nearly zero business), at a bargain rent. It was sad to see Bread and Roses close—but we still had Lord of the Rings, and some of the best doughnuts in the world.

And doughnuts were still in nearly everyone's budget, so Alicia was fine.

We worked under a cover story, cooked up by Floyd, that we were developing remote sensors for bass fishermen. (Cover stories are an old Silicon Valley tradition: The team that built the world's first digital video recorder worked for a year with a real bicycle repair shop as its front.)

We also used a dummy company (funded by the Ladies) to buy a bunch of computer and networking equipment (even desks and phones) dirt cheap from the liquidator brought in to start cleaning out PMT.

So in four weeks we had staff, space, and stuff. And by the last Monday in April we were ready to go.

And by noon that Monday I knew I was in trouble.

We started orientation promptly at 8 A.M. A dozen reasonably awake young programmers, plus Traci and Vince, looked back at me from around the conference room table. I handed out the RadioRemote handbooks and gave my talk.

You could say it went well.

Mine was a perfectly decent performance, the kind that would have gotten me an A or an A-minus back in business school.

And nobody laughed aloud at the idea that I was in charge. The handouts and work assignments all kicked in decently. The computers lit up properly, and the network ran like a charm.

By a little before noon, orientation was over and everybody was working quietly.

There was just one catch.

I'd forgotten my team wasn't just young, and new to startups.

Everyone in the room had also been thoroughly battered by their last horrific months with NDN. They were taking big paycuts, and a big gamble. Sure, they wanted to help save Larksdale, but the grapevine, made up of their friends in other tech centers, was already yelling that the startup glory days were over, that the smartest of the smart were leaving tech for law school, academia, or even public service. Maybe six months earlier (certainly, two years earlier) any dozen young software hotshots gathered together in a room would have been recklessly eager to launch their own company.

No longer.

They still had all the skills; they just didn't have the fire. They worked all that day, but in the neat, orderly way they would have worked for a big company.

And a neat, orderly launch was fine for a big company, or even a mid-sized one like PMT; but it would bankrupt RadioRemote. And the problem boiled down to that lack of fire—of fighting spirit. I'd seen Jake, who'd never been within fifty miles of a biz school, create it.

But I hadn't. I knew I'd have to, or RadioRemote was doomed.

I spent the afternoon with an ever-shrinking smile on my face.

And an ever-growing knot in my stomach.

By about 4 P.M. I was nervous enough to consider a screaming fit; by 5 I was idly logging onto Expedia and checking prices for one-way tickets to Nepal. And by 6, as people were drifting out the door, often after stopping by my desk to wish me a good night and to say they were glad to be working with me, I was wondering about job openings on the Space Station.

By seven when the place was empty except for Traci and me, and I was preparing to leave, Traci offered to walk me to my car. I'd been feeling a little grumpy about how closely she'd worked with Vince for most of the day. True, overall Vince had been a surprising paragon: He'd shown up on time and, by his standards, sharply dressed, and had spent the whole day—when he wasn't chatting with Traci—going from desk to desk giving encouragement. Still, I hadn't quite enjoyed seeing them so often together.

Still, I shook off my uneasy feeling, and told Traci, "Yes, please."

Traci stayed silent until I'd locked the building and switched on the alarm. We were hurrying along the street when she said, "You did a good job."

"I stank."

"All right. You did an *adequate* job."

"Or, more precisely, a really great job of stinking."

Traci halted right in the middle of the block. "You want to feel sorry for yourself or fix the problem?"

"All right, Miss I-know-everything. What do I need to do?"

"Throw away the MBA playbook. Work from *your* strengths."

"I should bake them a cake?"

"*No.*"

"Show them how a high-bypass jet engine works?"

"*Callie!* Come *on*. You've been telling me every day since forever that you *really* want to be a movie producer. *Put on a show!*"

She had me. This was the sort of annoying advice that at first seems the quick answer to your prayers, but on closer examination proves to be nothing but an invitation to work. Still, she was right. I let out a long breath—

"You think?"

"I think. You want me to come over and help you?"

Generally, growing up is a pain. This was no exception, but after a minute I shook my head. "Thanks—guess I've got this one."

She squeezed my shoulder. "See you tomorrow, Boss."

I grabbed a takeout dinner on my way home, then used the thirty minutes' saved cooking time to study my videotape/DVD collection for inspiration.

If that sounds like a lot of time to study a home collection, you've got to understand I devote about the same percentage of my income to movies that the U.S. government devotes to defense. I'd been thinking of using something *Raiders of the Lost Ark* for inspiration but had moved on to the war movies section when an idea struck like lightning.

A moment later I picked myself up, took the tape from the shelf, and got to work.

Now, business isn't *really* like war—but this was just too rich to pass up.

## CHAPTER THIRTY-EIGHT

# Me and the Siege of Peking

I didn't reach the office until eleven the next morning. That was okay—I'd called ahead and arranged for Vince to open the doors. In fact, it was good, since I figured my absence would inspire at least curiosity, and maybe suspense.

I'd spent the morning at Sam's Print & Copy, where I talked Sam into letting me use his fancy Mac system to capture an image from the videocasssette I'd brought. Then I got him to quote me an incredibly cheap price for transferring the image to two dozen T-shirts. Then I spent an hour and forty minutes biting my nails while he did the job.

By 11:15 I was going from desk to desk asking everybody to meet in the conference room in ten minutes. We'd cut a lot of corners in launching RadioRemote, but thanks to Vince's genius with gadgetry the conference room had a perfectly decent rebuilt video projector, which took inputs from my laptop and threw a sharp image onto the screen at the room's far end. As people filed in, I had the projector hot and the laptop ready to go.

I took a deep breath and told myself it was showtime.

Maybe I looked a little wild-eyed, but the interest level was far higher than I'd seen the previous day. It got me so pumped, I launched my remarks without pausing to agonize—

"All right. I know everybody's here to work and I appreciate it. But hard work's not going to get it done. We have to break all records. We've got to work harder, smarter, and cheaper than we ever did back at PMT, and believe me, I *know* how hard we worked there." I finally took a breath. "You all know me: I figure nothing's ever said better than it's said in the movies, so . . ."

I killed the lights and flipped on the video projector.

The screen behind me turned into a rough barricade facing a high wall in Peking, China, in 1900. Manning the barricades are a bunch of U.S. Marines, led by the redoubtable Charlton Heston, tough and gritty as ever. The Chinese Boxers, determined to drive the foreigners from Peking, come swarming down the pathways cut into the massive walls and are pushed back by the Marines in a desperate battle. After it's over, Heston, knowing it may be weeks before his force is relieved, asks how much ammunition the men fired, and hears, "I'd say about five thousand rounds, Colonel."

"From here on in, they get fifty rounds apiece, a day."

The incredulous sergeant roars, "*Fifty rounds!?* Hell, Colonel, that's just for warming up!"

And old Charlton fixes him with that icy blue-eyed stare and tells him, "You tell them to *start out* warm."

I switched the projector off and the lights back on. People were looking slightly mystified, but there's nothing like a good movie battle to get the blood circulating. Before anyone could speak, I ripped open a big brown-paper parcel and held up the top T-shirt. It had a choice, full-color shot of old Colonel Heston looking tough as nails, and over it, in big letters, the slogan:

RADIOREMOTE—START OUT WARM!

They started cheering, and I started throwing them T-shirts like I was a float rider in the Mardi Gras parade.

That was the turning point.

By lunchtime everyone in the building was wearing the shirts. All afternoon people kept disappearing, and then reappearing with the toys and posters and gadgets that mark a hard-charging tech startup. Before sundown the conference room table was covered with flowchart diagrams, and whiteboards had been propped up even in the snack room. When I went home close to midnight, almost everybody was still there working, except for Janet Carter, who'd fallen asleep over her computer, and Traci, who'd just switched hers off and was trying to get three of the programmers to join her in a Motown rendition of Stevie Wonder's "Yesterme, Yesteryou, Yesterday."

But the best news didn't show up until three days later.

I was working hard at my desk and didn't see it coming until it was right in front of me. I looked up and felt a loud double thud as my heart rebounded off my ribs and lodged in my throat. There, in his long duster coat, with his backpack clutched in one hand like a saddle, stood Jake. For once I avoided making a fool of myself. I just said—

"Howdy, Jake. Here to make a little money?"

"Nope. Here to make a *lot* of money."

"I'll show you your desk."

"I'm obliged. Hear you're showing Charlton Heston movies."

I got to my feet and started walking. I didn't want him to see how excited I was.

Life was looking up. We were starting out warm.

So it didn't really matter that I was already overheated.

The next morning, when I got to the office at six-thirty, everybody was already hard at work. On my desk sat a box, gift-wrapped, about fourteen inches by twelve and eight inches high. Half expecting it to explode like a trick cigar, I slipped off the ribbon and carefully removed the wrapping paper until I could see the box within.

It was ten thousand rounds of Remington .22-caliber long rifle ammunition.

The card just said: *Yee-ha.*

That Jake. What a romantic.

## CHAPTER THIRTY-NINE

# We Work While Larksdale Burns

The first thing I learned over the next few weeks was I *really* liked running the show. Especially in early June, when we were all giddy at having our own company. Even usually serious Jake joined a team effort to paint an undersea mural along our main office corridor one Friday to help our "we're developing high-tech fishing gear" cover story. I don't think Michelangelo would have worried about competition, but we had a lot of fun—and followed it with a twelve-hour working Saturday.

My private contribution to the general sense of wackiness was imagining myself captain of the dread pirate ship *RadioRemote,* raiding all along the high-tech coast. This wasn't entirely woolgathering; I still had my Hollywood dreams, and was considering updating *Treasure Island* as a story set among the buccaneers of high technology. Mostly, it was my secret joke, though I did once share it with Traci. "Callie," she said one early-June morning,

"Sophia and I think we should incorporate in Delaware. Better rules of corporate governance."

"Then do it," I replied. Then I squinted at her and slammed the desk. "And look lively, ya lubberly dog!"

"Oh. Okay. Only, Callie—are you nuts?"

"Arrgh!"

"I'll take that for a yes. Sign here, here, and here."

It was pretty easy then for me to be jolly, and Traci, tolerant. Our technology was exciting; the prospects for money looked wonderful; and we all felt we were saving Larksdale with our new, hip company. Motown-style singing (arranged by Traci) became a regular event every evening around six. Jake adopted an adorable puppy named Rachel ("She's a pure bulldog except for her back, which is Ridgeback, and her snout, which is boxer . . ."), who immediately became our mascot. And Vince had our softball team up-and-running (or in my case, mostly stumbling) pretty quickly. We lacked time to practice, but still played twice-weekly games.

Of course, the jollity couldn't last—if only because Larksdale was in such trouble.

It was hot weather, so, sure, we faced nothing as dramatic as people freezing in the streets. But with unemployment rippling outward from PMT, and bank repossessions starting to crowd the *Herald*'s real estate section, we would have been cold indeed not to feel the spreading woe. (Though I did find some of it almost gratifying: Patricia Farthingale's *Larksdale Style* folded after a single issue. I didn't gloat a lot at that news, but I'll admit I gloated a little.) It was alarming; we were becoming a town of vacancies, job wanted flyers, and canceled events.

Hands down, Larksdale's biggest losers on NDN stock were its most reluctant investors, the Ladies. Certainly they had other assets, and one June Sunday Aunt Dolly very kindly assured me we would have plenty to live on even if NDN "disappeared in a puff of smoke." And their V & V program was finally getting some traction. By mid-month they had a full slate of speaking engagements, while sales of their self-help manuals were slowly climbing. Gladys, who still brought their mail to meetings, said jokingly she would have to invest in a wheelbarrow if it got any heavier.

All that was reassuring, but even the Ladies couldn't afford losses forever.

They coped in different ways. Martha was stolid; Aunt Dolly, good-humored and practical. Sophia was simply human: Angry at her fortune's decline, she was not above blaming Milt for his part in it. She kept her own counsel, mostly, but anybody could see she and Milt were moving toward divorce. Sometime in May he'd started taking consulting jobs—all of them a thousand miles or more from Minnesota.

Despite the losses, though, the Ladies kept up their charitable giving. To the growing number of begging letters Gladys brought, they always replied they believed in self-help, not handouts, and would send a letter that included a list of local charities (never mentioning how many of them they underwrote).

But nothing the Ladies did was enough to turn the tide.

The third Saturday in June, the *Herald* ran the inevitable editorial: WILL THE LAST PERSON OUT OF LARKSDALE PLEASE TURN OUT THE LIGHTS? At that morning's meeting the Ladies set out an extra-fancy display of snacks—all homemade and decked out with early summer fruits. They had agreed to be brave. They also agreed that Deborah would write, for all of them to sign, a letter to the editor saying Larksdale was far from beaten. Bold gestures, but I lost my taste for the food after Sophia stood and summarized our situation.

It was now clear, she said (mostly to Traci and me), that RadioRemote was Larksdale's best hope; but with the Ladies' resources crumbling, we needed to bring in outside money—meaning venture capital. Sophia hestitated, glanced to Martha, then told Traci and me coolly, "We're guaranteeing funding through Labor Day. But if we don't have outside money by the end of September, well . . ."

That was, I realized with a catch in my throat, only ninety days away.

Ninety *dark* days.

With the stock market plunging, nobody was buying Initial Public Offerings of stocks. With no IPO market to cash them out, venture capitalists were in sudden retreat everywhere. Anyone reading the business section knew the VCs were funding ever-fewer businesses, and demanding ever-bigger slices of the pie for each rare dollar they *did* invest. Given the usual lead time to approve funding, I figured that within four weeks we had to hit the road and sell RadioRemote to a bunch of steely-eyed investors.

I realized my pirate days were over.

I announced the Ladies' decision to the team an hour after I heard it from Sophia.

Ideally, we at RadioRemote would have instantly become 100 percent business; but that never happened. We, after all, were 100 percent human; personal stuff kept creeping in. To be fair, Vince had been increasingly taking on serious business problems, and he kept on doing so. That was surprising, and impressive, but also, I thought, a little irritating because it meant his spending more time with Traci. And I couldn't say why that bothered me, except it reminded me I'd never asked Traci about her kissing him on New Year's Eve. Now, with nearly six months gone by, raising the issue would have felt goofy—but I couldn't help wondering if there were something between them.

Around 8 P.M. on the last Friday in June, Vince slapped a dopey Wisconsin cheesehead hat on his head and announced he was taking everyone to Chuck E. Cheese for pizza and games. Since we were committed to work through the weekend, a short break was certainly in order. I'd seen Jake nodding in agreement and switching off his computer, but, thinking I'd already tormented myself enough for one day, I buried my head deep in a stack of documents. I didn't need to moon over him outside of work, too.

A minute later Traci was leaning over my desk asking, "Aren't you coming?"

"I have work."

"Vince will be disappointed."

"Disappointment builds character."

"You don't care?"

I set down my pen. "What's all this interest in Vince?" I was backing into the long-avoided issue—and afraid I'd hear breaking glass.

"Nothing!" She shrugged uneasily. "I'm just saying he's a nice guy, and really smart—"

"Yeah, well maybe you should date him."

"Callie!"

"I'm serious. We could make it a movie. *Beauty and the Geek*."

Traci didn't laugh as I hoped she would. "Maybe someday you'll be sorry."

Whatever she was trying to tell me, I was in no mood to hear. I shrugged and grabbed my pen, and she headed for the door. I told myself, as she headed off for pizza and I resumed working, that until September, I was devoting myself to nothing but business.

* * *

I stayed at the office pretty late that night, but as I entered my apartment, the phone was ringing. It was Milt Green. Sounding awkward, he said he'd read the online *Herald*'s report that we were launching a business, and wanted to wish us luck. Now, don't ask me where I got off trying to improve anyone else's personal life, but I had the sudden impulse to help Milt and Sophia reunite by getting him involved in RadioRemote. As far as Milt knew, the business was indeed newfangled fishing sensors. Nobody had given me permission to let him in on the secret, but we were going public shortly, and once we started pitching to VCs, the whole world would know. . . .

So, after hesitating, I told him about RadioRemote.

I guess I made it sound pretty exciting. There was a long silence before he responded, "She didn't feel like telling me, I guess." He sounded so discouraged, I feared I'd blundered; but after another long silence he added, "Listen, Callie: If you ever have any business questions, if I can help, well, I hope you'll call me."

Of course, I agreed in a flash. I still wanted to say something kind, or helpful. But I figured romantic advice from me would be like anger management tips from the Hulk, so I left it at thanking him, and wishing him good night. I ended June telling myself I was all about work, but admitting grudgingly that personal issues were a part of life.

How big a part, I was about to find out.

CHAPTER FORTY

# Mighty Callie Strikes Out

RadioRemote moved into summer in high, even fighting, spirits. With the Ladies' deadline the great fact of our existence, work took up so many hours I lacked time even to think about small matters like the eerie silence from ICAAM in Hollywood.

Since we were about to drop our cover story in order to approach VCs, the Ladies (who'd previously kept a low profile) visited the office frequently. They weren't exactly shrewd judges of software, but they definitely baked a mean apple strudel and spread a lot of encouragement. Deborah and Sophia both got their sons to volunteer as interns (read "free labor"); since both boys liked gadgets, they seemed to have fun, certainly were a help, and added to our spirit of playfulness.

Still, work was the essence of the game.

Except for a mid-afternoon barbecue, we treated the Fourth of July as just another workday. As Vince put it with his newfound practicality, if RadioRemote didn't land new funding well before Halloween, we could all kiss our personal independence good-bye. So after the barbecue, we reopened the office, but later did step outside long enough to see the (very modest) fireworks show. Standing on the muggy street, I couldn't help but remember the previous year's festivities. I even missed Patricia Farthingale's grandstanding shenanigans—which shows you what a tiny holiday it was.

Jake, who had a boyish fondness for fireworks, was scarce that Fourth. He worked through all but thirty minutes of our barbecue, so he could leave before dark for the big show in Minneapolis. I wished he'd asked me along: I had much too much work in hand to go, but it would have been nice to have been asked.

After the Fourth came two solid weeks of nonstop work.

Then I had to make an executive decision.

During the jovial days of early June, Vince had signed up our softball team for the statewide Deeply Amateur Softball Tournament in Duluth. Of course, it wasn't exactly the World Series—and no one would mind if we canceled—but it was a commitment. And looking ahead, I saw no other excuse for a break between then and the Ladies' deadline at the end of September. So I gathered the team and announced it was a sad day for Minnesota sports: We were going to Duluth.

The decision was greeted with cheers.

Only Jake bowed out. He wanted to visit someone—I didn't dare ask who—in Colorado over the suddenly-free weekend, and seemed to consider himself at liberty to come and go as he pleased. I couldn't object, though, because none of us were taking the tournament very seriously; based on our season record and training program, hell would get an NHL franchise before we fielded a team with a hope of winning the tournament. So we headed north with a special game plan: get blown out of the tournament on day one, then spend the rest of the weekend kicking back.

The plan worked perfectly. Our Saturday morning loss, 11–2, left us free to lounge. The guys headed off Saturday afternoon for (we suspected) a bar in town. Traci, Alicia (who'd come along for moral support), and I bowed out, eager to enjoy an afternoon by ourselves, followed by an evening on the porch of Traci's lake-front cabin watching the glow of fireflies.

When we reached the cabin after dinner, a note for me was thumbtacked to the door. I recognized Vince's handwriting, but figured it was just an invitation to join him and the guys in Duluth, and stuffed it in my windbreaker pocket without reading it. This was girls'-only night.

We built a fire in the fire ring partly for atmosphere, and mostly for toasting marshmallows. The cabins were widely scattered, the night was dark, and it felt like wilderness. We reminisced awhile about high school, then Traci got us on the topic of college romances. That was unusual—Traci was usually so private; but she took us from there to romance after college, which in her case had always been a mystery. I'd barely thought this when Alicia demanded, "Yeah, what about New York? You never talk about it. We all thought you had the world's most romantic life."

I practically blushed for Traci—who, for all her veneer of elegance, was often shy.

Staring at the fire, Traci ran her hands through her hair, ruffling it as she did when nervous. But then she looked up and started talking.

"When I was young, I built up this idea. . . . I thought if I achieved enough, people would like me for what I *achieved,* not how I looked. Even later I kept the idea, and in college and law school I worked myself to death to prove it." She shook her head.

"Then in New York, I had a . . . thing with my managing partner. He was thirty-five and single, great-looking, and with a glamorous life, the Hamptons and all that; but what got me was his whole line about how ready he was to settle down and raise a family. He sure knew how to get to me. . . ." She made a pretense of skewering a marshmallow, abandoned it, and went on: "Anyway, one morning it was raining hard. I was making him breakfast, and like a dope I asked if I was special to him. I thought he would say 'sure,' or maybe what a great team we made. I was so desperate for a compliment, I would have written it for him. Why not? I'd been ghostwriting his briefs for the last year." She wiped again at her hair. With her hand sweeping slowly across her face, she seemed to be trying to hide. "Anyway, he puts down the *New York Times* and says, really sincerely, 'Are you kidding? You're like a hundred bonus points. I mean, even scoring with one of those hottie secretaries in Litigation is like, bagging a . . . a doe, or maybe a rabbit. But you, you're like . . . ' and he squints at my hair and says, 'Sleeping with you is like nailing a polar bear, out in the Alaskan wilderness.' "

Alicia stood to stretch her back—and also, perhaps, because she was upset. "Suddenly," she muttered, "dating women makes even more sense."

But Traci, having fallen silent, was watching me so intently I finally asked, "So, what are you getting at?"

Suddenly focused, she demanded, "Are you interested in Vince, or not?"

If I'd been standing, I would have reeled back. "No!" I blurted, too staggered to hedge. My bluntness stunned me. "He's my friend, and he makes me laugh—but I'm not."

"Well," Traci said, laughing shortly, "He's my friend, and he makes me laugh—and I *am*."

This was not the sort of line to be left ambiguous. In fact, it was so bizarre Alicia asked, "You're what?"

"In love with Vince."

I was stunned. This was like Jessica Rabbit dating Bugs Bunny. Weirder. "You're *not* serious."

"I'm always serious, Callie. And why not? What's wrong with Vince?"

"Well, I mean, he's a great guy—my best guy friend, by far—but he's not exactly a smooth romantic . . . and you always liked smooth romantics."

"We'll work on it."

"Could you see Vince taking a carriage ride in Central Park?" I persisted.

"Maybe."

"Yeah, *maybe*—except he'd replace the horses and wheels with, like, hovercraft running gear. You'd wind up—" I stopped in mid-sentence. I'd been describing the Vince of a year ago. The new Vince was . . . what? Reliable. Steady. And showing a remarkable talent for business issues. Still nice, still fun . . . but no longer so flakey.

Traci was still arguing. "Yeah, but would I be *bored*?"

"No," I admitted.

"Would he ever be *mean* to me?"

"I see your point." I was seeing it all too well, and feeling sort of queasy. I thought Traci was going to say, "Thanks." Instead, she just kept staring at me until I asked, "*What?*"

"You know Vince. He won't be happy until you tell him it's okay."

"You're telling me you couldn't, um, *persuade* him yourself?"

"If I did, it would break his heart." She shrugged. "You're his friend, Callie. He'd think he was selling you out."

Suddenly I felt incredibly irritated. I mean, there I was with my life falling apart: Jake unavailable, RadioRemote a risky longshot, and my future—dinky as it was—riding on one Hollywood job application where they hadn't even bothered to write for months. And I was supposed to give up the one guy who worshipped me? I almost shook my head and said, "I don't think so." Then I realized, to my deeper irritation, that I had to step out of the way of true love—if that was what this was.

So I swallowed my feelings and said—

"Okay. You want me to talk to him, I'll talk to him. You owe me one. Actually, you owe me about three."

Traci put a hand on my shoulder. "I owe you about *ten.* Thanks."

Perfect. I'd gone off to the northern lakes for a little spiritual consolation from my two best friends and ended up promising to kiss off my one faithful admirer.

When I finally reached Vince's cabin, it was nearly midnight, but he opened after about the second knock.

"Hey, Callie!"

I was irritable. "Don't 'Hey, Callie' me."

He jumped back about two feet. "What did I do?"

"You like her, don't you?" Suddenly this was getting funny. It was sounding like high school.

"Like who?"

"Traci, you idi . . . Traci."

"Oh." He looked off into the distance, looked back. "Well . . ."

"Come on. Speak up."

For once, Vince looked solemn. "Traci's not the question. It's just that . . ."

"That *what?*"

"Well, you've been my friend since forever. I was afraid—I might hurt your feelings. . . ."

I put a hand on his shoulder. "Look, Vince. You've been trying to *date* me since forever. Have I ever said yes?"

"Well . . . not really."

"Are there any conclusions you could draw from that?"

Vince thought about it for a long moment. Then he said, "You're not interested in me?"

"I'd say that's fair." I didn't know whether I was being amusing or not. I knew *I* wasn't having much fun. As for Vince, his expression kept switching between sadness and confusion. While sad, he asked, "We'll still be pals, won't we?"

"Sure. You bet. Forever."

Technically, I'd just kept my promise to Traci. But of course one topic remained. Sick though I was of being the entire world's lovable older sister, I kept my hand on Vince's shoulder. "Listen, friend. You're sweet, but if you're serious . . . well, it's time to step up to the plate. You know what I mean?"

I turned and left, with kind of a sinking feeling.

Halfway back to my own cabin, I was fishing in my coat for a tissue, and I came up with the note he had stuck on my door.

*Hey, Callie!*

*We're going for ice cream. Meet us at Beaudreau's, on Lime Street. It won't be any fun without you.*

That stupid Vince. I *told* him not to "Hey, Callie" me.

## CHAPTER FORTY-ONE

# Callie's Law and the Dog-and-Pony Days

Life around Vince and Traci was awkward, but they were scrupulously discreet. I doubled my efforts at RadioRemote, and that seemed to help, some. And I pretty shortly decided I couldn't agonize about Jake and Vince, both.

There's only one Lost True Love per customer.

By the end of July, though, I realized I had a bigger problem. There's an old engineering truism which, so far as I know, doesn't have a name. Since nobody's looking, I'm going to dub it "Callie's First Law," and it goes like this:

It's easy to build *one* of anything.

GM needed just over a year to build the world's first fuel cell-powered vehicle in 1964. It's nearly forty years later, and mass-produced fuel-cell vehicles are *still* a decade away. You could make the same point using manned moon rockets, television, or a zillion other inventions. Now, RadioRemote wasn't as complex a problem as the fuel-cell car . . .

But the law held.

Vince built the first model at home in his spare time. But turning his toy into a rock-solid product for Jane-Average-User meant thousands of development hours. Vince's blimp had been the only RadioRemote gadget in the world. No casual bystander, using a RadioRemote-enabled PDA, could have tried turning on his car heater out in the parking lot and accidentally sent the blimp flying out a window. But if they were mass-made, then each controlled object needed its own unique "address"—like an Internet URL. *Plus* there were issues of range, and cost, and security and . . . well, you get the picture.

All those problems could be solved; but solving them took time.

Time meant money, and money, as we already knew, was getting scarce.

In late July Sophia and I worked out what we'd need to carry us for the next eighteen months, by which point we could confidently expect to have, at the least, a licensable technology. Counting outsourced services from patents to prototypes, it came to about six million bucks.

*Six million.*

The traditional answer would have been venture capital funding. All through the nineties, VCs had been the money spigot for the tech revolution. At the peak of the boom (say, two years earlier), any halfway-decent idea (and many really bad ones) had been able to raise easily anywhere from 5 to 100 million bucks—plenty of money to work through all the technical problems between an idea and a product.

I wished those dollars were still available, but far too many of them had simply been flushed, invested in businesses that had gone public spectacularly and were now just as spectacularly flaming out. Don't get me wrong: the VCs were (mostly) still in business, but few of them were actually investing. By mid-July we had contacted about thirty different firms. More than a dozen were interested enough to talk with us, but we had no illusions. The number of startups actually being funded was dropping daily.

We still had to give it our best shot.

The last week in July I essentially turned day-to-day operations over to Vince and Jake so I could prepare for our dog-and-pony show, as it was called: the presentation we were going to take, starting the first week in August, to venture capital firms around the Midwest. Most of my prep involved boiling down everything—from our basic idea to the size of our market—to a single five-minute talk. Then Traci and I had to practice fielding every possible question and keeping calm while being grilled.

The Ladies weren't going with us on tour, but they helped a lot with prep: Not only did Sophia coach us, but the last weekend in July, all the Ladies teamed up on us with two straight hours of mock questioning. Just to crank up pressure, they held the session at Martha's with the windows closed, and the A/C off.

Deborah said they wanted to see us sweat.

They did.

Only after we passed the test did they bring out the usual snacks and (even better) crank up the air-conditioning. Then, to celebrate, Traci and I cleaned up and went into the Twin Cities to shop for power clothes for our presentations. I'm not usually big on retail therapy, but we needed every edge we could get.

Our first pitch was to a fairly small VC firm in St. Paul. Heading into it, we felt we had some things going for us. Above all, we weren't another retailing scheme, one of the zillion cookie-cutter ideas to take some regular business and put ".com" after its name—what Michael Dell of Dell computers had called "Wash-My-Car.com." During the late nineties, VCs had put up billions for those kinds of ideas, but by mid-2000, you could not give them away.

I had a bit of a secret weapon, too. I had taken Milt up on his offer to coach me behind the scenes, and for three nights at the end of July we spoke at length via phone. It made me sad, in a way, to realize he was giving me almost exactly the same advice I was getting from Sophia. If ever two people were a matched pair, they were. I wanted to tell them as much, but when I suggested to Milt that he simply team up with Sophia, he turned silent, then made me renew my promise not to mention our conversations to her.

I figured it was his life, and besides, I had enough on my plate without playing rematch maker.

So on Tuesday the first of August, we gave our first pitch.

And flopped.

It was the first flop of many—and not because we did a bad job. The simple truth was that VCs just then were looking for any excuse to say no. And say no they did. I won't recite the details: All of them were polite; two (in Chicago) seemed genuinely sorry to pass. They used every sort of excuse, from the catchall "market conditions," to the very specific pronouncement that our management team lacked startup experience. (That was perfectly true; but two years earlier, as Sophia pointed out, they would simply have *found* us a CEO.) Perhaps with Milt onboard we would have gotten closer—but in that market, even Milt would have provided no guarantee of success.

Of our dozen interested VCs, we burned through seven in the first ten days of August, and thereafter the rejections just kept arriving. By mid-August our "possibles" list had diminished to just two or three names. Yes, there were still more to contact, but the situation was decidedly grim.

I kept the problem to myself. It was always possible one VC firm would say yes where all the others had said no. But every day the numbers looked a little worse. And with the Ladies' funding cutoff date only six weeks away, and Larksdale daily looking grimmer (the August Town Council meeting had actually led to fisticuffs over school funding), I found myself slipping into despair.

I was at my desk about eight one late-August night when Jake said, "I need a word with you."

I switched off my computer. "Let's take a walk."

We were barely out on the warm street when it hit me with certainty what he wanted to say. "How much are they offering you?"

"Thirty grand raise. Moving package. Housing. Bonus."

"Jeez. I'll help you pack. Do they need a project manager?"

He gave me that crinkling look around the eyes, which was his usual equivalent to laughter. "Hold on. I haven't given them an answer yet."

I changed my tone a little. "Believe me, you're well out of this."

The intuition thing worked both ways. He asked, "How broke are we?"

I hesitated, then said "Pretty broke . . ."

Something had been bothering me about the scattered passersby, and now I knew what it was: Almost none of them had ice-cream cones from Dagmar's. Larksdaleans were watching even the spare dollars now. I sighed and said out loud—

"At this burn rate, under ninety days till we blow up."

"We can tighten up. Cut out the pizza parties, drop the—"

"Call it four months." I was suddenly, overwhelmingly tense. "Can we deliver the gold disk by then?"

"Hell, no."

"Hell, *no?*" I tried to smile, but barely said it without my voice breaking.

"Hey. You want me to talk to you man-to-man?"

"Man-to-man?" *Perfect.*

He put a hand on my shoulder. "You're in the saddle. Ride the damn horse."

"Even if I go over a cliff?"

"You're the one who wanted to be a cowboy." More kindly, he added, "If you do, you do. Listen . . . those Ladies are tough, and they know all about risk capital."

I was ready to swap this man-to-man stuff for a friendly hug, but Jake persisted. "Why not wait a month and see what happens? I'll stick if you do. Maybe the Ladies will shake loose some more cash. They've pulled off longer shots than this."

Funny: At first, all I heard was that he would stay. It took longer to get the part about how I wasn't the whole show, which was what I really needed to hear.

We had reached a bench underneath a large oak tree. As much as I wanted to forget all of my problems, and sit in the dark with Jake, I knew too much was riding on RadioRemote. Callie Whinefest 2000 was over. My stubborn streak reasserted itself.

"I'm heading back. You coming?"

"Reckon I'll sit here awhile." He grinned. "After all, I'm not management."

CHAPTER FORTY-TWO

# The Roof Falls In

My talk with Jake—and a subsequent team meeting—turned us into a tougher organization. Over the next six weeks the toys began disappearing, the games ceased, and people, while still trying to be polite (it was still Minnesota, after all), became short-tempered.

They weren't alone in turning short-tempered. I was losing a lot of my own (ahem!) sweet nature as September began. We were killing ourselves now, not to bring the whole system to market (that was impossible in the time we had left), but to make at least enough of a breakthrough that we could wow one of the few VCs still investing in startups. My mood got a big shove downward from a letter I got on the fifth of September. It read:

*Dear Ms. Brentland:*

*I regret to inform you that current market uncertainties (and the decline in Entertainment Industry tech spending) have forced us to suspend our search for an agent-trainee to help our producer and studio clients understand new technologies.*

*We hope the situation will become clearer in a few months. If it does, we will certainly revive our consideration of your work. Meanwhile, it seemed unfair to keep you from pursuing other opportunities.*

*Thank you very much for your interest in ICAAM.*

*Yours Sincerely,*
*Peter Goldfarb*

I hadn't merely gone from "Callie" to "Ms. Brentland." I'd had my back door into the film industry slammed in my face.

Not that I spent much time lamenting it. Compared with what other people were facing, my problems seemed small. As the days grew shorter, and autumn appeared in the cool winds around sundown, Larksdale began to sense just how nasty real poverty could be. Many people, it seemed, had been burning through their severance pay and were starting in on their savings, to keep their lifestyles alive. When the last of those reserves were spent, they would find themselves against a wall, indeed.

With failing fortunes and failing tempers came failing reason.

Some fool began yelling at Gladys whenever he spotted her around town. One day he cornered her in the supermarket and screamed that the Ladies were responsible for NDN's leaving and owed the whole town compensation. By freak luck (or act of Providence, as you prefer), Jake happened to be in the store and heard the commotion. With his usual friendly half-smile he suggested to the yelling fellow that maybe he'd rather step outside and discuss it with someone closer to his own size. That ended the matter for the moment, but it also brought home the fury beginning to build in the former Martha's Vineyard of the Midwest.

Things got so bad that when I read (on page eight of the *Herald*) that Patricia Farthingale had donated $2500 to keep after-school programs alive, I realized she must have been reaching down into her own, personal savings—and almost liked her.

The only thing running against total town-wide despair was a rumor which began in the coffee shops and doughnut stores, and by mid-month made it to the *Herald*'s pages: The rumor was that NDN was thinking of reopening PMT. Or else NDN was planning to use the PMT location for some new high-tech division.

What fueled this speculation was the fact that PMT's former building had not yet shut down. The three-person "final transition team," with custodial, security, and minimal support staff (including J'Nelle) was still there. Although nobody *really* knew what they were doing, many believed Larksdale's plunging labor costs (read, "desperate workforce") made it a natural place to move jobs from the high-wage D.C. area.

By September even the Ladies were wondering about the situation. Their theory (first put forward by Sophia, I think) was that PMT didn't want to book the losses that would be involved in a complete shutdown. For accounting purposes, NDN was better off paying the bills to keep minimal business alive in Larksdale, rather than admitting the entire plant was an unsalable write-off.

Still, even the Ladies had their curiosity.

For weeks they had been urging J'Nelle to try to get the scoop, and she had promised to do her best. But nobody expected her to risk her job to satisfy our curiosity, and though she kept her eyes open, she had learned absolutely nothing. Personally, I spent no more time wondering about NDN than I did lamenting ICAAM. I intended, as Jake had suggested, to ride the horse I was on just as far as I could.

But Callie's Law was doing us in. Certainly, we made progress, but as September wore on, we remained at least six months—probably over a year—from a salable product. And the VCs kept bouncing us.

Mid-September brought one piece of good news. Sophia called to say the Ladies wanted to make sure they gave RadioRemote the best possible shot, so they were willing to extend funding another sixty days. That was sweet, but I figured implicit in the deal was my promise that if I ever became certain we had no realistic hope of landing funding, I'd let them know ASAP, so they could cut their losses.

And their losses could be huge; even with every economy I could find, our burn rate was still almost $200,000 a month.

At the end of September (partly, I always suspected, because Milt pulled some strings) we were invited to pitch to a pair of the very biggest-name VC funds. We put together the absolutely best pitch we could, even including Vince to handle the tech questions, and on successive days the first week in October, we traveled to Chicago and then Dallas, and put on a song-and-dance that would have made Gene Kelly proud. I figured if there was a dime's worth of venture capital left in the country, we'd get it.

And both funds turned us down in record time.

When the ding letters arrived—both on the same day, October 10—I decided to face reality. I invited in my top three people: Traci, Vince, and Jake; spelled out the situation in detail; then asked them three questions:

—Did anybody think we could deliver a "gold disk" version of the RadioRemote software in the next forty-five days?

—Did anybody think what we had in hand would land us a licensing deal with a fair chance of recouping the 1.2 *million* dollars the Ladies had already sunk into the project—or at least of covering our expenses until we *could* recoup?

—Did anybody have an alternate plan, or a quick-hit product or service idea we could sell immediately to keep us afloat until we could somehow hit break-even?

We spent the next half hour trying desperately to invent a way we could stay afloat, and struck out completely. When we finished, we were the palest human beings ever seen in Minnesota, and that's saying something. We sat silently for almost fifteen minutes more, saying nothing.

Then I tossed my pencil onto the conference table and said—

"Okay. I'll call the Ladies." My voice was shaky with defeat.

As it turned out, the game was far from over.

Out at PMT something very Lady-like was about to happen.

## CHAPTER FORTY-THREE

# J'nelle Gets into the Game

In the months while Larksdale burned and NDN's stock crumbled in earnest, J'Nelle Baker had simply kept on working. She didn't like the work very much, and didn't like her boss even a little, but she needed the money and the Ladies had convinced her staying on might somehow prove useful.

J'Nelle's reward had been promotion to Lamont Patterson's personal assistant, the most trusted position not held by someone on the NDN transition team. All that summer, as the remaining staff dwindled, she had fielded Mr. Patterson's calls, booked his frequent flights out of town, screened his callers, handled his correspondence (he never used e-mail), and run his errands. Over most of that time Lamont Patterson had treated her with simple businesslike gruffness—less as a person than as a piece of office equipment. She had the faint notion that if she ever failed to respond to his instructions, he would bang her on the side like a jammed Coke machine.

Over these last two weeks, though, relations between them had worsened as the work expanded. J'Nelle was now regularly on the job from 8 A.M. until 8 at night. Mr. Patterson had given her one small consolation—a raise of $150-a-week—but even that came in an offhand remark, unaccompanied by even a word of praise or thanks. Increasingly, he was short, rude, and suspicious of everything J'Nelle said or did.

So J'Nelle spent early October hoping for some opportunity not for revenge, exactly, but for justice—justice for the Ladies and, increasingly, for herself.

The mid-October day she got her chance had been particularly miserable.

About 10 A.M. J'Nelle had been at the computer rushing to finish the fifth of ten letters for Mr. Peterson when he buzzed her to come to his office and pointed to his personal bar with its elegant crystal and expensive bottles. "All the glassware needs to be packed up. Call Supplies and have them send over whatever you think it'll take."

"Yes, sir. And . . . ?" J'Nelle was alarmed. This made it seem the long-delayed final shutdown was at hand. She worried both for the loss of her job, and because it now looked as if she'd never get the dirt on NDN.

Before J'Nelle could ask who exactly they would be sending to do the packing, Patterson interrupted, "And *pack it.*" He was nice enough not to bellow, "You moron!"

Somehow, that nicety did not greatly cheer J'Nelle. For once, she let her frustration show. "What about the correspondence? I'm only one person."

"Then you'll have to work like two, won't you?" Mr. Patterson paused, then seemed to relent. "Just get as far as you can while I'm out of the office between now and two. And put yourself down for a hundred-dollar bonus."

So J'Nelle—not quite ready to tell Mr. Patterson where he could ship his bonus and indeed his job—ordered the supplies and, in the half hour before they arrived, broke her personal speed-typing record. Strictly in her own mind, she also used some descriptive language she'd used aloud only once, in a big traffic jam in Los Angeles.

J'Nelle spent the next two hours on her knees, not exactly praying. With work piled up on her desk, she carefully folded Irish crystal into large sheets of light-blue tissue paper, then put the wrapped results into shipping boxes. By lunchtime her back ached, and by the time Patterson returned in mid-afternoon, it was killing her. As she returned to her desk, she wondered vaguely whether "going secretarial" would ever come to have the same meaning as "going postal."

Mr. Patterson ignored J'Nelle for the rest of the afternoon, and as she dug her way out of the pile of accumulated correspondence, she began to think almost dreamily of leaving the office, making the long drive home, and then soaking for about twenty years in a hot, bubbly bath. She was just improving this fantasy with chocolates, soft music, and Denzel Washington when it was all vaporized by the chirp of the intercom line, and Mr. Patterson's smooth, irritating voice.

". . . *right away,* J'Nelle."

She entered the inner sanctum. Mr. Patterson, slightly flustered, eyed her coldly and pointed to his private washroom's rosewood door. "You'll find a locked file cabinet in there. Shred everything in it."

J'Nelle sagged. She'd promised herself that hot bath and ten hours' sleep. Against her own habits of spartan discipline, she decided, for the second time that day, to protest, "I've already got at least three hours of work ahead, just on the letters."

"Then you'll have to work late." Mr. Patterson had let her finish only because he was occupied removing a small key from his key chain. Now, having pushed it across the desk, he was turning to the documents on his desk. "Order takeout, and turn in a chit. We'll pay. I don't want to see those papers here in the morning, right?"

A plan had been forming in J'Nelle's mind ever since she'd seen Mr. Patterson's flustered look. She had long intended to weigh in on the side of her friends, and against the bullies of NDN. Her wish had hit a brick wall of morality. She might look a modern, moderately hip young woman, but her upbringing, by parents who dragged her to church every Sunday of her preadult life and most Sundays thereafter, had been strictly old-school.

Besides, even though most of the security guards had been let go, video cameras were almost everywhere. J'Nelle, for all her motivation, had seen no way to beat the system.

Now, in an instant, Mr. Patterson's rude instructions turned the tide. J'Nelle's vague plan turned perfectly solid.

She was going to raid the documents.

She decided then and there with absolute certainty that whatever she was supposed to shred would be dirt to be used against NDN. And that was what the Ladies needed. And one way or another she was going to smuggle it out of the building. And the fact that Patterson, with his usual contempt for her exhaustion, wanted her to stay late not only hardened her determination, but simplified the plan.

For the next forty-five minutes J'Nelle worked to avoid suspicion. When the takeout arrived (the delivery boy was, as usual, accompanied by the security guard), she paid cheerfully and traded jokes about the weather. She ate the food, down to the fortune cookie, while seated quietly at her desk with fork in one hand and task checklist in the other.

And when Lamont Patterson, barely pausing to say good night, left his office, she was ready to move.

The cutbacks were certainly going to work in her favor. After months of staying late, she knew the routine of the one remaining night watchman who made his rounds every two hours. But she had barely told herself this when Mr. Patterson paused in the doorway and said over his shoulder, "I forgot to tell you. We put on two extra security guards, just in case anybody who was laid off tries making trouble. They'll be around every half hour or so. I'm sure you'll barely notice them, but if you do, don't let them bother you."

J'Nelle began thinking furiously.

How much had she learned in her year with the Ladies?

She was about to find out.

# CHAPTER FORTY-FOUR

## Agent J'nelle

J'Nelle waited twenty minutes, to make sure Mr. Patterson did not return, then hurried down the corridor to the janitorial closet and came back pushing the dolly. She considered doing a little discreet espionage in his office. But then she remembered the video cameras, and the rumors that many were micro-cameras, impossible to spot. The idea of staring in some new NDN/Golden West reality TV show like *Crooked Secretaries on Tape!* did not appeal to her. So, pushing the dolly, she crossed the fancy office and hurried on to the private washroom. The small lounge had been modernized, and the black file cabinet looked out of place, but it had to go somewhere.

For J'Nelle's purposes, the small room had two advantages.

First, it had a door that locked. Second, not even the most security-conscious company was likely to put video cameras in the president's private *washroom*.

She locked the door to the main office and got to work.

The first two file drawers seemed to hold only routine papers, but J'Nelle examined each page so carefully she actually forgot where she was, which was why the rattling of the doorknob made her jump about two feet skyward. She left the ground at a goodish velocity, and then relaunched with twice the force when a deep, rather tense voice demanded, "Hey! Who's in there?"

It wasn't Andy, the pleasant guard she'd befriended.

This voice was harsh and assertive. Her heart was battering frantically. She knew she looked so guilty any eager rent-a-cop would arrest her on sight for every crime from the Brinks job forward. Needing time, she hurried into the small bathroom and flushed the toilet, which responded with a satisfactory rush and gurgle. The door handle was being rattled, and she called, "Hang on! *One second!*" as she rushed to unlock the door.

The security guard who filled the doorway showed none of Andy's easy charm. He was a big, hard-faced detective type, who demanded, with bare courtesy, "Can I see some ID, please?"

"I'm J'Nelle Baker, Mr. Patterson's personal—"

"Are you listening? I said I need your ID." His tone was so caustic J'Nelle, who had heard that kind of tone before, decided he disliked her the minute he saw her complexion.

This was no time to back down. "No, *you* listen to *me*." She drew her security badge from inside her sweater, where it always hung from chain. She pushed it toward the guard. "I'm Mr. Patterson's personal secretary, and if you want me to call him, I will."

It worked like a charm. He stepped back. "Sorry. I'm new."

J'Nelle resisted the temptation to give him hell. She shut the door firmly and pressed the lock button as noisily as she could manage. Then she hurried back to the wash basin, splashed cold water onto her face, and held on to it until she stopped shaking.

* * *

J'Nelle made two discoveries.

First, all the gray folders forming the eight-inch stack at the back of the bottom drawer were stamped NDN/GWS-COMPANY CONFIDENTIAL.

And second, she had a problem.

If there had been only a handful of pages, she could have stuffed them under her big, puffy jacket and strolled to freedom. An eight-inch stack of papers, though, wouldn't make her look overweight; they'd make her look nine months pregnant. She would have to do some whittling down. Whittling meant reading, or at least skimming. She pulled the whole fat stack from the cabinet and carried it heavily to the sofa. Going fast as she could, she knew after twenty minutes she would have to smuggle out every last page.

For all her brains, J'Nelle was neither a lawyer nor an MBA.

Moreover, most of the papers used code words which meant nothing to her.

Still, she had touched perhaps two thousand corporate documents in the past three years, and when she began reading a thick, unsigned document labeled PROJECT GOLDEN PRAIRIE she knew that, as ordinary business, it made no sense. She also knew something else, and her heart began to slam with excitement.

Somebody was stealing something.

And it was up to her to steal it back.

To give the guards, who were undoubtedly watching for her on their video monitors, the illusion of a drone carrying out her job, J'Nelle loaded the dolly with a third of the unimportant papers. This was far fewer than she could have managed, but she needed an excuse for a series of trips. She needed to appear mindlessly busy while she figured out a way to smuggle out that big stack of documents.

Pushing the dolly down the barren path between cubicles, J'Nelle felt like a last survivor. The cubicles sat forlornly barren even of furniture. The emptiness distressed her, but also reminded her of the security cameras watching from above like cold angels. The cameras in turn reminded her to keep up her act. In the photocopy center she made a show of unloading the dolly, separating documents, and concentrating on pushing twenty or so pages at a time into the shredder.

She was concentrating, all right, but not on the shredder.

Then it hit her: *Call for backup!*

The idea that had come to her was so entertaining—and made her feel so much one of the Ladies—she needed great discipline not to laugh out loud. Back at her desk she fished out scissors and Scotch tape from a drawer. Then she hurried into Mr. Patterson's office. As calmly as she could, she grabbed six sheets of the light-blue tissue paper and the shallowest empty packing box, and strolled back into the private washroom. After a hasty ten minutes she had half the mystery pages stored in the packing box, and the box neatly wrapped in the tissue paper. She lacked a ribbon, but she made a folded-paper gift card from a sheet of memo paper and stuck it to the package. She inscribed it, and decorated it with little hearts and flowers.

Then she took out her cell phone and called Gladys.

* * *

Gladys said she'd need nearly an hour to reach PMT, so J'Nelle returned to the shredding with a vengeance. Destroying the rest of the unimportant documents took forty-five minutes, so she was just back at her desk when she got a call from the lobby.

"There's a Gladys Vaniman waiting for you."

"Thank you. I'll be right down," J'Nelle said. Then she grabbed the wrapped present and started for the door.

It was scam time.

Gladys positively beamed as J'Nelle came down the stairs and through the Plexiglas security gate into the lobby. She looked, J'Nelle realized, like Norman Rockwell's grandmother. J'Nelle held the wrapped gift aloft and sang out, loudly enough for the guards to hear, "Grandma! Happy birthday!"

In a moment she'd covered the thirty feet to where Gladys waited, and then Gladys had her arms around her. After they'd hugged, J'Nelle handed off the package, saying, "For you, Grammy. I'm sorry I have to work late."

Gladys took the package and gave J'Nelle a look much shrewder than the two onlookers realized. "Is this what I think it is?"

"Mmmm-*hmm*."

"Then it's just what I always wanted. And don't worry, we'll save you a piece of the pie."

Gladys rebuttoned her coat, adjusted her hat, and said, "I'd better let you get back to work. The whole family's proud of you, honey."

J'Nelle couldn't resist one last shot. Keeping her arm around Gladys's shoulder, she turned to the two guards, and said, "People say we look like sisters. What do you think?"

The mean guard turned notably redder and muttered, "Couldn't say, ma'am."

J'Nelle kissed Gladys's cheek and ended cheerfully, "Call you later, Grammy."

An hour later J'Nelle left the building. Before she did, she stopped at Mr. Patterson's desk and left a brief note:

*I handled the matters you mentioned.—J.*

Then she slipped one last time into his private washroom, where she carefully distributed the remaining four-inch stack of papers under her puffy blue coat, and secured it by yanking the coat's drawstring as tight as she could stand. As she went out the lobby door, she heard the mean guard tell the other one, "Geez. She'd be a babe, if she'd just drop about ten pounds."

CHAPTER FORTY-FIVE

# Things Heat Up

I was at my desk at RadioRemote at nine at night, trying to figure out how to make one dollar do the work of five. The phone rang, and it was Sophia, asking me to come by as soon as possible. I asked—

"Is it important?"

"You'll have to help figure that out," she said, sounding mysterious but excited.

I told her I'd be there, then hung up and switched off my computer. I was running as I left the building.

I reached Sophia's about a half an hour later.

The first thing she did, even before I had my coat off, was fill me in on J'Nelle's heist. By the time she finished, my jaw was dropped. My coat was on a hook, and so was I. We had to kill fifteen minutes over coffee before the others arrived. Then J'Nelle and Gladys appeared, and naturally *they* had to be served coffee and cookies. By this time I was fit to be tied. I swear: It's a good thing they didn't put the Strategic Air Command in Minnesota. If they had, we'd need about two and a half hours to scramble the B-2s: eight minutes to get airborne, and about two hours, twenty minutes to make sure everybody had enough to eat.

Finally we were all seated around the dining room table with the whole, reassembled stack of documents before us. I was reaching to grab one, but Sophia, ever the lawyer, put her hand atop the stack and warned, "Before we start, you ought to know our legal position is shaky. The laws protecting whistle-blowers are all over the board. Our being major shareholders is a help, but *still* . . . if NDN decides to come after us, it might get ugly."

Maybe Sophia had no idea how tempting this sounded. I was twenty-six years old, and all they could have put on my tombstone was SHE USED TO LIVE IN LARKSDALE and even then, there could have been an argument about whether I'd lived at all. I said—

"Quit hogging all the fun, and give me half the papers."

We did it Sophia's way, each of us reading through everything essential without sharing any comments, and then comparing our results. With eight inches of documents we could have been there all night and well into the next day, except J'Nelle's guess had been right: Project Golden Prairie was the smoking gun. A little after midnight Sophia looked up from the last page, took off her reading glasses, rubbed her eyes, and asked, "What do you think they're doing?"

I took a deep breath, and said—

"I *think* they're going strip all the cash out of PMT, plus use our perfect credit to borrow another twenty million dollars." I was shaking my head in amazement; the whole thing was like a particularly weird corporate ethics assignment in B-school. "Then they're going to use that twenty-five million as a down payment on the purchase of a hundred twenty-five million in tech services from *other* NDN divisions. *Those* divisions book a hundred twenty-five million in new revenue, so they hit their targets for the year, and the stock stops dropping and starts climbing."

Sophia nodded. But Gladys and J'Nelle were looking confused. So I said—

"In plain English? They're shuffling fantasy dollars and treating them as real. Their right hand is picking their left hand's pocket." *And,* I thought to myself, *they expect a bonus for dexterity.*

J'Nelle tapped the stacked papers and asked "But how can they expect to get away with it? Won't the auditors catch it?"

"Are they crazy?" Gladys asked.

"Maybe they're evil," J'Nelle replied.

"And maybe," I added, just to finish the topic, "they plan to take the money and run for the border."

In short, none of us really understood *what* they intended. Today, that makes us sound like dopes; but, remember, the first big corporate accounting scandals were just breaking. The scam seemed barely possible to us—but only barely. We sat marveling for so long I was startled when Gladys asked, "Are you sure there's no mistake? We've got to be absolutely positive before we act."

Gladys was right. It was one thing to swap guesses, and another to act on them. When it came to business, I was a rookie MBA, and Sophia, a lawyer. We didn't know enough to act.

We needed a pro.

Sophia turned to me and said quietly, "Give me the phone."

I put it in her hand. She swallowed hard, dialed, waited, and then said, "Honey? It's me. I'm sorry it's late—but I think I have a job for you."

The rest of us made our excuses and left.

# CHAPTER FORTY-SIX

# Hoisting the Jolly Roger

"Except for the candlesticks," Sophia said, with a nervous smile, as she and Milt entered the dining room, "everything on this table was stolen from NDN. If you object . . . well, I'll understand if you turn and leave."

"Object?" Milt smiled. When she saw how small his smile was, Sophia realized, with relief, that he was nervous, too. "I think it's great."

While Milt read the key documents, Sophia watched him. She saw him getting excited and returning to exactly those pages that had interested her. She liked watching his hands as they flipped pages and scribbled notes on a legal pad. She flashed back to when they had burned the midnight oil during the original fight to take over PMT. She had fallen in love with him during those crazy months. . . . Then she noticed with both sadness and affection that his curly black hair was going gray at the temples. She was thinking of a way to bring up those good old days, when Milt looked up. He was finished reading.

As he squared the pages, Sophia asked, "Well?"

"Well, for starters, this J'Nelle is now my personal hero. How she found this stuff out of maybe ten million documents beats me, but God bless her for it." He pushed the stack a few inches away, sighed, and rubbed his eyes. "And I can clear up one thing. They're doing it because of their compensation package. It's the only way for them to hit their targets."

"They'd risk jail for a bonus?"

"Honey, NDN pays its honchos like Hollywood stars. For the top guy we're talking twenty-five million in cash. Plus maybe five times that in stock-option gains, if they make their numbers."

"I still don't believe it. . . ."

"Say they get caught." Milt, his old fire returning, leaned toward her. Sophia felt her own excitement growing and thought to herself, *I love it when you talk business.* "If they catch the biggest fines in history, the CEO will still keep about ninety million dollars. Suppose they throw the book at him—which I seriously doubt—and he gets eighteen months. That works out to his keeping five *million* dollars a month for each month he serves in some country club prison. I'd do it, in a heartbeat."

"No, you wouldn't."

"Maybe not." Milt shrugged. "But plenty of people would say I'm a fool." He gave her one of his old, friendly smiles. "Now, before we hold forth on the state of business ethics, why don't you tell me what you and the Ladies really want? And," he added, "how I can help."

So Sophia talked. She told him about RadioRemote—and had her latest shock of many that evening when he admitted shyly that he'd been a secret supplier of startup advice for months. Finally she sketched out her half-formed plan to use the stolen documents to sue NDN to reverse the PMT sale, and to use the profits from a restored PMT to fund RadioRemote until it turned profitable.

"Sorry," Milt cut in before she finished. "You're right on the legal points, but it won't work. Go to court with this, you'll get a nice moral victory—maybe—but you'll lose PMT."

"But—" Sophia bristled; she was afraid he merely wanted to trash her plan.

"Sophia, the minute you blow the whistle, NDN'll get hit with enough shareholder lawsuits to tie them up till PMT's dead and buried." He waved toward the documents. "Anyway, there's a better way to use all this."

Sophia felt a sudden surge of excitement. "Meaning?"

"First, we have a quiet talk with Martin Davis about Project Golden Prairie. Then we offer him just enough for PMT that he figures the shareholders won't riot and the SEC won't step in. Of course, it's also an offer he would turn down cold if you didn't have him by the . . . in a hammerlock. But that's just how . . . where . . . you've got him." Milt, running with it, leaned back in his chair in his old comfortable way. "In fact, crazy as it sounds, the stock market collapse will be a huge blessing for you now. Software stocks like PMT are selling for eight cents on the dollar." He glanced back toward the stack of papers. "I figure certain facts entitle us to a discount. We should offer five cents on the dollar."

Sophia stared at him. "It's blackmail!"

"Damn right. Look, honey, broadly speaking I'm all for the rule of law. But you go public, and one of two things will happen: either nothing at all, because NDN's high-priced lawyers find a way to bury the truth or, more likely, to make Patterson the fall guy; *or* you get your huge civil and criminal blowup, and *maybe* Davis, Patterson, and the rest go to jail. Meanwhile, the lawyers suck up a hundred million dollars and PMT still disappears when NDN explodes."

He leaned forward, and the old fighting gleam was back in his eye.

"So what do you say, Soph? Do we hoist the Jolly Roger, and take back what's ours?"

There's never a cutlass around when you need one. Sophia's first instinct had been to pound the table and yell, "Arrrh, Matey!"

But the moment for joking passed. She was left with the warm feeling that this was the best proposal she'd heard since the night, long ago, he'd offered her a ring. Never mind, for now, English walking tours or Japanese martial arts. This was where they found their adventure.

She nodded her agreement.

They were neither of them inclined to do things by half measures. So she was ready when Milt asked, "How much money can the Ladies put together?"

"Rough guess? Maybe seven million, tops. It's been a lousy year."

"Tell me about it. But call it ten. I'm in, too—if you want it."

Sophia merely nodded again. She knew how absurd it was to be choked-up about a business proposition, but that didn't stop her from being choked up. After a moment she managed to say, "Okay."

They looked at each other longingly but stayed silent—the chumps.

Milt cleared his throat. "Okay. We've got the basic plan. Next step is for me to figure out our best bid, and you to find out exactly how much the Ladies are willing to risk. If the two numbers match, we may be back in business." He was standing, but with his fingertips still on the dining room table. "Thanks for thinking of me," he said.

It seemed they had decided to end on a businesslike note.

But the closer they got to the door, the slower they were moving, and the more they were turning to face each other. It would have taken only a single affectionate word. But they were both too shy. In the foyer they stood looking at each other, and the hopeful instant passed. Sophia opened the door; outside, autumnal rains fell on changing leaves.

Trying at least to leave gracefully, Milt said, "I'll help you get your company back."

She nodded, and he left.

She watched him for a few yards down the rain-swept path. When he was out of earshot, she whispered, "The company's not all I want back,"and softly shut the door.

CHAPTER FORTY-SEVEN

# Good Old Blackmail

The Ladies went for Milt's plan like the proverbial hungry dog after the pork chop. The vote came only five minutes after Sophia and Milt finished pitching it. Gladys loved the blackmail angle; Aunt Dolly was delighted to understand the issue (unlike the technical side of RadioRemote, which had mystified her); and the others, practical to their toenails, cared only that it was a way to reclaim PMT.

Milt had the only legitimate reason to see Martin Davis, so the next morning, without quite lying, he gave Mrs. Krantz, Davis's secretary, the impression he wanted to settle his employment contract in a civilized fashion. She put him on hold for three minutes and came back saying Mr. Davis would see him at 9:30 the next morning.

* * *

Milt's plane landed at LaGuardia well after dark; it was pushing eleven in the evening before he reached his room at the Plaza. He set out clothes and papers for the morning, showered, and fell into a blank sleep broken only by the wake-up call at 8 A.M. sharp. Rising, Milt had a vivid flashback to the miserable morning Martin Davis had dismissed him out on the street in front of NDN. Dressing, he made a point of keeping the image in mind.

It gave him the tough edge he needed.

Davis kept Milt waiting almost forty minutes. If it was an intimidation tactic, it misfired: Milt got tougher as the wait got longer. Gazing out the room's broad windows at a pelting rain, he reminded himself that this wasn't a regular business negotiation. It was a scam *disguised* as a business negotiation, and he had learned the art of scamming from the Ladies themselves. He was going to kick Martin Davis's butt.

So by the time he was sent in to see Davis, Milt was positively grinning.

Milt's first thought was that the past nine months had been hard on Martin Davis, who had acquired worry lines on his forehead and at the corners of his eyes.

Davis wasted no charm, waving Milt to a seat while saying, "I understand you think we can work out our problem without tying up the courts."

"I have a proposition"—Milt nodded as if he were agreeing—"that I think will solve your problems with PMT Software, and some other issues as well."

Martin kept most of the surprise, and some of the annoyance, out of his voice. "I thought you were here to discuss your termination package."

"In a way, I am." Milt spread his hands. "If we can reach terms on a PMT buyback, the employment issue will, let's say, just go away." He slipped the proposal from his portfolio case and slid it across Davis's desk.

"A PMT buyback?" Davis eyed the blue binder without enthusiasm. "Am I going to like it?"

"It'll solve a lot of problems. You'll take a big write-down, but nothing out of line with other stocks in the software sector."

"Which means we'll lose our shirt. What are you offering? Ten cents on the dollar?"

"Less."

Davis frowned and opened his mouth to speak, but Milt interrupted. "I don't say it'll be easy to sell to the board, but you'll get points, sooner or later, for facing up to market realities. And except for Web browsers and video games, NDN's not a software company. You'll get more points for refocusing the company on its core businesses." Milt managed to hide his secret excitement and sound exactly like a high-end business consultant.

Which, of course, he once had been.

"And all I have to do is write off—what?—a two-hundred-million-dollar investment?" Davis was shaking his head.

"People will understand. It's a tough economy."

"And a bad time to take big write-offs."

"Other people are writing off ten times that."

"And getting hammered for it." Davis was digging in his heels—and with cause. CEOs announcing write-downs were being roasted alive by the same analysts and journalists who a year earlier had promoted them into superstars.

Milt raised his hands as if giving up, and then said, "You're the one to judge the consequences. But you need to factor in Project Golden Prairie."

The room got very silent. Davis was either completely ignorant or one *hell* of a poker player. He eyed Milt mildly and asked, "I'm sorry? What was that?"

"Project Golden Prairie."

"Never heard of it."

Milt could play poker, too. He shrugged. "Then you have two choices, I guess. You can call up Lamont Patterson and ask him about it before the close of business today, or you can read about it in tomorrow's *New York Times*." He pushed the binder closer to Davis. "It's a helluva story, either way."

And with that, Milt—who'd been trained by the best, long ago—put his hands on the arms of his chair and started to rise. "Well," he added politely, "I've taken a lot of your time, and you've been very gracious." He pointed toward the proposal. "I think that's a fair plan for everyone. But it's your decision."

Davis made no reply. They shook hands briefly, and thirty seconds later, without really remembering the walk, Milt stood in front of the executive elevator.

After a long walk to burn energy and time, Milt was back in his hotel room by one-fifteen. He ordered lunch and left it untouched except for the coffee and two bites of the sandwich. The short afternoon seemed to take a hundred years to darken. It was five forty-five, and the sky had finally blackened, before the phone rang. Milt leaned back on his hotel bed, reached to the nightstand, and picked up on the third ring. The voice on the line was not a secretary, but Martin Davis himself. Milt relaxed the moment he heard the voice, even though it merely asked, "Green?"

"Speaking."

"I've spoken with several members of the board. They've made queries, and we're agreed that this Golden Prairie thing was simply a bit of noodling by Lamont Patterson and his friends out in Larksdale. Clearly, they were just playing with the idea and dropped it when they realized the legal problems."

Milt felt a moment's panic, but forced himself to say nothing. Had he guessed wrong in not attacking Patterson first? Well, it was too late now. If Martin was stonewalling, he was stonewalling. Then Milt knew better: CEOs did not make after-hours calls to deny what they intended to ignore. He settled back into his nice, soft Plaza pillows.

And waited.

At last Davis resumed speaking in a voice admitting defeat. "With that understood, we agree your plan might solve a number of problems. Only, we want these changes. A deal memo, signed by you, before noon on Monday. A one-million-dollar nonrefundable deposit, also in our hands by noon on Monday. And the price is twelve million, not ten, with the entire amount due-and-payable by Friday, twenty-two December."

Milt was thinking so hard and so fast he heard nothing for the next thirty seconds. Raising the money by December 22—sixty days, more or less—would be tough but not impossible. The twelve million sounded not like hardball, but like a minimum Davis had to have. And neither of them could stand a long negotiation.

Milt reached this conclusion just as Davis asked impatiently, "Well? Do we have a deal?"

"As far as I'm concerned"—Milt swallowed hard but felt victorious—"yes. If my principals agree, you'll have the deal memo and the check as scheduled."

They hung up more or less simultaneously.

* * *

Sophia must have been sitting beside her phone, because in the middle of the first ring she picked up and said sharply, "Yes?"

Milt thought of a lot of clever things he might say.

But he settled for "Shake out the piggy bank. If we can find twelve million, you've got your company back."

CHAPTER FORTY-EIGHT

# A Crisis—and Dolly's Wacky Idea

The wild excitement of a possible deal lasted more or less nineteen hours, from 6 P.M. on Wednesday, when Milt called Sophia, to just after nine the next morning, when, fresh off the plane from New York, he sat down with her to begin running numbers.

That was when economic reality hit.

Milt and Sophia worked almost nonstop on ways to finance a PMT repurchase, but the longer they worked, the tougher it looked, and by the time they summarized the situation at the start of the Ladies' usual Saturday meeting, they were positively gloomy. In our rush to put the screws to NDN, we'd unfortunately neglected to think about the screws being put to us by the economy.

Most obviously, there was NDN's plunging stock. Of course, actually selling the Ladies' shares was prohibited by the original PMT deal for many more months. But the stock was dropping so fast nobody would *lend* the Ladies even a fraction of what their holdings were supposedly worth. The same held for mortgaging houses. Larksdale was in the midst of a bursting real-estate bubble, and lenders were refusing to lend—or rather, were stretching out the process for so long that, for our purposes, it amounted to refusal. Nobody was saying the Ladies were headed for welfare; but they were far short of what they'd need to retake PMT and keep it funded until its earnings resumed flowing.

Martha and Dolly had already tried canvassing the former Ladies for investments, but with scant success. Mary Maitland's heirs, none of whom lived in Larksdale, had all passed; Agnes (with all her charitable commitments) could pledge only $25,000; and Skye Terrell's office said not very helpfully that Skye was traveling and could not be reached.

"In short," Milt ended, trying unsuccessfully not to sound discouraged, "under present conditions, we can easily make the one million down payment, but will likely fall at least two million dollars short of raising the remaining eleven million. Accordingly, we believe this meeting should either find a way to raise the two million dollars or vote to pass on the deal."

Milt had been reading—or at least, elaborating—from a single sheet of full-sized paper; now he folded it lengthwise and removed his reading glasses. Then he turned to Sophia with a sort of melting look that had no place in a business meeting.

Sophia responded by placing her hand in his.

Leaning a bit sideways to place her shoulder next to Milt's, she said, "Milt and I are working up a list of institutional lenders and investors to approach, and expect to have at least two dozen prospects before we start phoning them next week." She released Milt's hand. "Still, you know how we struck out with VCs, and this isn't likely to go any better. People are canceling deals by the hundreds.

"So we think it's important to start thinking outside the box. For example, we have the shell of a venture capital fund. We created it three years ago, most of you will remember, but never put it to use. It *might* be possible to act as our own VC, if we can find enough small investors who like the Larksdale approach. And I do mean small: The fund's charter allows us to accept investments as small as five hundred dollars."

Gladys raised her hand and asked pointedly, "Two million divided by five hundred dollars is how much? Am I doing the math wrong, or wouldn't it take four *thousand* small investors, at five hundred each, to make our target?"

"Four thousand is right." Sophia shrugged in concession. "And I haven't the vaguest idea where we'd find them. And of course, with that many investors we'd lose a good chunk of the money in administrative costs. I wasn't saying it was likely; I'm just trying to explore every option."

The Ladies gave a collective nod and cluck of sympathy for Sophia's efforts, but nobody seemed persuaded. A cloud of doom unequaled since NDN's first arrival began to settle over the room. In the silence I could hear the faint click of Dolly's knitting needles—which was why I noticed when they stopped. I glanced over and saw her staring blankly and drawing short, shallow, rapid breaths. I first thought she was sick; then I realized what was happening and said pretty loudly—

"I think Aunt Dolly has an idea!"

The Ladies, as one, swiveled in their chairs to stare at her. That was a tough break for Aunt Dolly, who now wore a deer-in-the-headlights expression. She opened and closed her mouth, and looked very pale. *If she has a heart attack,* I was thinking, *I'll never forgive myself.*

But Dolly rallied and, after a moment, said quite coyly, "I was just thinking. Why don't we go on TV?"

We all slumped a bit.

The Ladies had done media tours for books and knew they wouldn't serve here.

But Aunt Dolly's idea was different. Holding up her knitting as if it were Exhibit A, she told the jury, "Everyone's been saying I should try selling my hats and scarves and such. So last week I started watching all the shop-at-home channels. I thought they'd be pushing cheap stuff, like plaster kittens and slicer-dicers. Funny thing is"—she pointed a knitting needle for emphasis—"they were selling really *expensive* stuff, and selling it fast." She halted, and swept the room with a knowing glance. "In fact, just this morning, before I left, they were selling thousand-dollar computer systems with printers. And they sold over three hundred in *ten* minutes."

Now, if there's one thing the Ladies could do in their sleep, it was run numbers. Somebody had just raised $300,000 in ten minutes? That worked out to $1,800,000 an hour. The Ladies were suddenly on their toes: Those kinds of numbers hit them like a double jolt of Starbucks Mocha Moola.

Everybody had the same crazy vision. Seventy minutes' hard work, and we'd have our two million, plus something for expenses. It sure beat heck out of working for a living.

Martha said, "Go on."

Aunt Dolly's brief blaze of salesmanship was undimmed, though she surely realized the Ladies had figured out the plan for themselves. "I thought we could ask one of those networks if they'd like us to come on one of their shows and talk about conservative investing. We could push our materials, and Value and Values." A funny expression swept over her, and I realized with some amazement Aunt Dolly was trying to look sly. "And then, casually, we could mention we're trying to raise money for PMT."

Martha, turning generally toward Sophia and Milt, asked simply, "Well?"

We expected sharp, pointed legal and business advice. Instead, they behaved like those two Disney chipmunks who always defer to each other. In a cartoon it's cute as a button—and even here, it was sort of sweet—but we were in a hurry. Finally Sophia cut it off, by saying to the group, "You can't pitch stocks directly. All you can offer is a disclosure form, a prospectus."

Milt finished her thought: "But you *can* use advertising to offer people the prospectus. So I don't see how anybody could object to using a shopping program the same way. As long as you say, 'The offer to invest is made only in our prospectus,' or something similar, you should be fine."

Milt and Sophia had resumed gazing fondly at each other, but Martha, thank heaven, remembered this wasn't a wedding party at Niagara Falls. She hemmed loudly, firmly tapped a nearby desk with a paperweight, and said, "All right. We won't go to jail for trying it, and we don't have anything else. But it's all still a gamble, and we have to get a million-dollar bet down by noon Monday. I say we vote. All in favor?"

I held my breath. Even for the Ladies, a million bucks is real money.

It carried unanimously.

## CHAPTER FORTY-NINE

# The Ladies Go Live

Sophia was jarred awake by the phone early Monday morning. She had been researching venture capital firms until 3 A.M and was very groggy when she mumbled, "H'llo?"

"I have Morton Abercrombie for Sophia Peters Green," a young man's chipper voice replied.

"'Kay," said Sophia, slightly flummoxed. She cleared her throat, and a moment later an older, gruffer, but still polite voice came on.

"Sophia? Mort Abercrombie here. I'm a producer at America's Shopping Channel. Milt Green gave me your number."

In a curious style, which Sophia described to herself as "friendly good manners, but at Internet speed," Mr. Abercrombie rushed on to explain that ASC would be interested in doing a half hour with the Ladies on its morning *New Ideas for You* show, which generally pushed a mix of curious new products and hot new books.

"We know your materials aren't all new," he said. "But everybody's looking for a way to stay afloat in this stock market, and we have a feeling some conservative advice might go over pretty well."

The range of Milt's contacts still amazed Sophia, and she had a rush of warm feelings just thinking of him. She also realized she had neither the time nor the inclination to handle a shopping show. She had in hand not only the lenders and venture capital firms to approach, but a whole laundry list of documents to prepare, escrow accounts to open, and so on, before the Larksdale Ladies Investment Fund could actually begin taking in money. In a moment of remarkable good sense she punted, "You really want to talk to our media director. Her name's Callie Brentland."

Then she gave Mr. Abercrombie my number.

Pegging me as manager of the Ladies' impending road show was very kind of Sophia, who was thinking partly of my interest in the entertainment industry. Of course, it takes some imagination to see Midwestern Ladies peddling stock-market tips as "entertainment," but who was I to argue?

So that was how I wound up, an hour later, yacking with Mort Abercrombie.

When he started slinging questions, I did my best to give short, snappy, and reasonably professional answers. I doubted this was how Steven Spielberg got his start, but I was still delighted to have the chance, all the same.

"How many Ladies are there?" he asked.

"Depending upon how you count, as many as nine."

"Too many, Callie. We can't use more than one or two . . .

three, absolute tops. Say we'll fly in three, in case one of them freezes up. Why don't you fax their pictures and bios? We'll pick three—with your input, of course," he added hastily.

I had a brief, comical image of a bunch of forties cheesecake shots of Gladys and Aunt Dolly with gardenias in their hair—but figured I'd amused Mort enough for one morning. I said—

"I can shoot some digital snaps and get them to you, with the bios, by, say, tomorrow afternoon."

"Great. Assuming we decide to go forward, when can we schedule you?"

"Your studios are in Florida?" Fun was fun, but suddenly I thought of my crazy workload at RadioRemote. "How about in two weeks?"

A brief pause. "This is television, Callie. How about next Wednesday?"

That would be eight days.

I figured what the heck.

"Unless we hit a glitch, Mr. Abercrombie, that should be perfect."

"Great! We'll have a solid week to promote their appearance. Once we have the Ladies' materials in hand, we'll get back to you with our picks within a day."

That was way better than "Don't call us; we'll call you." As soon as I had the phone back on the cradle, I picked up again and called Vince.

He could take the pictures.

And I was going to find those gardenias and forties bathing suits.

CHAPTER FIFTY

# NDN Strikes Back

The Ladies' shot at buying back PMT changed everything at RadioRemote.

First, of course, it meant I needed to convince the team we had strong hopes of a new lease on life, without betraying the secret of J'Nelle's discovery. I called them together two minutes after Mort Abercrombie's Monday morning call and said the Ladies were going on TV to solicit money to buy back PMT—that one way or the other, we'd know by Christmas if we were still in business, but we were funded until then and so owed them our very best shot. They cheered up immediately and looked, on average, about ten years younger.

The Ladies' new plan also handed me two new jobs: helping Traci and Sophia write the prospectus and other materials for the Larksdale Ladies Investment Fund, and arranging the Florida trip.

As the meeting broke up, I asked Jake and Vince to stay behind. Over the next four hours we reorganized RadioRemote into three teams focused on our three main technical problems. I gave Jake charge of two, and Vince charge of one. I told them to make their own decisions and not to bother me during regular business hours for anything less than a building afire. We'd meet every evening from eight until as late as necessary.

Then I jumped on my two new jobs.

Between Monday and Tuesday afternoon I fielded probably a dozen calls from Morton Abercrombie, his assistant, and various folks at the Ladies' publishers—and made, probably, three dozen calls to the Ladies themselves. I also spent hours each day closeted with Traci and Sophia (who'd begun sharing Traci's office) working on our proposed PMT offer.

So I didn't exactly have to worry about filling my empty hours.

I wasn't complaining. I'd already learned my emotional life has more backup systems than an interplanetary craft. With ICAAM out of the picture, I switched over the Shopping Channel and Florida for my entertainment industry fantasy. With Vince no longer my ardent suitor, I simply reemphasized my daydream that Jake would realize I was perfect for him.

And always, I had work.

Late Wednesday I was on the phone with Mort Abercrombie again, to hear his final guest choices. To my surprise, the first person he bounced was Traci, as both too beautiful and too well educated for his audience. He said they definitely wanted Gladys and Aunt Dolly, the two "sweetest-looking" of the Ladies, but would give me my choice of number three.

I favored J'Nelle, but we had not even sent Mort her file for fear of tipping off NDN. I told him Deborah was our best-spoken member, which was true, and avoided mentioning she'd likely bayonet anybody who got in our way. He said she would be fine, and that he looked forward to meeting us soon.

Readying the Ladies for prime time (well, okay, morning TV) and their takeover bid took every spare minute the rest of that week. The really shocking thing, though, was how well RadioRemote ran without my minute-by-minute supervision. The team wasn't living in fantasyland but was giving the job everything they had. I'd made it clear that nothing, including paychecks, was guaranteed beyond December—but that didn't slow them a bit.

Thursday afternoon Vince's team found a way to use Java applets to solve our remote-object interface problem, the first of what we'd called our "big five" problems to be cracked. Jake was less flashy; but that same afternoon he declared his people in such solid shape he was taking off his first long weekend in months, to visit a friend. Like an idiot I had to ask—

"A *sick* friend?"

"Well, she's pretty inventive"—he flashed me his half-suppressed little smile—"but I wouldn't call her 'sick.' "

Sure, I had no one to blame but myself. Still, it meant I could kiss off sleep for that night, which I devoted instead to imagining Jake's new girlfriend as a cross between Annie Oakley and Cleopatra. Otherwise, though, I put my head down and worked to get the Ladies on-air. It was exciting and fun, but with Jake gone and Vince devoted to Traci, a bit lonely.

By Friday noon I considered the Florida trip a lock.

And then everything seemed to blow up.

Friday afternoon Sophia got a call from Washington, D.C., and was informed some obscure Securities and Exchange Commission committee had decided the mere *discussion* of a stock offering in "a venue frequented solely by unsophisticated investors" constituted a "possible breach of Federal regulations" and could not be allowed without at least six months' deliberation. They did not threaten legal action, but based merely on their warning, America's Shopping Channel, with many apologies, had canceled our invitation.

Nobody would admit it, but fingerprints were all over the knife in our back.

And they were NDN's.

Sophia's first move was to call Milt, who had studied or worked, over the years, with a lot of people who went on to big careers in government. "I don't see how they can do it," she fumed. "It's prior restraint, and it's illegal—"

"Honey, NDN owns an amusement park, six thousand hotel rooms, and film and TV studios in Florida. They don't *need* legal grounds."

Sophia made an exasperated sound and asked, "Well, what can we do about it?"

"Let me make a few calls."

With Milt on the job, Sophia came to my office to tell me to keep organizing the trip, but to be prepared to have it canceled. I wasn't nearly as calm as she was. "Nice to know we can trust them, the bastards!"

"Callie," she said, "if we could trust them, we wouldn't be blackmailing them."

Then she turned and left.

Saturday and most of Sunday passed without a word. I started thinking we'd been whipped by NDN's well-connected lawyers.

But if NDN's guys had gone to prep school with half the guns in D.C., old Milt had gone to Harvard with the other half, and he had the minor but decisive advantage of having the law on his side. He worked the phones all weekend, reminding his former classmates of what Jefferson said about this, and Franklin said about that, and, to make a long story short, on Monday morning the head of the division that had pulled the plug on us gave his *new* decision. It was agreed that as long as they merely *mentioned* the prospectus—and did that carefully—the Ladies were good to go.

Our invitation was reinstated almost immediately.

After that scare, the rest was easy.

The Ladies' publisher agreed to pick up half the travel tab, and to provide an escort to drive us around Delray Beach, Florida, where ASC had its studios. All the other details were routine. Aunt Dolly and Gladys both suffered minor attacks of nerves once they learned we were on, and I spent the rest of the day reassuring two aging ladies—

"Kids, you're going out there a nobody, but you're coming back a star!"

On Sunday Jake e-mailed that he was extending his trip an extra forty-eight hours. By Monday night I couldn't wait to get out of town.

Unfortunately for us, NDN wasn't out of dirty tricks.

## CHAPTER FIFTY-ONE

# Dancing in Florida

At five-thirty Tuesday morning, on our way to the airport, the Ladies were in high spirits. Aunt Dolly in particular looked better than I'd seen her in years. The operation hadn't yet made her thin, but now her bulk looked solid, not sickly. Gladys had been on the upswing ever since helping J'Nelle boost the NDN documents, but that morning they both acted positively giddy. Gladys was wearing a red-orange dress that looked as if somebody had gone down to a bar in hunting season, shot a Tequila Sunrise, and skinned it.

Deborah noticed the new mood as soon as she joined us in the car, and asked me, only slightly sardonically, "So? Ready for summer camp?"

Actually what I was *really* ready for was a ten-hour nap.

Luckily, our flight, counting time on the ground in Atlanta, was nearly six hours. I lost consciousness shortly after takeoff, barely roused myself to refuse a couple of meals, and did not really regain consciousness until I heard the landing gear coming down and the captain announcing the temperature on the ground was a sunny 86 degrees. We'd left Minnesota with hints of autumn already strong, but we stepped off the plane into a cloud of warm, moist air. Compared with Larksdale, Delray Beach was a sauna, but in a very pleasant way. Since my body had tried a nap, and decided it liked the idea, as soon as we were settled in our rooms (I was sharing with Deborah), I threw myself down on one of the beds, grunted, "Call me when we're famous," and fell fast asleep.

Through half-closed eyes, I saw Deborah standing over me.

I groaned, but she answered unsympathetically, "You've been sleeping for two *hours*. Get up, we're going out for dinner."

"I'm not hungry."

"Who are you, and what have you done with Callie?"

"Callie died from exhaustion. Go away. I'll eat room service later."

"When did you become a stick-in-the-mud?"

"You're the first person ever to call me a stick." I rolled over and closed my eyes. "Bless you."

Deborah poked me in the back. "Hey! You're the den mother; we can't go without you." She poked me again, not very hard. "Come on. Gladys found a piano bar."

I opened my eyes again and realized the sky outside the room was dark.

"Curse you, piano bars are prohibited by the Geneva Accords." I swung my feet to the floor and sat up. "If anybody plays Wayne Newton songs, I'll kill 'em."

"You knock 'em down; I'll stomp 'em. No jury would ever convict," Deborah agreed, and pulled me upright.

The evening proved to be a hoot.

At Gladys's piano bar the player had a great supper-club voice and knew every old standard Gladys and Deborah threw at him. I decided this guy Gershwin had a big career ahead of him. After an hour of classics we ate dinner at a Cuban restaurant, a first for me, and I caught up on a whole day's missed calories.

We ended at a little beachfront courtyard club where the band played Afro-Caribbean-salsa music. The air still hung balmy and fragrant, moonlight filled the patio, and if you listened hard between songs you could hear the ocean. The courtyard crowd was a little thin when we arrived, and Aunt Dolly said she wanted to walk off her dinner, so I followed her down onto the beach.

We strolled along the hard sand for a hundred yards or so before I noticed that in the reflected neon from waterfront buildings her cheeks looked wet. A breeze had whipped up, and I supposed the bits of blown sand were bothering her eyes; but when I asked her about it, she said softly that my parents—her sister and brother-in-law—had honeymooned in Florida, long ago.

We talked about my parents, and by the time we were done, the sand must have been getting in my eyes, too.

Once Aunt Dolly and I were back at the courtyard, though, we all danced our heads off: Gladys with half-tempo grace; Deborah as if she'd been born in Rio; and Aunt Dolly and I with, let's say, a lot of enthusiasm. Early on, Aunt Dolly let it slip that we were in town to do a TV show, and from then on, we never lacked for partners. By a little before midnight, in sleepy Delray Beach, we were part of a giant conga line snaking around the courtyard.

And we *all* wound up with gardenias in our hair.

We were definitely ready for our close-ups.

## CHAPTER FIFTY-TWO

# Fifteen Minutes of Fame

Our escort from the Ladies' publisher picked us up at sunrise the next morning. None of us looked the worse for wear, and the Ladies all wore the pricey, tasteful suits we agreed upon before leaving Larksdale. I had time for about two breaths of warm air between the hotel lobby doors and the escort's minivan.

My first thought was that the America's Shopping Channel's studio was bigger than Paramount Pictures, but once we cleared the security gate, I realized most of what I was seeing was warehouse space and loading docks for the merchandise they shipped. As we entered the studio building, I was struck mostly by how few people worked there: It was handsome but it was small, and from the reception area back it had clearly been designed to be as automated as possible.

Morton Abercrombie proved to be half a head shorter, and much broader-shouldered, than I had imagined him. He looked as if he could play Gimli the dwarf in a film version of *The Lord of the Rings*. I stayed in the background while he chatted with the Ladies, a process clearly meant to judge which of them belonged on air. Sure enough, a minute later, he said, "Ladies, this has been a pleasure," and then turned to a young woman with a clipboard and told her, "Alice, will you take Gladys and Deborah, here, to makeup?"

Aunt Dolly looked briefly—but only briefly—disappointed.

We both knew she'd been dreading going on camera since she'd agreed to do it a week earlier. By the time Gladys kindly asked her to come along to makeup for moral support, Dolly was her usual contented self.

While Dolly went with the others, I phoned Sophia. It was mostly a courtesy call, but I also wanted to test my ability to reach her quickly in case of trouble. She said the other Ladies (and probably the entire RadioRemote crew) would be gathered around TVs to watch the show.

Things move quickly in television; fifteen minutes after the Ladies left, they joined me in the greenroom, all dolled up, with their hair styled and their makeup camera-ready. Gladys was beaming, Deborah looked a little uncomfortable, but they both looked sharp and professional. Alice joined us as well, clipboard still in hand, and reminded us it was a live show, so they should watch their words.

Mr. Abercrombie appeared in the doorway and signaled me to join him. When I did, he eased me out into the corridor and said conversationally but very softly, "Wanted to make sure we're on the same page. The producer thinks it's better if we skip the stuff about your new company and just push the books and tapes and such."

I tried to sound only moderately surprised. "I thought the SEC cleared us."

He shrugged. "The producer still thinks—"

"Aren't *you* the producer?"

He stayed cool, too. "I'm just one of many."

I flashed him a conspiratorial smile. The objective now, I decided, was to get the Ladies on-air, no matter how briefly. "I'll certainly tell them what you said."

"I appreciate it." He thought about shaking my hand, thought the better of it, patted my shoulder, and started off for, I supposed, the control booth.

The greenroom clock said we had about ninety seconds. I gestured for Deborah and Gladys to huddle up with me. Then, pretending to brush lint off Deborah's lapel, I leaned close and said, "If you bring up RadioRemote, they're going to pull you off the air. What do you want to do?"

Gladys, sounding surprised, answered, "Why, what we came here for, of course."

"You won't mind getting bounced on your fanny?"

"Well . . . we're too old to start a riot, so I say we form a conga line and go out dancing."

Deborah nodded agreement and whispered, "I'll talk fast."

That worked for me. "Good enough," I said. "I'll see the engine's running on the getaway car."

Alice called them out onto the set.

I called our escort and asked her to pick us up early.

Despite being so primed for action, Gladys and Deborah both smiled sweetly at Alice as they sat to have their lapel microphones clipped on. The show's host, a very pleasant woman named Emma Blackstone, was making calm chat even while fiddling to make sure the Ladies' materials were properly displayed on the coffee table before them. The studio clock was sweeping up on the hour. I desperately wanted to listen in on the proceedings—or even better, call Sophia—but time was short and I had a more important task.

I needed to scope out our defensive position.

Security at ASC was—this, remember, was in happier days—fairly light. There'd been a guard at the gate and another in the lobby, but that was about it. Also, the studio's high-tech design, as I'd already noticed, meant very few people were involved with the show. The cameras were robotic, and there didn't seem to be a floor producer. Alice, the young assistant, had already exited the studio through the greenroom. No glass producer's booth overlooked the set; so unless Emma Blackstone was wearing an earbud I couldn't see, the only communication between her and the producers ran via TelePrompTer in one direction and video monitor in the other.

Very modern—and very handy for us.

Unless I was entirely wrong, Morton Abercrombie had only two ways to pull us off the air. He could run (or phone) to the central production booth, wherever that was, and order the cameras switched off, and/or a wind-up message sent over the TelePrompTer. Or, he could dash to the studio itself and personally flash Emma Blackstone the cut-throat signal.

Now, my guess was that giving the signal personally would be a lot faster and would be Mort's first choice. And the only way into the studio that I could see ran through the greenroom—which meant he had to come through me.

And Aunt Dolly.

We couldn't exactly barricade the doors, but I had an idea.

Even seventy pounds lighter than she'd been a year before, Aunt Dolly was still formidable. Properly positioned, she could protect our flanks by placing *her* flanks in the doorway from the corridor to the greenroom. So instead of watching the start of *New Ideas for You,* I stepped over to Aunt Dolly, who was facing the silenced TV monitor. I gave her the situation, nodded toward the doorway, and ended—

"Nearly as I can tell, the best way for Abercrombie to yank the show is to walk from his office and signal Emma Blackstone from here. Every minute will help. Can you stall him?"

She grinned. "Can Green Bay's offensive line stall a pass rush?"

I took that as a yes.

The clock came up on the hour. The Ladies were on the air. I told Dolly, "Bless you," and started for the studio doorway. I reached it just in time for the last of Emma's guest intro: ". . . a $49.95 kit which includes *Investing the Larksdale Way,* a set of three . . ."

Maybe Gladys saw the worry on my face, because almost at once she interrupted politely, "Well, actually, Emma, we have something *much* more exciting to talk about."

Emma knew instantly something had gone terribly, terribly wrong, because on a shopping show not even world peace is more important than whatever they're selling. But she had barely swung in surprise toward Gladys when Deborah leaned forward to upstage her and told the camera, "We have an investment idea that's . . ."

I heard a faint *thunk* behind me and, turning, saw that Dolly, standing in the doorway, had removed one of her shoes and dropped it on the floor. Then, as I watched, two things happened simultaneously:

—Dolly cried, "Blast!" and bent over to pick up the shoe, and:

—A fiery-looking Morton Abercrombie bumped into her from behind.

Dolly responded neatly by keeping her head down and her attention focused on the errant loafer, while also clamping one large hand onto Mr. Abercrombie's shoulder. Then, saying, "Oops! Oops, *oops*!" she began hopping on one foot while trying to tug the shoe back onto the other. The main result of her hopping was to push the surprised Abercrombie back out into the hallway.

After a moment's confusion Abercrombie rallied.

With a medium-polite cry of "EXCUSE *ME*!" he tried to shoulder past her. But he was fighting out of his weight class, and it took another ten seconds or more before he was able to use his lower center of gravity to begin regaining lost ground. He was moving forward with the slow relentlessness of a street sweeper when Aunt Dolly countered by retreating and turning sideways, so that the two of them were both wedged tightly into the doorway. Between Dolly and Mr. Abercrombie, you were talking some *serious* wedging: It looked like rush hour on the Tokyo subway—at the sumo wrestler's stop.

I went to help.

Between Dolly and me, they would have needed earthmoving equipment to get Abercrombie through the doorway. Alas, I was too slow off the mark. By the time I closed in, he was in the clear and accelerating rapidly.

I still managed to get in front of him, grab his shoulder, and say energetically—

"Oh, Mr. Abercrombie! I'm *so* glad you're here. Could I ask you about—"

"NO!"

And that was the turning point for the Battle of the Greenroom.

Abercrombie was moving with speed; he swept by me, and

before I was completely turned around, he was in the studio doorway, waving his arms like a madman. I was right behind him and could hear Deborah, speaking with great enthusiasm. "So, really, if *you* think RadioRemote is the kind of woman-owned speculative investment that would interest you, the best thing to do is to get our prospectus. You can do that today by . . ."

She was staring firmly into the camera while Emma Blackstone, mystified and miffed, tried unsuccessfully to squeeze a word in edgewise. Mr. Abercrombie was now frantically giving Emma the universal "cut" signal, repeatedly drawing his right index finger over his own throat.

I was looking over his head and could see Emma's sharp blue eyes take in Mr. Abercrombie and then, it seemed, the TelePrompTer. "I'm afraid our guests have to leave us early," she began, only a little flustered. She angled this so that it would shut Deborah up, but Gladys jumped in, saying cheerfully, "No, we don't! We're having a wonderful . . ."

And with that covering fire, Deborah resumed her recitation of the ways to reach us.

But Emma Blackstone was no cream puff.

Completely ignoring Gladys, she said, "And now we're joining in progress a special edition of *The Cosmetic Life* with Doris Fayne."

Deborah was still giving out our Web address when the red lights over the robotic cameras went out.

Radio Free Larksdale was off the air.

I gathered up the others, and we sped from the building. Deborah kept glancing back regretfully, as if she would have liked a rematch; but Dolly alternated between reprising her "Oops! Oops, oops!" routine and telling us, "I'm back—I'm really back!" Gladys confined herself to a restrained smile, but her eyes glowed, and as we dashed across the parking lot, she gave us a rousing, wordless version of the theme from *Chariots of Fire*.

As for me, I was just glad when we cleared the guards at the front gate, and were headed for the open country.

Since we were already checked out of the hotel, we called the airline from the van to book an earlier flight. A little under two hours later we said good-bye to our escort and got the hell out of Dodge.

Nobody from ASC was there to see us off.

CHAPTER FIFTY-THREE

# An Eerie Silence—and Then . . .

Despite the thrills of our Florida adventure, the results were scarily small.

Oh, we got a decent number of Web site hits and requests for prospectus forms, and even sold a few thousand copies of *The Complete Larksdale Guide to Hard Times Investing*—but overall there came a thudding sound of failure. RadioRemote continued to burn through money like . . . well, money, and our progress, while as rapid as could be expected, was just not fast enough.

Every time we solved one problem, two more appeared.

Still, we pushed on through November. It became a test of character, of Larksdale spirit, not to quit. Maybe we were foolish; but we were driven by pride and hope and the idea of saving our town. It was easy to say, "Well . . . one more week."

And there always seemed to be one more reason to carry on.

On November 20 Vince declared the secure-address issue

solved. Milt and Sophia kept finding new venture firms and angel investors to approach. Everybody loved our idea and was ready to invest—just as soon as we solved our technical problems, and the market improved.

Then, before we knew it, Martin Davis's deadline was just two weeks away.

And we finally accepted we were weren't going to make it.

Friday afternoon, the eighth of December, after getting turned down by the richest VC firm in America, we admitted we were done. The time had come, as Jake put it, to call in the dogs and put out the fire; the hunt was over. Without venture backing, the Ladies—even if they emptied every piggy bank—were still a good two million short.

We could not buy back PMT.

I'd never seen such crushing gloom as marked the Ladies' faces that Saturday morning in Martha's living room—and that was with Sophia and Gladys missing. When they arrived, I guessed, the room would plunge into an emotional black hole.

I didn't blame the Ladies. If we pulled the plug immediately, at least they'd keep their houses and enough money for comfy retirements. Risking that on about a one-in-fifty shot we could launch RadioRemote in time was clearly nuts.

We all knew what was expected.

I was supposed to stand and propose shutting down RadioRemote as unworkable. That was the solution creating the fewest hurt feelings and the least guilt all around.

It was the Minnesota way.

As home of the immortal Harold Stassen, who ran (and lost) for President more often than anyone else in American history, we have a long and noble tradition of concession speeches. And I was ready to make one.

Still, I was glad when the doorbell rang and gave me a few minutes' delay.

Lots of traditions are easier to admire than to follow.

When I opened the door, there stood Sophia and Gladys, red-cheeked and puffing, carrying (or rather, dragging) a canvas bag about five feet long and eighteen inches in diameter. It was stained and dirty, and its metal grommets were dark-oxidized. The bag and the two ladies both were flecked with snow. Gladys rapidly lowered her end to the ground, leaving Sophia looking like a low-rent and very tired Santa Claus, a good image of what seemed in store for us in the upcoming holiday season. As Gladys's end neared the ground, Sophia staggered under the extra weight.

I told them as cheerfully as I could—

"You're just about in time for the memorial service."

I grabbed the lowered end of the bag, while asking—

"What's this?" Then I lifted it and guessed cement.

"The missing mail." Gladys was stepping ahead of us into the foyer. "Seems our regular mailman has been on vacation, and our forwarding got fouled up."

That explained why we hadn't received a single letter for a week. It also *ought* to have suggested pretty strongly we were getting way more mail than usual. But I was far too focused on the knot in my stomach, and the overwhelming pain of failure, to pay attention. And I was having trouble with the mail bag. It seemed to weigh a hundred pounds, at least. Staggering as I hoisted my end, I told Gladys—

"You're stronger than you look."

As we walked inside, I eyed Sophia closely. Her face was red and puffy. She saw me looking at her and whispered, "I *really* hate losing." Then she added more forcefully, "I can drag the bag. Give me two minutes, okay?"

We lowered the bag to the floor. Then I put an arm around Gladys's thin shoulders and, leading her away, told Sophia—

"See you in there."

None of the Ladies were looking at the others, and they very definitely weren't looking at me. Nobody wanted to be the one who asked for a decision. I didn't blame them. I said without explanation that Sophia would be in shortly, and walked to the snack table. I'd been there only a moment when Traci stepped up beside me. She tried to smile, but the corners of her mouth were trembling. Pulling herself together, she declared, with forced energy, "I say we sell lemonade."

"Swell. At twenty cents a glass, ten million glasses, and we're golden."

"Twenty cents? I say we spike it and sell it for four bucks a pop."

I refused to be cheered up. Traci saw it and fell silent. Sophia had just entered the room. Traci leaned close and whispered in my ear, "Go get 'em, champ."

By the time Sophia was seated, I'd moved to the spot by the fireplace whence people usually addressed the group. Upon consideration, and with due respect to Harold Stassen, I figured short and sweet was best, so I said—

"First, I want you to know that we gave RadioRemote everything we had. But the simple truth is, without PMT's resources, or their equivalent, we're not going to make it. We're out of cash at the end of the month and couldn't possibly have a product on sale before next September. So, I suggest, respectfully, that we pull the plug: Give everyone thirty days' pay, settle our bills, and turn out the lights."

That was it. I waited silently. There were no questions.

Martha said, "Ten minutes' recess, and then we'll vote. If . . ."

Caught in my own misery, and wondering whether "Taps" had lyrics, I missed Martha's last remarks plus another minute or two. When I zoned back in, everyone was gathered around Sophia, who had opened the mailbag and spread a few dozen envelopes on the coffee table. I realized with a small shock they had effectively decided RadioRemote was dead, and I hadn't even heard the vote.

Sophia selected an envelope. The other Ladies watched with polite interest—while I watched them in confusion. I had expected a lot more agonizing. I realized the Ladies had been around a lot longer than I, and were simply more used to life's disappointments, but still . . .

Then I got a hold of myself. What had I expected? A suicide pact where they all threw themselves on a flaming pile of RadioRemote brochures?

Not the Larksdale way.

Certainly, Sophia had regained self-control. Her color was better, and she seemed quite calm as she opened an envelope and extracted a couple of pages of pale yellow paper. "From the Hagenbloom sisters, in Quiet Valley," she said, then read aloud:

*Dear Sophia and Friends,*

*This letter leaves us in fine circumstances, and we hope it finds you in same. Of course, winter's in the air already, and some dry bits of snow, but after such a hot summer and pleasant fall, we can hardly complain . . .*

I cleared my throat noisily—rude of me, but I couldn't help it. When you've fallen overboard in a heavy sea, you don't really care about what a swell meal they're serving in the main dining salon. Sophia hesitated, then plunged on quite firmly:

*We're both . . .*

Traci groaned aloud. I didn't blame her. I mean, our world was collapsing, and here we were having a kaffeeklatsch. There's such a thing as being *too* Minnesota.

But then something curious happened.

Sophia shuffled papers to get to page two, then suddenly froze.

A pink rectangle of paper had fluttered out from between two sheets of the letter and landed in her lap. She snatched it from the air, glanced at it, and her face took on about the strangest look I'd ever seen. Appearing stunned, she began studying the paper as if it were a lost Chinese manuscript.

Sophia opened her mouth.

She closed it.

The she examined the letter narrowly, and then, as if nothing much had happened except that fifty naked Hobbits had just performed the finale to *Oklahoma!* there in the living room, returned to the letter. She read on silently to the end of that page while we all strained forward and bit our knuckles and then, turning to the second page, she resumed reading aloud:

*Lastly, you'll see we've sent you our check, which we hope you will invest in your new business. Please don't worry whether we can afford it. Thanks to all your help with the wind leases, it amounts to about exactly one of our quarterly royalty checks, and sixteen more multimegawatt turbine groups are planned to go up next year, so we'll soon be almost doubling that. Plus, of course, this was by far the best canning season either of us can remember in nearly half a century. So please don't hesitate to invest it for us in your company. And know that we remain,*

*With All Fond Wishes,*
*Yours,*
*Emma and Muriel Hagenbloom*

Sophia, still in a sort of a daze, seemed to think this covered the whole matter quite nicely; but of course the rest of us were climbing the walls. I couldn't decide whether the check was for enough to buy a large jar of preserved kumquats, or . . . well, I knew *something* had given Sophia that just-hit-over-the-head-with-a-hammer expression.

Finally Deborah burst out, "Well, for crying out loud. *How much!?*"

Sophia, rather shakily, handed the check to Deborah, who glanced at it, yelped, "Holy . . .!" and lunged for the canvas bag. Gladys, meanwhile, had grabbed the check from Deborah, and no sooner had she seen it than she began to make a strange gurgling noise deep in her throat. This was starting to look like some bad thirties horror movie, *The Curse of the Pink Check*.

Even before the check reached me, I realized what had happened: The Ladies, the reigning queens of unsuspected small-town wealth, had just been out-Ladied by two sisters from North Dakota.

It was a sad day for the honor of Minnesotans, but I figured we could live with it.

When the check finally reached me, I saw we were $250,000.00 closer to our goal.

I grabbed an envelope and started ripping.

Every ten seconds or so someone would shout out something—a hearty cry of "Two thousand!" or a wry lament, "A pie recipe." The entire bag of letters had been spilled out and mounded high onto the big round coffee table, and the Ladies plus J'Nelle, Traci, and I were all opening.

A fair number—say a quarter, or a third—contained no money.

But there were an astounding number of hits.

Nothing came close to the one from the Hagenblooms, but still, after nine or ten minutes, the total I was running in my head was pushing $400,000.00. We were in a frenzy.

For fifteen minutes the only sounds heard were the ripping of envelopes, the shuffling of papers, and the frequent half-shouted numbers. Sure, we realized it was probably a fantasy; the prairie might hold *one* pair of rich sisters crazy enough to invest in us big-time, but we needed more like *eight* pairs.

Then, suddenly, Deborah's voice rose over the others, "HEADS UP! Everybody look for an envelope from BISMARCK NATIONAL BANK!"

She was waving a ragged, yellowing, old-fashioned airmail envelope, the kind with the red-white-and-blue borders they stopped using about thirty years ago. The charge in Deborah's voice kicked what been a state of high excitement up nearer to frenzy—a good bit, I guess, like what happened that California afternoon in 1849 when some grizzled mill worker yelled, "Hey, Look! GOLD!"

I vaguely remembered having seen a business envelope under a bunch of personal envelopes at the far side of the table; but before I could lunge for it, Gladys fished it from the pile and waved it in the air. As she brought it back down, I saw she had her fingers crossed, and I automatically crossed my own. I figured it couldn't hurt. Then she got it open, with J'Nelle's help, and they both were struck dumb. It was absolutely weird: Where the first silence had been rather wild, this was almost religious. You normally didn't see this kind of reverence outside a Nativity scene. I was half waiting for the heavenly choir to sing "Hallelujah" or "Roll Out the Barrel" or something. They passed the check from hand to hand, each in turn looking at it wordlessly.

Then the check reached me, and I was struck dumb, too.

Silas Butteroot, Deborah's irritating old buzzard, had ordered his bank to send us—or rather, Deborah, apparently the only person in North America he trusted—a certified check for $1,000,000.00, with a memo saying it was for purchase of a 10 percent stake in RadioRemote.

Suddenly the fantasy was looking a lot less fantastic. We were still half a million short; but we'd raised around a million, five in twenty minutes. Anything seemed possible. The Ladies dove after the remaining stack of envelopes as if somebody was giving away money. Which, I suppose, somebody was.

The place sounded like a Jerry Lewis Telethon, with us all calling out donations every few seconds. I found a pair of checks for five hundred dollars, three or four simple letters wishing the Ladies luck, and one crank letter that doesn't rate a mention. Eventually I stood to stretch my back. Somebody called out, "Five thousand!" but the pile was looking a lot smaller.

Then we hit a dry spell, and the pile shrank silently for two minutes or more.

I tried to convince myself we really could raise the last bit with bake sales or spiked lemonade or something, but still felt the exhilaration seeping away. The Ladies had succeeded by strict fiscal discipline, and if we fell short by any significant amount, I figured they'd still want to pull the plug.

Then J'Nelle jumped to her feet and, waving a check, called out, "Fifteen thousand, from Iowa!"

It raised the mood, but scarcely two dozen letters remained on the table. I have the habit of running numbers in my head and knew we were still short. But I wasn't the only one who could run numbers. A moment later Deborah gave a soft grunt of annoyance or impatience and said decisively, "Forget it. My fingers hurt, and I'm hungry. I'll put up the last two hundred grand. Let's have dessert!"

And that was that.

The other Ladies eyed Deborah with a strange blend of approval and annoyance. I wondered whether they were annoyed with her for acting unilaterally, or with themselves for having hesitated. It didn't matter.

We'd crossed the two million mark.

The Ladies were back in the game.

Deborah was back at the chocolate strudel.

And I needed to get back to work.

## CHAPTER FIFTY-FOUR

# Making It Happen

We had eleven days before the deadline.

At work Traci and I had to keep the impending PMT deal secret until it closed. The Ladies believed the best way to win support for it was to present people with a complete package. You show them something half-baked, and it's just human nature to want to help with the cooking.

The cooking was growing more complex by the minute—although most of us realized it only when Martha spoke at the Ladies' emergency meeting, held the Thursday after The Great Day of the Mail.

Martha announced she had banked the money to repurchase PMT. Then she said something shocking. "I realized last night we're making a big mistake." Coming from Martha, this was one notch south of a Federal indictment. You could have heard a dime drop into a jailhouse pay phone. "We're planning to buy back PMT for a song, which is good business as far as it goes, but ignores the human side. In particular, it ignores the hurt feelings of all the people who've lost their shirts."

"It was their own darned fault," Dolly said loudly.

"Certainly." Martha nodded. "But when did anybody's sense of guilt ever affect their sense of entitlement?"

"In church?" Gladys asked, with what might have been irony.

"Perhaps. But we can't run a company with two thousand angry employees who feel they've been robbed of their life's savings, even if we didn't do the robbing. They're our friends and neighbors; we don't want them to suffer."

Martha's point was clear: If the Ladies revived PMT using their own, fresh money, most former PMT employees would be wiped out. Sure, they would still own their NDN shares, but those were next to worthless. And sure, any hard-nosed business person would say it was their own damned fault for ignoring the Ladies' advice and taking NDN's bait in the first place. Still, they *were* our neighbors—and most of them, our friends.

The Ladies debated for half an hour before finally agreeing they were obliged to help the rest of Larksdale recover at least part of its lost wealth. So the question now became: Where could they get the dough to re-fund PMT's stock purchase plan? They sat in perplexed silence until Sophia, calmer than most of us—or maybe just knowing Martha better—finally asked, "What do you propose we do, Martha?"

After a sharp glance at the gold clock on the mantel, Martha said slowly, "*Weelll,* I propose we . . ."

Which was when, with really unnerving timing, the doorbell rang.

* * *

I answered the door. On the steps, snow swirling around her, stood a slim woman of about thirty-five, dressed like a banker except for an overcoat of some high-tech material with a thick mock-fur collar. She looked like J. P. Morgan's hip great-great-granddaughter. Offering me her hand, she said "I'm Elizabeth Terrell."

I must have gaped blankly, so she elaborated: "People used to call me Skye?"

The light went on: I had always imagined her as she must have looked fifteen years earlier, with pink hair, an army jacket, and a surly attitude. I took her arm and pulled her inside so energetically I practically yanked her off her feet. She really was a slight creature. But once inside, she led the way back to the living room as if she'd last entered it fifteen minutes, instead of fifteen years, ago.

I was excited: Martha would not have staged all this to small purpose.

The Ladies actually gasped as Skye crossed the room to hug Martha and ask, "Am I in time?"

"Absolutely."

If it had been anyone other than Martha, I would have said she was choked up.

After briefly pressing her lips tightly together, she told us, "Let's welcome our long-absent co-founder, Elizabeth Terrell."

Of course, Skye, like all the Ladies, was about equal parts sentiment and toughness. She might have been sniffling when she turned back to us, but she got right to the point.

"For those of you who don't know me, I was . . . sort of an honorary Larksdale Lady in the founding days. Since then I've lived in Silicon Valley, where I was a partner in"—she named one of the biggest venture funds—"and then founding partner of Athena 21st Century Ventures, which went liquid four months ago. So I'm looking for investments. Now, we closed Athena because we expect a real tech crash, but I'm willing to consider RadioRemote. *Especially* with PMT attached to pay the bills."

Over the murmurs and whispers in the room, she went on firmly, "Martha faxed me RadioRemote's package yesterday, and I have to say it beat the usual Christmas card. Anyway, here's what I propose. You sell me a twenty percent interest in RadioRemote for $10 million. You use some of that for operating capital, but most of it to underwrite a new stock purchase plan for your new, or rehired I guess, employees. The plan will be structured so that any rehire who sticks with you at least two years will be restored to eighty percent of their old stock holdings."

"You're valuing us at *fifty million?*" Gladys asked. "In *this* market?"

Skye looked slightly flustered. "I know those are generous terms. But it's my personal money and I . . . let's say it includes retiring an old debt to the people who helped me long ago." She toughened up and ended, "Anyway, I think we'll make *a lot* of money, which, at least when I was a member, was always one of the main points of the Larksdale Ladies."

During the brief silence that followed, Skye turned to Martha and asked humbly, "Okay?"

I thought Martha was going to answer, "That'll do, pig."

But all she said was "Okay."

The Ladies took under three minutes to embrace Skye's plan—after which the original members all left their chairs and embraced *her.* A few minutes later I nearly slipped quietly out the front door, but I noticed Skye seemed a bit lost. It's not easy to go home again, no matter how friendly home is.

After the other Ladies said good-bye, Martha invited Skye to stay as long as she liked. Skye touched Martha's shoulder and said, "I won't impose. But I'll come by early and take you out to breakfast before I fly back, if you like."

A faint disappointment crossed Martha's face, then was gone in an instant. "That would be lovely."

I walked Skye to her car. "Do you read Jane Austen novels?"

She looked a little startled. "Yeah." She smiled. "Deborah started me on them."

"Do you eat vegetarian food?"

"Almost nothing else."

I took her by the arm. "In that case, I've got somebody for you to meet."

I called to ask Alicia if she'd care to meet the famed Skye Terrell. Sounding excited, she said if we'd come to the small restaurant where she was guest-cooking that night, she'd make a special meal just for the three of us.

Midlothian, Larksdale's last surviving expensive restaurant, was nearly empty, but Alicia met us at the door. I guess technically she and Skye were just shaking hands, but it looked to me as if they fluttered together like a couple of doves.

About twenty minutes into dinner they were leaning across the table toward each other. "Well," I said softly, in my best Randolph Scott tones, "reckon my work here's done."

Nobody heard me.

They were leaning still closer when I excused myself and headed home.

I walked past empty shop windows to my car. It was winter,

it was cold, and I ought to have been grim, but I was absolutely excited.

Not only was I feeling like the Mother Teresa of romance, but the Ladies were back in the saddle, and riding to Larksdale's rescue.

With those jolly thoughts in mind, I doubted anything could have raised my spirits higher.

But I was wrong about that—because waiting at my apartment was a blinking light on my answering machine, and a message asking me to call Peter Goldfarb, the hiring partner at ICAAM, as soon as possible.

CHAPTER FIFTY-FIVE

# We Race for the Deadline—and My Life Gets in the Way of My Life

I rose early the next morning—easy enough, since I hadn't slept all night. Instead, I had exercised my body by flopping around the bed, and my brain by trying to solve the unsolvable: how to spend the coming year in Larksdale and California simultaneously.

At exactly 9 A.M., California time, I called ICAAM in Beverly Hills. My heart was pounding, but Peter Goldfarb sounded very genial. After he offered me an ICAAM internship for 2001. I almost sank myself by blurting I wasn't sure I could leave Larksdale so soon. That's not what you tell the world's most important talent agency. Luckily, before I could blow it, Mr. Goldfarb said official letters would go out shortly, and he'd look forward to my response. He was taking it for granted I would grab the offer.

I thanked him and got off the phone as quickly as I could.

The whole call had probably lasted sixty seconds.

I spent the next thirty minutes in a dazed flurry of action, so busy trying to sort out my options I was showered, fed, dressed, and out the door before I realized what I was doing.

The Ladies had established a secret war room in Martha's house for all the document drafting and business planning involved in the repurchase of PMT. Sophia and Milt had moved in stacks of computers, and the place was humming. Deborah and Traci also worked there about sixteen hours a day, as did three high-priced imported securities lawyers. Traci had started calling it Bletchley, after Bletchley Park, the country house the Brits turned into an intelligence center during WWII.

Our deadline for delivering the check to ADN was 10:59 P.M. Friday, Larksdale time—one minute before midnight on the East Coast. We had five days to complete what an ordinary team of experts would have wanted five weeks to do. Not only did we need to run our due diligence—and convince ourselves PMT really could be reestablished in Larksdale—but we had lately realized Skye Terrell's huge cash infusion had not necessarily solved the angry worker issue. *We* knew giving PMT employees back 80 percent of their original investment was highly generous, but people can be awfully persnickety about money.

So even with Larksdale melting down, we couldn't count on our buyback being greeted with open arms. It was going to take some very careful selling to make the whole deal work. Plus, our best guess was that PMT needed to have the doors open and product updates appearing within forty-five days of our taking it over, or it would start losing key clients.

That should have been plenty to occupy my brain.

Certainly it was enough to keep other people from obsessing about their personal problems. Milt and Sophia, for example, were working together at full speed without having faced the question of whether Milt ought to move back home.

For almost an hour that morning I did my best to focus on work.

I couldn't do it. I had to decide about moving to Beverly Hills.

When Traci looked up from her desk, I whispered, "I need to talk with you."

She set down her pen. "Sure. Have a seat."

"Not here."

She frowned, then shrugged. "Where, then?"

"The greenhouse."

Martha's property actually held two smallish greenhouses, set side-by-side. We endured a frigid December wind walking to them, but inside the nearer one the air hung warm, damp, and earthy. I had not slept in thirty-six hours; when the warmth hit, I actually staggered.

A couple of stools were set near a potting bench; Traci, anxious to resume working, didn't sit, but I had to. Maybe it was the way I slumped, but her attitude changed. She checked to see the bench was clean, then leaned against it and asked quietly, "What's up?"

"ICAAM has a place for me."

Traci looked briefly pleased, but then, perhaps hearing my confusion, asked, "How do you feel about it?"

The high walls of Martha's property largely sheltered the greenhouse, but now some renegade wind rattled the glass panes, and a moment later sleet began hitting, with hard little clanks against the glass roof.

"If I knew how I felt, would I be asking you?"

"*Are* you asking my advice?"

"Yeah. I don't promise to follow it—but I do want to hear it."

"Okay." She stood up straighter. "I'll miss you like crazy, but you should go."

The knot in my stomach tightened. "Why?"

"Because Jake and Vince and I can handle things if we stay small. Because Milt will handle things if we take back PMT. But mostly because you'll go nuts if you stay here. You're just not a small-town girl, Callie. I know, because I *am*."

She put her hand on my shoulder, but so swiftly it felt like a poke. "If you love movies, go make them." She stood looking down at me while I sat in a disheartened stupor and tried to think.

I decided she was half right. But if I quit, I would have nothing to show for my two years back in Larksdale. And I'd be abandoning my friends. I shook my head, and felt my decision take shape as I spoke—

"I'm going to try stalling ICAAM long enough to see whether RadioRemote will work. If I have to, I'll ask them to take me next year. If they won't, I'll pass on my so-called Hollywood dream. I'm not bailing out mid-project. Period."

Traci grinned at me. She'd been so solemn since the Vince thing, I'd forgotten how jovial she could be. And she started clapping, slowly, just three or four times. "Good for you. Today, RadioRemote; tomorrow, Paramount Pictures." She offered me her long, graceful hand, so very feminine in contrast to her hearty manner. "Put 'er there."

As we shook, the greenhouse door opened. Sophia stuck in her head, held out a cell phone, and said Martha wanted me.

Traci, using that as her excuse, slipped around Sophia and out the door. A call from someone in the same house seemed amusing; or maybe I was just cheering up from having decided. I held Sophia's phone to my ear and said—

"Hello?"

"Callie, why isn't your cell on?" Martha demanded. Working with the Ladies was like having six extra moms.

"Sorry. I left home in a huge rush."

She inhaled pointedly, as if about to give me her view of such carelessness, then exhaled in a sigh and asked, "Can you drive me to an appointment?"

The storm outside had grown rather fierce. I assumed she was worried about the roads.

"Sure. I love driving the Cadillac." I did. Hers had all the gadgets.

But she sounded apologetic. "We'll have to take your car. I want to be inconspicuous."

"Oh. No problem." I was suddenly sharply curious. Martha wouldn't call me away from work for an Oreos-and-milk run.

"It's important. You don't mind?"

"Not a bit. Three minutes."

As I left the greenhouse, the gray sky was dotted with those soot-black little clouds that mean a bad storm is coming. The wind was still swirling, tipping and freezing everything in the garden.

Despite that, I felt awfully good.

CHAPTER FIFTY-SIX

# I Drive the Getaway Car

I reached the main house expecting a full briefing, but all Martha gave me was the name and address of the person we were heading to see. The name *definitely* got my attention, but when I asked for details, she became a clam.

A very patrician clam, but a clam.

By the time we were buckled in, the storm had subsided to a cold, steady sleet. That was great luck in Minnesota in December, and it let Martha relax and enjoy the drive to a part of old Larksdale with lovely Victorian houses. All had been large at their inception; in the last year many had been extravagantly expanded. I saw what Martha meant about using my car to be less conspicuous; as we rolled slowly down the icy avenue, I felt we were being watched out of half the front windows.

It was a very socially-alert street.

Which made perfect sense when you realized Patricia Farthingale lived there.

We pulled into the drive of the largest house (a mini-mansion, shielded by an ironwork-and-hedge combination) and parked well out of street view. The secret-agent feel invigorated me, but no sooner had I shut the engine off than Martha said, "Wait here."

She must have seen the disappointment on my face, for she gave me a rare smile. "It's better this way. Patricia has her suspicions about a certain incident one Fourth of July."

Alone in the car, I restarted the engine and began speculating about possible reasons for this visit. While perhaps not as stunning as Nixon's trip to Communist China, it certainly was *odd*. I turned the car to face back down the drive and that led me to a fantasy about getting ready for a fast getaway, perhaps driving for some big-time mobster. I kept the engine running, partly to humor that imaginary getaway scenario, but mostly so I wouldn't freeze to death.

No matter how active your fantasy life, Minnesota is still Minnesota.

I had just gotten to the point where an all-points-bulletin for Martha "Two Guns" Crittenden was being broadcast, when the passenger's door opened.

Martha wore a look of grim satisfaction as she climbed back into the toasty car. As she buckled her seat belt, she said, "We have a deal." When I pressed for a few minor details—like what *kind* of deal—she changed the subject to the new herbacious border she intended to plant. I pushed a little, but all I got were random observations on the merits of organic mulch.

So much for being the getaway driver.

The ride back was about as exciting as driving Bob Vila from a *This Old House* taping.

I dropped Martha back at headquarters and headed to RadioRemote. The mood there had been growing tense; people realized they were just four days away from either triumph or their last paycheck. During the short drive, I considered telling Jake about Hollywood's hottest agency wanting my body.

I hoped it might give him ideas.

But when I got to the office and passed his desk, I overheard him on the phone telling someone he loved her. I averted my eyes and walked on, vaguely hoping he was talking to his mother.

And that his mother's name was "Darlin'."

So much for romantic fantasies.

I desperately needed a nap, but went straight to my office, sat down, and worked like there were very few tomorrows.

## CHAPTER FIFTY-SEVEN

# Showtime

For the next forty-eight hours I did a fair job of keeping my head down and concentrating on work, with my time going far less to the secret planning at Martha's (now nearly done) and far more to RadioRemote, where morale was terrible.

Morale was terrible almost everywhere in Larksdale. In shop windows GOING OUT OF BUSINESS signs were three times as common as holiday displays. Those stores still *in* business were running massive holiday sales—but losing all their shoppers to the discount malls. All we needed was for the Grinch to come sleighing down Main Street.

Morale hit an all time low at RadioRemote, where people had stopped worrying about Christmas bonuses, and started worrying about their next paychecks. Too many of them, including sweet, recently married Janet Carter from my old PMT group, had bought their first houses with NDN stock as collateral—and were facing losing home and stock alike.

Worst of all, the Ladies were still keeping their rescue plan secret, including their frantic efforts to arrange a mass meeting Friday night to vote on it.

The tension was crushing. At noon on Wednesday, when Deborah called to say they'd hit a snag, I was so frazzled I snapped at her, and she was so frazzled, she snapped back and hung up. Two minutes later we were on the phone again apologizing, but *still.*

That was why I felt such a rush of relief when, Thursday morning, Deborah called and said without preface, "It's on." Her voice held the suppressed excitement of someone announcing a floating craps game, an after-school fight, or maybe a space launch. She didn't have to say what was on; she just added, "Friday Night. Larksdale High Auditorium. 8 P.M."

"So I can spread the word?"

"Absolutely. Tell 'em everything you know. We'll still have a few surprises."

And she hung up.

I hung up, too, and when I looked around my office, it suddenly looked quite beautiful. I raced out to the bullpen, and it looked beautiful, too, but with far better cause. For the last hour Alicia and Luís, her assistant from Lord of the Rings, had been setting out catered goods for our First Annual RadioRemote Holiday Party. Our budget was minuscule, but Alicia had worked magic. Two turkeys already sat flanked by a vast array of fragrant side dishes. As I approached, she was pulling a foil cover from a large silver tray, on which sat what looked like a cross between a dark fruitcake and a cannonball. No cannonball, though, ever smelled as sweetly delicious as that thing.

"What on earth?" I asked, pointing, momentarily distracted from my mission.

"Authentic Christmas pudding, *à la* Charles Dickens."

Alicia set the foil aside. "I followed the recipe from an early Victorian cookbook. Except I replaced the beef suet and added ginger."

People were already crowding the serving area like cartoon characters being drawn helplessly through the air by strings of aroma. I held out a hand to stop Alicia from pouring brandy onto the pudding. Once the party started in earnest, I could kiss off any speechifying. Getting between the whole staff and the buffet was like trying to halt a stampede, but it was now or never. I put a hand on Vince's shoulder to steady myself, scrambled onto the nearest free desk, then called out—

"All right, everybody! I don't want to hold up the feeding frenzy, but there's *REALLY* important news!"

"You're starting the RadioRemote Ballooning Club!?" somebody yelled.

Over the laughter I yelled back—

"Very funny. Remember two minutes ago, when you used to work here?"

I drew a chorus of boos and cheers, all good-natured and about evenly divided. I waved my hands for silence—

"All right, everybody, this won't take long, but you'll want to hear it: The Larksdale Ladies want to use *us* as a base to *buy back PMT,* and—"

A general gasp of excitement turned into a noisy, jubilant demonstration. But since time mattered, I shushed them and hurried on—

"You'll get an e-mail shortly with the details. Point now is the Ladies won't buy PMT without a motivated workforce, one holding no grudges over NDN. Sure, they can count on us, but we're, like, twenty out of two thousand. So if you have *any* friends or family who worked at PMT"—of course, all of them did—"you need to get them to a meeting. Friday night, 8:00 P.M., Larksdale High auditorium."

They were still listening, but starting to eye the food. I wrapped it up as energetically as I could—

"Okay! This deal can be a huge Christmas present for us, for PMT, and for all of Larksdale. Let's make it happen!"

It wasn't exactly Churchill's "We will fight them on the beaches" speech, but they were smart enough to see their own interests. They did their clapping while jostling toward the roast turkey, but I knew them. Once they'd stuffed themselves, they'd hit the phones and stay at it till they dropped.

Meanwhile, everybody needs to eat, and I was ready to eat enough for everybody.

Alicia was unwrapping additions to the salad end of the buffet.

"What's that?" I asked.

"My own invention. All-natural Jell-O, with mango and coconut."

"Too healthy. No chocolate-caramel brownies?" With the start of the drive to reclaim PMT, my diet and workout plan had linked arms and jumped off a cliff.

"Luís is out getting them from the van."

"God bless us, every one," I said reverently.

Vince added, "Amen." He swept a hand toward the far end of the room, near the Christmas tree, where Traci and Chad Harley, our six-foot-eight quality-control specialist, were laughing and hanging mistletoe from the ceiling, and asked, "Join me in the first kiss?"

Something had certainly done wonders for his self-confidence, and it was pleasing to note he was quite snappily dressed. Maybe it was the turkey and stuffing talking, but he was starting to show a kind of Jimmy Stewart boyish charm I hadn't noticed before. I guessed with a sudden twinge of jealousy that *Traci* was the one improving him.

I told him he had a deal, in a couple of minutes.

Then I turned in earnest to filling my plate until it looked like a relief map of the Himalayas, and started munching my way toward K2. I should have been obsessing about selling the PMT deal, but I wasn't. As I looked around the room, I saw that for the first time in ages, people were happy.

Alicia herself was positively glowing. The food's success, and the compliments, were surely part of it; but this was different. I wanted to phrase it artfully. The best I could think of was to ask—

"So? Planning on seeing more of Skye?"

She blushed. "We're meeting up later."

I was now golden as a matchmaker as well as a manager. I turned away whistling. I was feeling downright noble. Across the room Jake was raising his glass to a small group of carolers gathered by the Christmas tree. Nearer to me, Vince (still Vince for all his fashion gains) had climbed up on the photocopier table, announced, "Hey! I can fly," and stepped off. Landing, he said offhandedly, "Oh. Guess I can't." Then he went to join Traci, and I realized, with a somewhat stronger touch of jealousy, I wasn't really first in line for the mistletoe anymore.

"Callie?" A small hand touched my shoulder.

I turned, and Alicia said, "Thanks."

"Merry Christmas, kiddo." I grinned and started for Luís and the brownies. After that, I figured, I could round up Jake and head for the mistletoe. The holidays, after all, are when and where you make them.

But thirty minutes later we were all working the phones.

We were happy—not crazy.

CHAPTER FIFTY-EIGHT

# We're B-a-a-a-c-k!!!

The auditorium was packed to standing room only. There was so much noisy confusion we were forty-five minutes behind schedule before we started. That worried me: We'd picked the start time to allow for introduction, discussion, and vote, plus a one-hour safety margin—by 10:59, we had to send the money electronically to NDN's account or the deal was off.

Our safety margin had now shrunk to a mere fifteen minutes.

The Ladies had worked out the program privately, but their logic was clear: For Gladys or Deborah to make the pitch would have been too much of an "I told you so" gesture. Aunt Dolly wasn't a public speaker, and Skye was unknown to nearly everyone, so that left Martha. When we finally got underway, Milt introduced Martha while the rest of us, wearing wireless mikes but keeping quiet, sat in a wide semicircle on the stage. I was so far stage left I was almost off-stage. At my elbow sat a small table holding a wireless laptop I'd use only if things went well.

Martha, in her slow, careful way, laid out the deal, along with the Ladies' concerns. She concluded by saying, "Remember: Nothing you say here, no vote you cast here, will have binding force or be held against you. We just want to know how you feel, so please speak your conscience."

I'd love to say from that moment forward, it was all one long fest of friendship and kindness. Unfortunately, the first five guys on their feet were all from some ten-minute-old organization called the New PMT Committee. Their faces were darkened by anger and even at a distance I found them scary. I won't repeat all they said; their overall point was they were mad as hell, and if they couldn't find a guilty party to lynch, the Ladies would do in the meantime.

But these first five—and two others who followed—were merely warm-ups. As warm-ups (or maybe, heat-ups) they worked just fine. Listening to them, the crowd was finding a channel for its pent-up anger.

A chorus of *yeahs* and *rights* built to a roar.

And then burly Stan Farthingale took the wireless mike.

It had been uncomfortable up on stage even before Stan spoke, but once he took the wireless mike, I got angry in earnest. Stan had that effect on people.

"ALL RIGHT," he bellowed. "We all KNOW this isn't going to fly." His tone softened to irony. "I'm not saying 'the Ladies' are wrong to try it. They see some easy pickings, and maybe this deal of theirs"—he dismissed it with a wave of his free hand—"maybe it has *some* bits of generosity. But what I *really* see is if we go along with it, then, when the deal closes, these *Ladies* suddenly own . . ."

Stan kept yammering. For almost ten minutes he grew steadily angrier, but apparently no more tired of hearing his own voice.

The clock, meanwhile, was speeding past 10:50. At last Martha whispered something to Milt, who nodded and leaned toward the podium mike. "Stan, Martha wants to know if you'll yield the floor for three minutes to a new speaker."

Stan barely paused to hear this, then demanded, "Who the *hell* is it?"

His language brought a low murmur of disapproval.

"I don't know, but Martha's been darn nice about listening to you. How about returning the favor?"

Stan, against a rising tide of disapproving grumbles, looked fierce.

Milt persisted, "How *about* it, Stan?" His voice was still calm, but irritation showed in the way his brows had knitted together. Milt still had standing in whatever weird, tribal hierarchy the PMT guys used, so Stan backed down enough to insist, "I'll get the mike back?"

"You'll get it back, Stan. Absolutely."

Stan hesitated, looked to his friends, and finally shrugged. "Sure. Why not?"

Milt nodded to Martha, who said into the microphone, "In that case, it gives me great pleasure to introduce the new executive director of the Larksdale Ladies Community Foundation . . .

*"Ms. Patricia Farthingale."*

For pure dramatic impact it's hard to top stunned silence.

Perhaps a dozen people had begun, automatically, to clap, but they fell silent almost as soon as they began. I was as stunned as anyone else—anyone else, that is, but Stan Farthingale.

Poor Stan.

His jaw dropped. Reflexively he looked down at the seat beside him, as if wondering why his little woman was not there. Finally, understanding, he slapped his suddenly pale forehead, but by then, Patricia Farthingale had reached the podium.

She kept it short and sweet.

Looking straight at Stan over about fifteen rows of seats, she said clearly into the mike, "Stanley, this offer isn't just more than we deserve, it's more than we're ever going to get, unless you sit down, shut up, and let us say yes in the next ten minutes. So honey: Don't be a fathead."

Maybe Teddy Roosevelt could have kept on talking after being called a fathead by his wife in public, but Stan was no Teddy Roosevelt. He just stood there, rocking on his heels. And in that moment of silence Traci, using her wireless mike, yelled, "Call for the vote!"

I spoke my one line of the evening—

"Second!"

Milt was swift. "Moved and seconded that we vote! By voice: All those in favor of a repurchase of PMT Software say Aye!"

The AYEs nearly blew the roof off the auditorium.

My big moment was at hand. We were going to send the NDN payment electronically—via secure wi-fi link—from my laptop. Vince had set it up, and that made it bulletproof. All I had to do was switch on the local link to the video projector, bring up the right screen, and then—on orders—hit the button moving the money. My fingers felt fumbly, but I did what I had to do. The screen lit up behind us, and, finally, I looked over to where the Ladies had huddled. Traci, on the edge of the group next to Skye, looked to Martha. Martha nodded. Traci nodded to me and called, "Push the button, Max!"

The clock was swinging up on 10:58.

A full minute, at least, till the deadline. Unless I got struck by lightning, or tripped and fell off the stage, there was no way I could blow it.

I hit the button.

Up on the screen the account transmittal ledger (with account numbers discreetly blocked out) showed that eleven *million* dollars had moved from the Larksdale Ladies Investment Trust, Ltd., to NDN.

People started cheering and then the screen went absolutely black.

My heart shot up into my throat and felt inclined to keep rising; it seemed just possible we'd suffered some kind of crazy, fluke system crash in mid-transmittal and had blown our chance. I was trying desperately to remember exactly what had been on the screen before it blanked, when—

The theme from *The Magnificent Seven* boomed from the speakers, and there, flashed across the video screen, in giant letters, red-white-and-blue, the words:

*WE'RE B-A-A-A-C-K ! ! !*

The place, I must say, went bananas.

Upon consideration, I decided not to have a heart attack, after all.

That Vince. What a card.

## CHAPTER FIFTY-NINE

# Afterward

Maybe the Martha's Vineyard of the Midwest was gone forever, but good old Larksdale was making a comeback. People strode out of that meeting into the cold night in very good spirits, and very few of them seemed to mind walking together.

Behind the auditorium, in a parking lot of snow-dusted and long-unwashed luxury vehicles, Sophia caught up with Milt as he reached his car. "Hey!" she called. When he turned, she said, "Just wanted you to know we . . . *I* appreciate all you did."

"I goof up a lot," Milt said, his hand on his car door. "But I keep my word."

Sophia had a warm, long-forgotten feeling that he always fed her straight lines.

"And I keep mine. I said I'd love, honor, and cherish you as long as we both shall live. Are you coming home?"

Milt let go of the door handle. "You've taken me totally by surprise."

"Really?"

He nodded. "And you wouldn't want me back without my bag, would you?"

This wasn't quite what Sophia had expected. "How long will you need to get it?"

He pushed a key chain button, and the trunk popped open. Then he grinned. "About ten seconds."

About the same time, a quarter of a mile away, I was starting up my Taurus. I felt entirely happy. The PMT repurchase hadn't been my deal, of course, but I'd done my part. With the company back in the Ladies' hands, there would be money to perfect RadioRemote; and I'd suddenly decided that, given a little time to come to his senses, Jake would quickly realize I was his one-and-only.

Between this lovely notion, and the *Riders of the Purple Sage* CD on the car stereo, I nearly missed the soft tapping on my window.

When I finally heard it, I turned and saw Jake.

Naturally, my heart jumped. I hit the power window Down button, and then started to open the door, but he said, "Don't get out." The snow was sticking to his hair and the sheepskin collar of his jacket.

He shivered slightly, and I said out the window, "Come in here, then."

He shook his head. "Long drive ahead."

Even I knew that was bad news, and I didn't want to listen when he went on, "Laurie wants us to get a place together outside of Boulder. Guess I'll try it. Probably nuts. I never was any good at sticking around." He brushed snow off his jacket. "You made me consider it, though."

I didn't believe that last bit—and didn't want to hear any of it. I changed topics desperately. "The Ladies put on a heck of a show, huh?"

"You're why they had a show to put on. You did a helluva job. You even made me toe the line." He flashed that brief, held-in smile. "Keep that up, and you'll be the first female Bill Gates." He reached in the window and stroked my hair. "Or the next Steven Spielberg. You might single-handedly bring back the cowboy movie, gal. You'll make 'em heroes, instead of guys with chilblains and cracked ribs."

He meant it kindly, but fame and riches seemed a lousy consolation prize.

"The job's not done!" I was losing control.

He rubbed his cheek. This was hard for him, which, I realized, was all the consolation I was going to get.

"My part is. So long, Callie."

I swallowed hard, but nodded without crying. When a cowboy's work is done, he should ride off into the West. If a sunset isn't handy, a snowstorm will do.

If a dream has to end, it ought to end like a dream.

I had my eyes closed and my head down. No footsteps crunched on the snow, and for a moment I vaguely hoped he had changed his mind. But then I got a quick kiss on the cheek and heard a slightly husky voice say, "Take care of yourself."

And then he was gone.

## CHAPTER THE LAST

# *My Hollywood Ending*

By early January Milt and Sophia were happily back running PMT, though Milt soon announced they would be staying for only two years: Once their son started college, they were off to see the world. The Ladies, securely behind the scenes again, returned to doing good deeds. J'Nelle got stock options and a full-ride college scholarship, straight through to MBA. That much was simple justice, she had risked an awful lot; but at the second meeting in January, the Ladies added a bonus. Remembering that J'Nelle had once said she preferred joining them to a new car and a trip to Europe, they gave her both. Traci and I got smaller rewards, but still more than enough to make us very happy.

At that same meeting Traci announced she was not returning to PMT, but considering offers from law firms as far away as Chicago. When I asked about about her small-town dreams, she said she had to set them aside for a few years while she made her fortune. Then I took a risk and asked how Vince felt about her moving. To my amazement, she answered, "Callie, sometimes we mistake love for friendship—and vice versa." She put a hand on my shoulder and added slowly, "It's a *common* mistake."

I didn't have a reply.

The last NDN people left town on January 15. I didn't get to kick J. Brian Henley's backside aboard the plane, which I guess proves nothing's ever perfect in this life, though some things are darned good.

At the end of January, Deborah called me into her office and, not quite looking me in the eye, said that with RadioRemote a real business some changes would be needed. In fact, they had already been made. The Ladies had hired a Silicon Valley legend named Lance Beauford McCauley. He was forty-six, and in the previous ten years he'd taken four start-ups public, landing two on the Big Board. The Ladies figured he could do as much for RadioRemote. Plus, with Milt leaving, McCauley had the chops to eventually run the whole show.

They offered me a generous deal: group manager with a 20 percent pay raise, a fat stack of stock options, and direct report to Lance McCauley himself.

I told Deborah I understood completely, and that she and the other Ladies were doing the very best thing for all concerned. Deborah called that the sweetest lie she'd heard since she was six years old and her mother told her she'd be a beautiful woman someday. We shook hands. I went home, took the phone off the hook, and cried for two straight hours.

Or rather, I cried from 6 P.M. to 7:45.

Then I remembered AMC was showing *Fort Apache* and *She*

*Wore a Yellow Ribbon* starting at eight. If I hurried, I could get the popcorn popped before the titles rolled. The day I can't pull myself together for a John Wayne double bill, I won't be depressed; I'll be dead.

By bedtime my nerve had returned.

And the next morning I faxed ICAAM my acceptance.

Three weeks later I stood at Martha's buffet table for my going-away party.

That morning the Ladies served what they called a "pancake breakfast," which meant pancakes. And plump sausages. And thick bacon. And thicker ham. And waffles with fruit compote and whipped cream. And hot cereal. And cold cereal. And coffee with cream, and a big wedge of coffee cake to top it all off so you don't go home hungry . . . and small glasses of orange juice for any health nuts in the crowd.

It was great fun, but with every passing minute I was growing antsier. Finally, as the group broke into smaller conversations, I took Traci aside and said—

"I was thinking . . . number two to Lance McCauley wouldn't be so bad. Maybe . . ."

She put a shushing finger up. "*Your* Hollywood ending is your ending up in Hollywood."

Just then Vince walked in, late but looking extremely sharp in a suit he surely hadn't bought in Larksdale. He was, I realized, appearing ever more like the tech mogul he would soon enough be. Before I could talk with him, though, the Ladies intervened. Since we were barely a week from my birthday, they brought out the traditional birthday strudel, complete with candles and a thoroughly embarrassing rendition of "Happy Birthday."

The singing was so bad, and left me so emotional, I didn't know whether to laugh or to cry. I guess I did a little of each. When Traci let it slip they intended to close the festivities with a chorus of "Auld Lang Syne," it sounded like more than I could take.

Which was why, well before my scheduled departure, I decided to go.

I'd already said a sniffly farewell to Aunt Dolly the night before. I still hadn't spoken to Vince, but didn't really know what I wanted to say to him. So I found Deborah and told her I wanted to slip away like Bilbo Baggins at his birthday party, and since I didn't have a magic ring, I'd need some help. She said she'd cover for me, and I headed for the front door as she was asking the Ladies' attention for a story, which, knowing Deborah, was about something Winston Churchill had said during the Boer War.

I thought I'd made a clean getaway, but just as I took my coat from the closet, I heard Vince calling my name. When I turned, he said with his old shyness, "Southern California actually ships more high-tech than Silicon Valley. Little known fact."

I couldn't help smiling. "Yeah. Little known fact."

"So I figure I'll be out there pretty soon. Maybe I'll see you there?"

"Okay," I heard myself saying. "That would be nice."

Then he kissed me, more on the mouth than on the cheek, and to my surprise it was very nice. And then, with his newfound finesse, he smiled faintly, helped me with my coat, and opened the door. It wasn't quite the end of *Casablanca,* but it worked for me. He'd said exactly enough.

So I went out the door with warm feelings about my time in Larksdale. It had brought me not only closeness to Aunt Dolly, but my shot at RadioRemote (which, after all, I hadn't run so badly), and two years to make friends, including the Ladies, I'd keep forever.

The snow was swirling magically—but about halfway down Martha's long drive, I slipped and smacked down on my fanny. When I looked back, the big house was half whited-out by the snow. It suddenly looked awfully tempting, but I picked myself up and continued, sore and slipping on the ice, to my car.

Still, my high spirits had been replaced by a sinking fear that I was making a terrible mistake.

I spent a long minute in the car thinking about all that had gone wrong: about losing control of RadioRemote, and how I'd never see Jake again, and how I had never really fit in anywhere—even in Larksdale, which I loved with nearly all my heart.

Soon I was worrying that Hollywood would chew me up and spit me out, just another Midwest girl who wasn't even pretty.

I was about two seconds from abandoning my trip.

But then I remembered a story they teach, sometimes, in engineering school.

In the fifties the U.S. and the Soviet Union competed fiercely to be the first into space. For the first years of the race the U.S. got hammered, as our rockets misfired, pinwheeled, and fireballed on the launchpad. The Air Force, which had been running the disastrous program, was down to its very last, do-or-die shot. They gave the launch command; the missile lit up, and for about three seconds, rose perfectly . . . then it stopped, settled back onto the pad, crumpled, and exploded. Instead of flying six thousand miles, it had risen a little over thirty feet.

The control room plunged from wild cheering to wrenching, silent despair.

Then the project's brilliant young chief scientist (who would go on to build a world-class aerospace conglomerate) called out to the Air Force officer in charge, "Well, General, now we know she flies. We're just working on the range."

That's me. No matter how often my dreams blow up on launch, I know how to fly.

I'm just working on the range.

I put the car in gear and headed for California.